SALVATION

THE CAPTIVE SERIES BOOK 4

ERICA STEVENS

BOOKSHELF

Books written under the pen name
Erica Stevens

The Coven Series

Nightmares (Book 1)

The Maze (Book 2)

Dream Walker (Book 3)

The Captive Series

Captured (Book 1)

Renegade (Book 2)

Refugee (Book 3)

Salvation (Book 4)

Redemption (Book 5)

Vengeance (Book 6)

Unbound (Book 7)

Broken (Book 8)

The Captive Series Prequel

The Kindred Series

Kindred (Book 1)

Ashes (Book 2)

Kindled (Book 3)

Inferno (Book 4)

Phoenix Rising (Book 5)

The Fire & Ice Series

Frost Burn (Book 1)

Arctic Fire (Book 2)

Scorched Ice (Book 3)

The Ravening Series

The Ravening (Book 1)

Taken Over (Book 2)

Reclamation (Book 3)

The Survivor Chronicles

The Upheaval (Book 1)

The Divide (Book 2)

The Forsaken (Book 3)

The Risen (Book 4)

Books written under the pen name
Brenda K. Davies

The Vampire Awakenings Series

Awakened (Book 1)

Destined (Book 2)

Untamed (Book 3)

Enraptured (Book 4)

Undone (Book 5)

Fractured (Book 6)

Ravaged (Book 7)

Consumed (Book 8)

Unforeseen (Book 9)

Forsaken (Book 10)

Relentless (Book 11)

Legacy (Book 12)

Coming 2021

The Alliance Series

Eternally Bound (Book 1)

Bound by Vengeance (Book 2)

Bound by Darkness (Book 3)

Bound by Passion (Book 4)

Bound by Torment (Book 5)

Bound by Danger (Book 6)

Coming 2020

The Road to Hell Series

Good Intentions (Book 1)

Carved (Book 2)

The Road (Book 3)

Into Hell (Book 4)

Hell on Earth Series

Hell on Earth (Book 1)

Into the Abyss (Book 2)

Kiss of Death (Book 3)

Edge of the Darkness

Coming 2020

Historical Romance

A Stolen Heart

Special thanks to my husband for all his patience and support, my parents for always being there, my siblings, nieces and nephews who make life more interesting and fun, my friends for their laughter, and Leslie Mitchell from G2 Freelance editing for all her hard work.

CHAPTER ONE

BRAITH'S SHOULDERS HEAVED, his chest tensed, and his arms were sore from the amount of damage he'd rendered. His vision was blurred by a hazy cloud of red that coated his eyes and made it nearly impossible to see. He'd never experienced anything like it.

When he'd lost his vision, the world around him had consisted entirely of blackness. Then Aria had come into his life and brought the illumination back, brought color back, and given him the gift of vision again.

Now the blackness had become the deep hue of blood. Instead of being completely blind this time though, shadows still moved across his field of vision, and he could make out the blur of other obstacles in the clearing.

He couldn't see them clearly, but he knew Gideon and Ashby had retreated far from him; David, Daniel, and William were standing by something solid, perhaps a rock, maybe a tree. Only Jack was brave enough to remain anywhere nearby. He didn't know what caused this shadowed haze, he'd never been able to keep his vision this far from her, but it had been steadily improving when they were apart. He thought it was due to the increasing amount of her blood within him.

She had strengthened him, and he'd let her down. He'd lost her.

He never should have agreed to her going into that town, never should have let her go. However, there was no *letting* Aria do anything. One way or another she was going to go, and he'd vowed she would have the freedom to spread her wings. He'd been trying so hard not to squash her wild and beautiful spirit with his heavy-handed, overbearing manner.

He'd been concerned about her safety, but he hadn't thought it would be overly risky for her in the town. The weather had driven most people inside, the dark servant's cloak would cover her, and though she'd been his blood slave, few people within the town had ever seen her, and even fewer would remember her. Or so he assumed.

He'd been an idiot.

His entire body shuddered as he grasped a small tree. His muscles rippled as he ripped it from the ground and hurled it through the air. Gideon and Ashby scrambled to get out of the way as it bounced in their direction. Braith stood, shaking as he tried to gather some semblance of control, but he was quickly spiraling toward something dark and dangerous.

This dark spiral was worse than when he'd fed from his kind, worse than when Aria first left him in the palace. The only thing allowing him to hang on was the fact he knew she was still alive, and he could find her. Soon.

Now. Spinning on his heel, he stormed across the clearing toward the town.

Jack moved to intercept him. "Braith you have to calm down, think about this rationally. We don't know where she is."

"I can find her," he grated.

"Yes, yes you can, but if you go charging after her, you'll ruin every aspect of surprise we have. Until we know who has her, and where they have taken her, you have to stay in control; you're our leader..."

Jack broke off mid-sentence when Braith moved toward him. Apparently, Jack's survival instinct was firmly intact as he held up his hands and took a couple of steps back.

A muffled sound in the woods whipped Braith's head around. He strained to make out the figure emerging from the forest, but it was nothing more than a dark shadow amidst the red. Even his heightened sense of smell seemed to be failing him, or it was buried beneath the crushing wrath and worry consuming him.

"Max," Gideon murmured.

"Max," Braith snarled. Lost in the confusion, the boy hadn't returned with William and Daniel.

Max's blurry figure staggered; he fell to his knees and attempted to get back up, but fell back again. David, William, and Daniel fled the safety of whatever they had been hiding behind to reach Max's side. They helped Max back to his feet and hoisted him between them. The cloying scent of Max's blood hung heavily in the air, but Braith couldn't see the extent of the damage done to him.

"How bad is he injured?" he demanded.

"He'll survive," Jack assured him.

An extreme thirst for blood was beginning to ravage his veins as he stalked toward Max. "Where have you been?"

"I followed them," Max croaked out. "I had to make sure I knew where they were taking her. I broke away when they entered the gates of the palace walls."

Braith's hands fisted as he fought the urge to rip everything around him to shreds to assuage the volatile monster looking to burst free of him. The palace, his father, it was the worst possible fate for her, but if he got to her soon...

He *would* get there soon. He would tear the palace apart with his bare hands if it became necessary.

"The soldiers will take her straight to father," Jack muttered.

"Not soldiers," Max inserted. "Soldiers don't have her."

Something in the boy's voice briefly pierced through Braith's cloudy haze. He nudged Jack out of the way as he struggled to focus on Max. "Who? *Who* has her?" he barked.

"It was your brother."

Braith felt as if he'd been kicked in the gut; Jack let out a low curse. "Caleb?" Braith managed to choke out.

"Yes."

This time it wasn't rage that overtook Braith, but a fear so intense it left him momentarily immobile. Caleb would destroy her; Caleb would break the spirit Braith had sought to keep free.

He didn't know who he hated more, himself or his brother. Red suffused his vision once more as a bellow of anguish ripped from him.

Broken. He felt broken, but nowhere near as broken as Aria would be when Caleb finished with her. Even if he could reach her right now, it may already be too late for her.

DANIEL SPREAD the papers out before him; his nimble fingers ran over the lines of the street and homes he'd hastily sketched into the plans. Jack kept one eye on the drawings, and the other warily focused on Braith. His brother was wound to the point of breaking.

This silent, seething Braith was more frightening than the one who ripped trees from the ground and snapped them in half with a flick of his wrist. This Braith was a ticking time bomb waiting to explode.

If they didn't get into that palace soon, Jack was worried

Braith would turn on them to get to her. He prayed Braith's reason, and ability to lead, would win out over his determination to reach Aria and the unraveling Jack could sense slithering beneath his brother's still exterior. He'd been hoping and planning Braith would be able to keep it together without Aria, but he sure hadn't expected *this* to happen.

The worst thing he ever could have imagined happening to Aria was Caleb getting his hands on her. It made him sick to think of what his father and brother would do to her, made *him* feel like heedlessly rushing into the palace to get her back. She didn't deserve such a hideous fate.

"We can split up through the streets," Daniel stated.

The drawing wasn't Daniel's best, but then he hadn't exactly had the time to put the detail into it he usually would have. The other group they'd planned to send into the town to survey it, had become more of a rescue team when they stumbled across Daniel and William trying to escape the king's soldiers.

Daniel's fingers trembled as he pointed to the two main roads of the town. His left eye was nearly swollen shut, and his cheek bore a nasty bruise that Jack suspected shaded a broken, or at least a fractured, bone.

Beside him, William was pale and his face nearly as bruised. His lip was split open, and dark stitches had repaired it. Max had fared slightly better than the brothers, but he'd focused on staying with Aria instead of trying to fight through the soldiers with Caleb. If it hadn't been for Daniel's sensibility, Jack was certain William wouldn't have returned at all.

"The town won't divide us as much as we thought," Daniel said. "The roads are big enough for us to move through in large groups that won't be easily taken down by the people, and whatever vampires remain there. Though, I suspect that after today the king will increase his forces within the town."

"Or he'll pull them all behind the palace walls and into the palace town to strengthen his forces there," David murmured. "We know he cares little for human life; it is the palace he'll look to protect the most."

"David's right." Braith didn't lift his head to look at them as he remained focused on the ground. "The king may send some troops into the woods to search for me, but from here on out the full force of his might will be concentrated within the walls surrounding the palace."

"How will he know you're here?" David inquired. "Just because Aria was discovered doesn't mean he knows you're here, or that any of us are here."

Braith's jaw grated back and forth; his hands clenched on his biceps. "He may suspect there is a militia within these woods, but he'll *know* I'm here because he will smell my blood in her."

Jack was motionless as he awaited David's reaction to Braith's blunt statement.

David blinked once, twice, and then his mouth parted. "I see."

Daniel's fingers tapped on the drawing as his focus turned to Braith. "I also believe we should raze the town as we move through it."

Jack did a double take at Daniel's words. Braith's head slowly turned toward him; even behind the thick glasses, Jack could see the burning ruby coals of his eyes. A chill crept down his back; he wasn't entirely sure it was Braith standing over there anymore, or if it was something far more hazardous and feral.

"There are humans in that town," Braith reminded him.

Or perhaps Jack was wrong; his interest piqued as he studied his brother. He was showing signs of concern and reasoning beyond Aria again. Was it possible Braith would keep it together? Was it possible Aria and Braith could be separated?

He felt no hope at the realization. If Aria survived this, the worst thing Jack would ever do in his long life was take her away from Braith again. They had all done things they didn't want to do though, and they would all do far more before this war was over.

Daniel was paler than normal, but his eyes were unwavering. "That town is a death trap. If the king doesn't pull all his soldiers from the town, and they somehow get the chance to come up behind us, there will be nowhere for us to retreat to if it becomes necessary. There are far too many homes and places for them to hide and wait for us. It should be burned as we move through so they can't set a trap for us."

Jack was taken aback by the ferocity of Daniel's words. Gideon quirked an eyebrow as he nodded approvingly. Xavier's head cocked a little, and a small smile played across his lips as he surveyed Daniel, William, and David with the same strange look he'd been studying Aria with ever since he'd met her. Jack found it bizarre, even for Xavier.

Daniel's gaze darted to his father. David was as pale as his son; his lips were pressed firmly together as he stared at the hastily scrawled plans.

"There are innocent casualties in every war, and it needs to be done," David confirmed.

"They aren't that innocent," William growled. He tugged at his hair as he strolled around the table and continued toward the edge of the woods. "Burn it then. Burn it all, and I'll make sure we burn that bitch who turned Aria in with it."

"William," David's tone of voice was low and warning, "this is not for revenge, no matter how badly we want it to be, that is not what we are about. We *will* limit the amount of innocent bloodshed."

William shot him a dark look; his busted lip curled into a sneer, but for once he held his tongue. David stared at Braith for some confirmation, but when none was forthcoming, Jack responded. "We will."

David didn't look overly relieved, but he didn't press the

7

issue. Jack anxiously watched Braith as he approached the table and plans. The other aristocrats stood behind him as they awaited his decision. They sensed something off in Braith, but for now they seemed to be willing to trust his judgment. Jack didn't know what would happen if Braith refused to see reason and put them all in peril, didn't know what would happen if Braith turned on them to vent his wrath.

"If we set the town on fire it will also provide an effective distraction for you to slip into the tunnel you spoke of," Daniel continued.

"We'll take what weapons we can from the town and level it as we go," Braith declared as he settled his glowing eyes on William. "I will have the girl who recognized Aria though; she is mine."

William's jaw clenched, and a muscle jumped furiously in his cheek.

Please stay quiet, Jack pleaded silently. It wasn't William who spoke though.

"The girl who grabbed Aria isn't in the town anymore," Max informed them.

Braith's nostrils flared. "She *grabbed* Arianna?"

Jack stepped forward, but he had no idea what he was going to do if Braith lost control again. He didn't even know who Braith would go after first if he did go berserk. He certainly couldn't stop him, and he would likely be killed in the process if he tried. Max nodded. "Yes, she seemed to know Aria from the palace. I don't know how..."

Max broke off as Braith rested his hands on the table and leaned forward. The muscles in his forearms and biceps rippled beneath the simple, short brown tunic of the rebel people that he had taken to wearing in the woods.

"Was she a blonde?" Braith growled.

Max glanced anxiously at Jack; he nodded in response to

Max's unspoken question. Unfortunately, lying to Braith wasn't going to help in this situation.

"Yes," Max said.

Jack felt a crack as a sizzle of power shot through the air like a lightning bolt. He'd never experienced anything like it, not even when his father was at his deadliest had he radiated a destructive force as strong as the one emanating from Braith. Even the aristocrats took a step back as the hair on Jack's arms stood on end.

He'd known Braith could destroy their father if it became necessary, but he wasn't entirely confident Braith would survive it. Jack wasn't sure if Braith would be able to return from the depths he would delve into if he completely lost it and allowed the monster within him to rule.

Jack remained immobile while Braith became as still as stone. He sensed the impending unraveling in the air, but Braith somehow managed to keep himself restrained. Though, Jack suspected a few more trees would be destroyed when this meeting ended.

"Lauren." Jack had no idea who that was, but the name appeared to leave a bad taste in Braith's mouth when he spoke it. "Where is she?"

"She went to the palace with your brother," Max said.

The strange stiffness overtook Braith once more. "We'll move on the palace tonight."

"Not tonight," Jack inserted quickly, half frightened he was going to have his head ripped off. "We require more time to plan, more time to maneuver, Braith. Not all the humans have weapons yet, we're still working on carving the stones for arrowheads, and we have to gather supplies to be better prepared and trained. Not all the vampires we recruited from the outer villages have arrived. If we go in before we're fully prepared, we'll lose."

Jack tried to ignore the crimson eyes glaring at him from behind those lenses. It was a disconcerting, awful spectacle that left him a little rattled. For the first time, he realized the cruelty Braith was willing to unleash and inflict on others for Aria.

Braith was retaining control because he knew where she was and that she was still alive. Although they all suspected what might be happening to her, it wasn't confirmed, and Braith was confident he would get her back. If something were to happen to her before then...

There would be no control, and there would be many deaths before Braith was stopped.

Jack had been wrong; his plan with Aria and Gideon never would have worked. Braith would hunt her to the ends of the earth and back. They never would have gotten far enough away from the rampage Braith would unleash.

And when he found her...

Jack shuddered at the thought of what would happen then. It wasn't a side of Braith he ever wanted to encounter. Braith hadn't killed him when he'd taken Aria before; he wasn't fool enough to believe he would be so lucky a second time.

That was a problem for another time though. For now, they had to keep Braith calm enough to see reason, to wait and organize, and to get them successfully into the palace so they could get Aria back from Caleb.

"She's my daughter," David said.

Though David spoke, Braith's gaze lingered on Jack before he turned away. To David's credit, he didn't flinch when those glowing red orbs turned on him, but his eyes did widen slightly.

"I want her back as much as you," David continued. "I can't bear to think about what she's going through, I've already imagined every horror known to man when she was in the palace before, and she was lucky that time. From the way you talk about this Caleb..."

He broke off as his voice hitched. His throat worked as he fought back his tears. "She is *my* daughter, I *created* her, the circumstances of her life and her family have formed her, and one thing she understands and accepts is sacrifice. She *knows* we won't be coming for her, at least not right away, and she will forgive us for it. She won't forgive us if we fail because of her."

"You don't know Caleb," Braith grated.

"I don't, but I know my daughter, and she will put the greater good above herself," David stated.

Jack glanced at Gideon when he shifted nervously and lowered his head.

"She would never forgive us if we rushed in and ruined everything. I want her back as badly as you do, but we will fail if we aren't prepared. If we lose because we're careless, what will they do to her after...?" It took a moment for David to regain his composure to continue speaking. "I know you understand her; it's why you let her go into town in the first place. She won't be caged, and she can't be broken, no matter what they do to her. We must be organized, and fully equipped, if we're going to have any hope of getting her back alive."

Braith remained still for a moment, then faster than the human eye could see he picked up the table and heaved it. The massive slab of oak flew through the air before shattering against a tree across the clearing.

Daniel and William jumped back as papers and debris scattered about their feet. David closed his eyes as his head bowed. He'd stated his opinion, but Jack could tell he still hoped Braith would choose the course of action they all knew to be wrong.

"Get the supplies and make sure those vampires are here soon!" Braith snarled before he disappeared into the woods.

CHAPTER TWO

Jack nervously glanced at the aristocrats gathered near the woods with Frank to the side of them. Their eyebrows raised as they watched Braith fade into the woods with Xavier trailing behind. Jack didn't know what the strange vamp expected to learn or see with Braith right now, but he thought Xavier might be the bravest of them all. He wasn't going anywhere near his brother again for a while.

Gideon opened his mouth to spin some tale but closed it and threw his hands in the air. "Oh, what does it matter anymore?" He turned away from them and walked over to join Jack. "Cat's pretty much out of the bag anyway."

"The cat shredded that bag," Jack muttered in return.

"He cares for the girl more than you let on," Calista said.

Jack met Calista's dark eyes but didn't speak. As the oldest amongst the group of aristocrats surrounding her, she would speak for them.

"How deep is their bond?" she asked.

"They are close," Jack hedged.

Calista lifted a sleek eyebrow as she clasped her hands before her. In the dim glow of the moon, her dark skin gleamed. "Many will not accept her, not as a human."

"Braith is aware of that fact, as is the girl." Jack ignored the startled looks from her father and Max. Daniel and William remained unspoken and expressionless.

"This information would have been useful before we agreed to join in this endeavor; before we threw our support behind a leader who is volatile, and attached to a *human.*"

Apprehension trickled through Jack; they couldn't back out now.

"The girl has agreed to leave when this is over," Gideon inserted forcefully.

The aristocrats pondered this revelation while David and Max absorbed it.

"Go where?" David demanded as he broke the heavy hush.

"She realizes that, as a human, she cannot be our queen, and she is also aware most humans do not survive the change," Gideon continued as if David hadn't spoken.

"It doesn't seem as if Braith would agree to let her go," Calista said.

"As he has just proven, Braith will put the greater good and *our* needs above his. He may not like it, but he has agreed it's what must be done. He has chosen to lead us over his desire to rescue the girl, and the girl has also chosen the greater good over him."

Jack winced at Gideon's blunt words; he sometimes forgot what a cold bastard Gideon could be. The aristocrats turned to each other and talked in hushed whispers as Frank edged closer to Daniel and William. Jack's hands twitched; it took all he had not to look at Gideon in case he revealed that what Gideon just said was a blatant lie. He had a feeling Gideon knew it too; he had to after everything that happened.

"You knew about this?" David hissed at his sons.

"Yes." William didn't back down from the glare his father shot him. "I planned to go with her."

"And when were you going to let me know about it?"

"We haven't exactly had much of a chance to talk in private."

When the aristocrats split apart, their gazes focused on Gideon. "We have made it this far; we *will* see this through. But only if we have your word the girl will leave after this is over," Calista stated. "Or your word she will not remain human if she chooses to stay and become queen."

Jack didn't look at the humans; he was terrified of their reactions to this statement. *Stay quiet,* he pleaded, knowing Max or William would be the first to erupt.

"I agree to those terms," Gideon murmured.

"It is not your agreement we care about," Barnaby inserted. "It's Braith's. These terms will be met Gideon, one way or another."

"They will be met," Gideon assured them.

"How can you be so certain?" Calista demanded.

"I've spoken privately with the girl, and she has agreed to forfeit her life if it becomes necessary to separate them."

Somehow, Jack managed to keep his face impassive after Gideon's revelation. David wasn't so quick as his mouth dropped, but it was the stunning lack of surprise surrounding William and Daniel that rattled Jack most.

Jack seized Max's arm and squeezed when Max stepped forward. He would shatter the boy's arm if it silenced whatever words Max was about to spew. Max's mouth pursed, but he wisely kept quiet.

The aristocrats exchanged another look before nodding. "Make sure this happens as you say, Gideon, or we will hold *you* accountable," Calista vowed and her eyes momentarily deepened to blood red.

Gideon's face was serene as he nodded his agreement. "That is acceptable."

"No child of theirs will be acknowledged as an heir if it is born while she is still human."

"There will not be a child; I can guarantee that much. At least it will not be Braith's child."

Jack almost swung his fist into Gideon's face. It was only the fact he had to snatch William back and throw him at Daniel that stopped him from doing so. His stomach twisted as the implications behind Gideon's words sank in.

It would not be Braith's child, but that didn't mean it wouldn't belong to another member of his family. Jack shuddered; he had to forcefully loosen his grip on Max's arm before he accidentally shattered it.

The proud thrust of Calista's shoulders highlighted the length of her slender neck and elegant features as she leveled Gideon with an unwavering stare. "You sound certain."

"I am completely certain it will not be Braith's child."

"This will only matter if Caleb doesn't destroy her first," Barnaby reminded them.

"Very true," Saul agreed as he slipped his hands into the sleeves of his robe.

"Would be a pity, I rather liked the girl." Calista shrugged as she rolled her shoulders and stretched her back. "I am hungry now though." The others bobbed their heads in agreement. "Will the three of you be joining us?"

Jack shook his head, not at all surprised by their abrupt change in discussion. "Not right now."

"Suit yourselves." Calista nodded to the others, and they fell into step behind her.

Jack waited till they were out of earshot before he turned on Gideon. "What was that nonsense about an agreement between you and Aria?"

Gideon's gaze didn't waver; there wasn't a flicker of remorse in his hazel eyes. "Aria came to speak with me; she agreed their bond would not develop further. She was also aware that if we are unable to separate them, it may mean her death."

Jack's mouth dropped; Max took a threatening step forward, but Jack jerked him back when Gideon's eyes focused harshly on him.

"I never agreed to that. I would *never* allow such a thing!" Jack shouted.

"That's why she came to me."

A low curse escaped Jack as he released Max's arm.

"My daughter will not be sacrificed in this!" David snapped.

"Your daughter has already been sacrificed for the greater good. You have already agreed she wouldn't want us doing anything reckless and that winning this war is far more important than any one life."

"She has *not* been sacrificed!"

"Caleb has her in his possession. She may be alive, but you must accept that she will not come out of there the same. Caleb is not Braith; he will *not* be kind, especially if he has any idea how much Braith may care for her."

"Jesus, Gideon," Jack muttered.

He wished the vampire had one ounce of tact in him. Gideon didn't understand the close bonds between these people, much as Jack hadn't when he arrived to spy on them. However, Gideon had to realize that though Braith and David had backed off, for now, they wouldn't stay that way if they were pushed.

David was as white as a ghost; William and Daniel remained quiet, but their faces had become nearly as pale as their father's.

"Your daughter was strong enough to realize her life isn't worth the lives of so many others, including yours. You should be strong enough also," Gideon said. "If Braith ever found out about our agreement, my life would be forfeit too. I was willing to accept that, and I still am if it becomes necessary."

Jack groaned; he was tempted to rip Gideon's tongue from his relentless mouth. For a moment Jack thought David was going to fall over, and then he rounded on his sons.

"You knew what she intended!" he exploded.

"Not this much of it," William admitted as he glared at Gideon. "But we knew she planned to leave after the war. I was going to go with her."

"And you? Were you going to leave also?" David demanded of his eldest.

Daniel shook his head. "No, I intended to stay."

"This was the only option dad," William said softly.

"Letting her die is an option?"

"We didn't know about that part." William's gaze flickered resentfully to Gideon again. "But I suspected Aria might do something this drastic if it became necessary to sever her bond with Braith."

"The needs of many outweigh the needs of one—or two."

"For God's sake, Gideon, shut up!" Jack yelled at him when all the humans turned to glower at Gideon.

"And Braith, what of him?" Max inquired.

"He can't know about this, *any* of this," Ashby said as he moved from the shadows. His face was hollow and ashen, but his shoulders set in determination. "I know better than any of you what the two of them are going through, but Braith cannot know about this plan. He'll destroy us all, and he'll storm the palace with little thought to anyone else, and he'll get them both killed in the process."

"You know I disapprove of this whole situation more than anyone, but what do you think is going to happen to him when this is over? What will happen to him if Aria dies? In case you haven't noticed he's a little unstable right now, and she's still alive," Max retorted.

"And in case you didn't notice, he still chose the right path. Braith has been raised since birth to be a leader, he'll be unsteady in the beginning, but reason and *centuries* of preparation will eventually win out." Max's lips compressed, his gaze turned to the woods as Gideon continued to speak. "Especially if there's no way for him to get her back."

"I'm not going to let you kill my daughter!" David exploded.

"Are you telling me your daughter is a stronger person than you are?"

David's hands fisted as he began to shake.

"Gideon, stop talking!" Jack snapped. He stepped forward to block David if he flew off the handle and attempted to attack Gideon. "I am not going to let that happen, David." He shot a pointed look at Gideon. "I *never* agreed to Aria dying. I will take her; I will keep her safe—"

"I thought Braith could track her anywhere if his blood was inside her," Max interrupted.

"We're hoping to dilute his blood with another vampire's, probably the three of us to confuse Braith further."

"And if it doesn't work?"

"Don't!" Jack thrust a finger at Gideon when he opened his mouth to speak again. Gideon glowered at him but remained silent. "We will cross that bridge when we come to it."

"You're not promising to keep her alive."

"I will keep her *safe*," Jack vowed. "I swear it. She's important to me as well."

David shook his head. "So her life is sacrificed no matter what."

"None of us like it," Ashby agreed. "At all. This was not an easy decision, and it was not made carelessly."

Max stared blankly at him before turning to Gideon. "I don't trust you."

Gideon lifted an eyebrow as he quirked his head in a small nod. "Fair enough, I'm not exactly certain about you either, but you must realize we're not doing this to be cruel. You heard what Calista said; they will not accept her as a human. They admire her, hell, *I* admire the girl, but admiration does not make her a vampire."

David turned away; he walked to the edge of the clearing where he leaned tiredly against a tree. "She's my daughter; she deserves happiness. I *want* happiness for her, more than anything."

"We all do, dad, but they're right; *Aria's* right, there are sometimes when our wants no longer matter," Daniel murmured.

David wouldn't look at them; Jack could smell the scent of tears in the air as his head bowed and his shoulders shook slightly. "If she is to leave after so be it, but we have to get her soon. She can't be kept in there—"

"We'll get to her soon," Jack promised.

Max shook his head ardently. "No, *now*. You didn't see what Caleb was doing to her; I don't think he'll keep her alive..."

"He'll keep her alive," Jack asserted.

"He was draining her!"

David finally turned away from the tree; tears didn't streak his face, but his eyes watered.

"He'll keep her alive," Jack insisted.

"How can you be so certain?" Max demanded impatiently.

"Because he'll smell Braith on her, *in* her. He won't kill her."

"So he'll torture her?" Max accused.

Jack's eyes flitted nervously to David as he stepped away from the tree. William and Daniel were beginning to shake as their jaws clenched and a muscle jumped in William's cheek.

"Abuse her?" Max asked. "I know you're one of them, Jack,

but you have no idea what goes on in there from a human's viewpoint. Aria was lucky last time, but by all accounts, Caleb is a sadistic son of a bitch."

"We *will* get her back," Jack assured him.

"Braith has to know what Caleb is doing to her. He has to be aware of everything before he decides to wait," Max insisted.

"I'll break your neck before I allow you to tell him that," Gideon vowed.

"Gideon, shut the *fuck* up!" Jack barked in frustration. "Max, we can all guess at what might be happening, but you can't shove it in his face. He may think he knows, may think he realizes it, but if you confirm it, there will be no stopping him. If there is to be any chance of getting her back alive we have to do this right."

"I don't like this," Max said.

"None of us do, but I need your word that you won't do anything reckless, yours too, William." He added with a pointed look in William's direction.

"I won't," Max muttered resentfully.

William shifted uncomfortably, his jaw locked and unlocked before he bowed his head and reluctantly voiced his agreement. "I'll do what Aria would want me to do. I won't ruin our chances of succeeding."

Relief flowed through Jack, and his shoulders slumped. Jack studied Gideon as he contemplated whether he should tell the vampire he didn't believe any of their plans would work, or that the only reason Braith was remotely sane right now was because she was still alive. He decided to remain quiet though; he didn't trust how Gideon would react if he realized there would be no separating them.

CHAPTER THREE

THE SENSATION in Aria's fingers was one she often associated with warming up too fast after being out in the cold for too long. A sharp tingling woke her from the darkness that had claimed her for an unknown amount of time. Her heart seemed sluggish, and it ached as it worked to pump blood through her body.

She was dying, she was sure of it.

She didn't want to die. She'd told Gideon she would, but now she was terrified by the possibility. She'd meant the words when she said them to Gideon, but that was when her death would have been quick. That was when it would have been for others, for her family. There was no reason for her to die now. For the first time in years, she felt like a child, she felt every bit of her seventeen years, and she longed for more of them.

Mostly she wished she could have said goodbye to Braith and her family.

Her tears were cold against her already icy flesh as they slid down her cheeks. "She's awake."

She hadn't realized there were others in the room. She was

ashamed of herself for crying, but she couldn't lift her hand to wipe them away. Aria didn't have it in her to face Caleb right now. Even under Braith's protection, she'd feared Caleb and the cruelty the middle brother radiated. Now she was his to do with as he pleased.

"Give it to her."

The other voice was unfamiliar to her, but she didn't have time to ponder it as hands seized her hair. A small cry escaped her, but she held most of it back as she was hauled up from the floor.

She didn't have time to take in her surroundings before something metal was thrust between her lips and her head tilted harshly back. The foul taste hitting her tongue caused an explosive reaction to erupt from her.

She struck out at the hands holding her when the thick liquid was forced down her throat. She gurgled and choked, but her head was kept tilted back. The liquid pooled against the back of her throat until she was forced to swallow.

Bile surged up her throat; tears unwillingly burst free as more poured down her throat. Once, when she was a child, she'd eaten a handful of berries that she'd mistakenly believed to be blueberries. The taste alone had made her vomit. But this, this was worse.

She'd gladly eat those revolting berries again before swallowing one more drop of the viscous liquid spilling down her throat.

She was abruptly released, and her head was thrust forward. She staggered but was unable to keep her balance. Falling back to the floor, her shoulders heaved as she panted, choked, and dry heaved.

She felt like she was dying even as heat spread through her numb limbs and strength gradually returned to her weakened extremities. Sobs stuck in her chest; fresh anguish twisted through her body as she realized what it was they had given her.

Blood. Caleb's blood.

It tasted nothing like Braith's. Braith's was sweet and soothing when it filled and strengthened her; it was right in so many ways. Though Caleb's blood had renewed some of her strength, it felt hideously wrong in her body, it didn't belong there, and although her body was absorbing its healing properties, it was also revolting against the influx.

A scream built inside her; she had the irrational urge to rip her skin off to release the blood that didn't belong there.

Her hands wouldn't sit still on the hard floor as they jumped and danced over the marble beneath her. She tried to steady herself, but it felt as if she were no longer in her own body but someone else's entirely.

This was only the beginning of the suffering to come. Caleb could do this to her over and over again, and he would because her reaction had just revealed how appalling his blood was to her, how miserable it made her feel.

"Apparently, someone only likes big brother's blood."

Aria's eyes flew open. For the first time, fury and indignation tore through her. Her eyes narrowed as they focused on Caleb; her jumping fingers curled into her palms. He appeared unreasonably dignified in his refined clothes as he smirked at her.

He was somewhat shorter than Braith, but broader through the chest and shoulders. His dark hair tumbled in waves around his face, and his green eyes would have been pretty if they weren't so icy. Caleb's nose was a little larger than Braith's, his lips thinner, but there was no mistaking they were related.

Caleb knelt before her and seized her chin. He turned her head first one way and then the other. Aria's jaw clenched, but she didn't give him the satisfaction of trying to pull away. He squeezed her chin until she flinched, and he threw her face away in disgust. Her lip curled as she slowly turned back to him; she itched for her bow.

"Enough. Bring her here," someone else commanded.

Aria was so busy glaring at Caleb as he hauled her to her feet that she didn't immediately notice who he was dragging her toward, and then her gaze traveled to the dais. Foreboding slammed into her when she saw the man casually sitting on the large throne, a throne meant for a king.

The King.

Aria's legs almost gave out on her. Sheer will kept her on her feet as Caleb pulled her forward. She'd never seen him before, but she knew him instantly because he looked so heartbreakingly like Braith.

His hair was that same black shade, but his features were different in subtle ways. His nose was sharper and his mouth crueler as it curved in a sneer. Though she knew how merciless Braith could be when pushed to his limits, there was a depravity about this man Braith could never possess.

She shuddered at the thought of what Braith was like now, without her.

The king rose to tower over her. This close to him she was able to pick out the other differences between this man and his son. There was no sparkle within this man's callous green eyes; the king's forehead was higher and his cheeks broader, but she was still unnerved by the similarities.

His gaze raked her from head to toe and back again. She felt exposed, judged, and found lacking.

"I smell my son on you, *in* you," he stated.

Aria remained still, uncertain what he expected of her. If they planned on killing her, she felt she would be dead.

The king rested two fingers against her cheek. Pride kept her face impassive as he turned her head first one way, then the other.

"He has also fed from you, recently, and on what appears to be a fairly regular basis," the king murmured.

She remained immobile as his fingers slid over her neck and then her collarbone. Bile rose in her throat; goose bumps broke out on her chilled flesh as his fingers brushed against her breast and a leering grin crossed his full mouth.

Caleb was the threat she'd known upon coming here, but the other one was now standing in front of her, touching her far too much for her liking. The king was the one with all the power; the one who would now control her fate.

"You willingly allow this?" he asked.

He required an answer; she just wasn't sure what she was going to say to him. Her heart hammered, stammered, and then leapt into full-blown panic mode as his fingers wrapped around her throat, and he leaned closer to her.

"You *allow* this?" he hissed.

He wouldn't tolerate her disobedience or willfulness. She was alive for some reason she didn't understand, but he would kill her without hesitation if she didn't at least pretend to play along with him.

"I do." Her voice was as strong as she could make it considering the hold he had on her.

He smiled, but it didn't reach his eyes. "Delightful."

She was ashamed of the tremors shaking her as his fingers trailed over the bare flesh of her arms. She would have preferred death to having this man touching her in such a way.

"Simply delightful. Will my son come for you?"

The lump in her throat had become uncomfortable. "I..." she swallowed heavily. "No, he will not."

She wasn't sure if it was a lie. She knew Braith would be furious, devastated, he would blame himself, but she had to trust he would do what was right. It was what she had hoped for, what she'd plotted with Jack and Gideon for after all.

No matter how badly she longed for Braith to storm in here and take her away from the foul creature across from her, he couldn't be careless. Braith had to think this through; he had to realize he couldn't throw everything they'd worked for away. He had to accept the fact she was most likely a lost cause.

And so did she.

The king's face was suddenly in hers. "You *really* don't think so?"

The quirk in his eyebrow and a shifting in his eyes caused alarm bells to ring in her head. Not only was he powerful and sadistic, but she was beginning to realize there may be a little insanity lurking within his twisted mind. His fingers encircled her wrist; she thought he was going to break it to punish her for some offense he thought she'd made.

"No," she said forcefully. "I don't believe he'll come for me."

"If that is true then you are of no use to us; maybe you should change your answer."

Her teeth clenched as she grated the single word. "No."

He pulled her a step closer to him; their noses almost touched. "I think you should. There is a reason my son left here, a reason he gave up everything he knows. What *are* you to him, and what do you know?"

"I'm nothing but an ex-blood slave and a rebel, teenage girl. What could I possibly know?"

"Your pulse is racing."

"I'm frightened," she admitted.

"As any normal teenage girl would be, I assume."

"Yes," she confirmed.

"Why is my son with you?"

"I... I don't know."

His hand clenched on her wrist; pain lanced up her arm as he twisted it back and grasped her middle finger. Her eyes widened as she gazed at the massive hand wrapped around her finger. She was unable to stop herself from flinching as he pressed his nose to hers.

"You're lying," he said.

A startled cry escaped her when he snapped her finger back. He grinned maliciously at her as the distinct crack of bone reverberated through the massive hall. Sweat beaded her brow; her breath came in rapid pants as nausea swelled up her throat and tears burned her eyes.

He squeezed remorselessly as he pulled her downward. Aria strained to stay upright, but he was far stronger than her, and her broken finger throbbed relentlessly. The king loomed over her as he drove her to her knees.

She should be afraid, and she was, but righteous fury also built in her chest and a self-respect that refused to let her cower before him. He had managed to force her to her knees, had maimed her, and she was sure he would do far worse to her before he finished, but she managed to tilt her chin up and glare back at him.

"You're far more than what you let on, and there is something between you and my son. Perhaps even both of my sons; it was Jericho who led you from here the first time."

Sickened by him, she leaned away as he bent close to her neck and sniffed her like a dog.

"But it is only Braith I smell in you, and myself, of course."

Aria started in surprise; she turned to meet his shrewd green eyes. It wasn't Caleb's blood they'd forced into her, but *his*.

"Do you know what that means?" he asked.

She knew what it meant, but she couldn't put the appalling realization into words. It didn't matter; he continued without her reply.

"It means I can find you *anywhere*. It means that what once belonged to my son now belongs to me. If you somehow manage to escape these walls again, I will hunt you down and destroy anyone with you. I will shred everyone in your life, and then I will shred you."

His fingers lingered over her cheek; she couldn't stop herself from turning away from him. "There are things I will do to you that not even an animal should have done to them, but I'd prefer to do them in front of my son. I will save up every little torment, every little pleasure I have planned for you, until then. I know you're lying to me my dear, he *will* come for you."

She couldn't tear her gaze away from his. The cruelty in his eyes mesmerized her; she was trapped by the horror of his promises, and the glimmer of his insanity. His hand wrapped around her brutalized finger again, and he bent it back bit by bit.

"Oh, and what superb torture it will be," he murmured.

His other hand brushed against the tears streaming from her eyes as he bent the broken appendage farther than it was meant to go.

"Is he out there now, near the town? I imagine he probably wasn't far from you, but Caleb says there were only three other humans with you."

"No," she breathed. "No, he wasn't with us. I haven't seen him in a while."

A snarl curved his mouth; his fingers pressed on the marks on her neck. "These are from Caleb." A small cry escaped her when his fingers dug into Caleb's bites before drifting over to Braith's marks. "Who left these on you then?"

"I don't know where he is!"

"Oh, maybe not right now, but you did, and he was close to you. What were you doing in the town?"

"Looking for food."

"What exactly are you to my son?"

For the first time his casual, sadistic demeanor slipped. In its place was pure wrath as his eyes briefly shimmered red.

"No... nothing," she stammered out.

Faster than a striking snake, he sank his teeth into her inner wrist. A startled yelp escaped her; she tried to jerk her wrist back, but he clung to her as he bit deeper. Much like the blood Caleb had forced into her, her body seemed determined to reject this invasion from someone who wasn't Braith.

Flames and heat licked through her veins from where his teeth embedded in her arm. This was worse than when Caleb bit her; her head bowed as she felt crushed beneath the torment engulfing her.

Just when she thought she couldn't take anymore, and her entire being was going to splinter apart, he pulled away. He rose over her as he leisurely wiped away the blood staining his mouth.

"Delicious," he murmured as he licked his lips.

He snatched a goblet up; before she could react, he shoved it into her mouth and poured its contents down her throat again. He jerked her back when she tried to scramble away and grabbed her hair when she shook her head to keep from consuming the blood. Seizing her hands, he clenched her wrists together while he held her head steady. Nausea burst through her as he forced the blood into her mouth and wouldn't release her until she swallowed it.

Though tears rolled down her cheeks, and she was struggling not to start sobbing in devastation, she managed to thrust her shoulders back and at least try to appear defiant. He watched her with a maliciousness that caused chills to run up and down her back.

"I'll enjoy every minute of what I'm going to do to you. I'm going to break you *and* my pathetic excuse for a son."

He pulled her roughly up and spun her around. For the first time, Aria was able to take in the massive hall they were in, was it the dining hall? But that made no sense, what were all those...

"Oh," she breathed as realization and abhorrence suffused her.

The tears streaming down her face were no longer for herself but the people in this hall. Only they weren't people, not anymore. They had once been alive and breathing, perhaps at one time they had even been happy and loved before they entered this nightmare.

Aria's head spun; she couldn't take everything in at once. It took her a minute to comprehend they weren't all humans, that there were also desiccated remains of vampires pinned to the walls, hanging from the ceiling, the rafters, and sitting at the massive table. The vampire's faces were pulled into macabre grins that revealed their pointed fangs, while the human's faces were warped into different expressions of torment and woe.

A scream rose in her chest and lodged itself there. She tried to keep it suppressed while her mind underwent a fracturing that left her barely hanging onto consciousness as her legs trembled.

How they had gotten like this, she didn't know. She assumed it had something to do with blood or lack thereof. Is this what happened when a vampire was drained? Did they become shriveled, somewhat preserved raisins? But why wasn't their flesh rotting away? She realized she didn't want to know the answer to that question; she suspected it was as awful as the sight before her.

The ones at the table seemed fresher. There appeared to be more fluid still left in their flesh. Their skin, though graying and wrinkling inward, still had some color to it. Then the eyes of the desiccated vampires moved as one toward her.

Despite her every intention to appear as stoic as possible and retain some semblance of dignity when it was being stripped away from her, Aria let out a startled shriek as she jumped back.

The king released a low chuckle. "I see you like my handiwork; I have a prime spot at the table picked out for you."

Cold sweat trickled down her neck and slid down her back. She was starting to realize she was only at the tip of the iceberg when it came to this man's evil. All pretenses of dignity and stoicism vanished.

She dashed to the side. The king hadn't been expecting the movement, nor had he expected her to be as quick as she was. She sprinted forward, determined to at least attempt an escape as she dodged two guards. Aria was briefly reminded of the time she tried to allude Braith and Jack. She'd stayed free from them for longer than she'd expected, but she was drained now and weaker.

She felt a dark presence rushing at her. She tried to switch direction, tried to get her body to move as fluidly as it usually did, but her legs wouldn't cooperate. Caleb hit her with the force of a sledgehammer.

The breath burst from her lungs as she tumbled head over heels across the marble floor before colliding with a chair, and one of the *things* in the chair. Dry bits of flaky skin broke off beneath her hand. Its eyes followed her as she scrambled backward. If its gurgling, twitching movements were any indication, this thing was starving.

"It seems that Merle is thirsty," the king taunted.

Strange noises filled the air; it took Aria a minute to realize they were coming from her. Merle's jaundiced blue eyes rolled in his head as Aria was hauled back to her feet. She didn't care who held her or what they did to her; she yearned to be out of here. One way or another, dead or alive, she wanted free of this nightmare.

She was losing it, she knew, but she wasn't entirely sure how to keep it together anymore. Not in here, not with these monsters.

Aria fought against the king as he wrapped his arm around her waist and carried her back to the abomination named Merle. He seized her still bleeding wrist and held it above the thing as it issued eager, enthusiastic sounds. A single drop of blood fell, not on Merle's mouth but on the center of his forehead, where it quivered and shook. It was one of the cruelest things she'd ever witnessed as Merle's eyes rolled crazily with hunger and he twitched violently in the chair.

The king lifted her wrist and gently licked the blood beading there. "And all Merle did was vote against me when I decided to start the war. That was over a hundred years ago dear. Imagine what I will do to my son, my *heir* who betrayed me. I cannot wait for him to come play with us, oh the things I will do."

Revulsion twisted through her as he pressed a kiss against her cheek and briefly nuzzled her before he dropped her unceremoniously back to the ground. She almost fell but managed to catch herself in time.

She was righting herself when the large doors across the hall were thrust open, and a tall, beautiful blonde strode inside. The blonde never even looked at the bodies surrounding her, but beelined straight toward the king and Caleb. Her eyes, however, did scathingly rake over Aria.

Thrusting her shoulders back, Aria defiantly met the woman's hostile glare. She'd only encountered Braith's sister, Natasha, once before when she'd first been brought into the palace as Braith's blood slave.

"It's true then," she said flatly. "She has been recaptured."

"Obviously," Caleb retorted dryly.

Natasha chose to ignore Caleb. "And Braith?"

Aria's gaze darted toward the doors as another tall, willowy blonde walked through them. She didn't stride forward with the same purpose as Natasha but instead slipped through the shadows as she moved to stand behind her older sister.

Aria's heart leapt at the appearance of Melinda, Ashby's bloodlink, Braith's youngest sibling, and Aria's only ally within this place. As swiftly as her hope rose though, it fell. There was nothing Melinda could do to help her, not now anyway, not without being caught. She was on her own for now. Aria kept her face impassive as Melinda's dove-gray eyes met hers briefly before they promptly slid away.

"I have dispatched guards to search the woods. I am sure he is close," the king responded.

Dread pulsed through Aria; it took everything she had to remain outwardly calm. Of course, they would search the woods and the town. She hoped the others had retreated into the caves, but even then there was a chance they would be found. A small tremor worked its way through her body.

Caleb's eyes gleamed as he perused her. "He'll come for her."

A cruel smile twisted Natasha's mouth. Apparently, Natasha was as twisted and sick as her father and brother were. "Wonderful."

It took everything Aria had not to look at Melinda to see her reaction. She remained immobile though, unwilling to draw any more attention to herself.

"And Jericho?" Natasha asked.

"I'm sure he's also somewhere nearby; they'll both be punished accordingly," the king informed her.

Natasha reminded her of a praying mantis inspecting its prey as she rubbed her hands eagerly together. "I can't wait."

"Make sure she is returned to the dungeon, Caleb, and don't take too much of her blood. I have more questions for her; questions she will eventually answer. You may have your fun, but she is not to be broken, not yet anyway. I want her to be alert and screaming when Braith arrives, and she is not to be raped."

Aria started in surprise as her eyes swung to the king.

"Oh, it will happen my dear, but it will not be Caleb," the king said with a smirk. "I suspect it will kill my son to watch *me* take you, and I intend for him to be here to watch *our* first time together. You may even enjoy it."

She somehow managed to swallow back the bile such a thought caused to burn her throat. She was rapidly beginning to change her mind about the idea of dying. Aria would gladly welcome death over having this man invade her body in such a way and having Braith be forced to watch.

The sadistic gleam in Caleb's eyes frightened her as he came forward to claim her. Aria lifted her chin, appearing far more dignified than she felt as he practically dragged her from the hideous room.

CHAPTER FOUR

Xavier was a dark shadow against the bark of the tree; a shadow Braith could barely differentiate from the woods. He'd spent a hundred years in the dark; had thrived in it when others would have failed, but the near darkness now was a stark reminder he'd lost the only person who mattered to him.

And he'd lost her because he was an idiot. He'd lost her because of some bitch he tossed from the palace for abusing Aria in the first place. He should have killed Lauren instead of allowing her to live.

In truth, he was the one who caused this awful mess. He despised himself for it, but he couldn't change it now no matter how much he would like to.

He swore that if he ever got her back, he would spend the rest of their lives trying to alleviate the impact of his sins. He *would* make this up to her if he could, if she could ever forgive him, and if they didn't destroy her first. The red haze of his vision darkened as he fisted his hands in frustration.

Stay in control; he reminded himself. *Stay in control; it's the only way you'll get her back alive. Stay calm.* If there was any chance of getting her back and winning this war they had to be ready, or they would fail.

It was nearly impossible to remain composed though. His skin crawled and fire boiled in his belly. He was on the verge of completely unraveling and letting the monster within take over.

His fangs tingled with the urge to drive them into the necks of his father, his brother, and every other person who dared touch her. He craved their deaths with a ferociousness he'd never experienced before. He wanted their bodies littering the ground at his feet, and he wanted it *now*.

If Braith weren't certain he would be killed before he could get to her, he'd have gone after her without the rest of them. If he thought they would set her free in exchange for him, he would gladly walk up to the palace gates and hand himself over.

He would die for her, but his death would do nothing to save her from this, and she would never forgive him for ruining everything they had worked so hard to achieve. He'd never forgive himself either. There were too many lives at stake; too much was at risk. There were people he cared about...

That was the worst part of it all. He had come to care for them. Ashby pissed him off, but Melinda loved the idiot, and he wasn't entirely obnoxious. Jack infuriated him to no end, but he was still his brother, and Braith had always been fond of him.

He'd even come to like and admire Aria's family. He couldn't let them all down. He couldn't bring himself to destroy the only chance at happiness and peace they'd ever hoped to attain; that *Aria* had ever hoped to achieve. She would forgive him for not coming for her immediately, but she would never forgive him if he ruined everything.

Aria was alive; he could feel it in his bones. By now his father had realized she was important to him, he'd probably detected his blood inside her, and seen the marks Braith left on her skin.

He would use her against Braith; he would torture her until she was broken beyond repair, but his father would hold out on the worst of the torture until Braith was present. He would make sure Braith witnessed the worst of what they did to her. At least that was the hope Braith clung to. Otherwise, he would leave these woods and go to the palace now, and then he would ruin everything *and* lose Aria.

He wouldn't allow that to happen to Aria, even if it meant giving himself over to the darkness lurking within him, and which was so close to consuming him now. He had to keep it at bay until they were ready to move. He could give in to the darkness when he found his father and brother; he could let it rule him to destroy them. Maybe, if he and Aria both survived, he would be able to salvage whatever was left of himself after.

He experienced no compunction about killing his father and brother. They wouldn't feel any about torturing him, killing him, and making the only thing he cared about suffer. The only difference was he would make their deaths quick; they wouldn't return the favor with him.

"What do you know?" Braith demanded.

"What do you mean?"

"Don't play stupid with me, Xavier. You know more of our history, and of the human's history than any of us. I see the way you watch Aria, the way you study her. If I thought it was because you had any interest in her as a woman, I would have put a stop to it long ago, but we both know women are not what you desire. I know you're not watching her because it's *me* you're interested in."

"How do you know that?"

"Xavier," Braith's patience was reaching its end.

Whatever crush Xavier may have had on him had vanished years ago when Xavier accepted Braith wasn't interested in men.

Xavier shrugged. "You are a good-looking man..."

Braith leaned into him until Xavier stepped into the tree behind him. "Do *not* play with me, Xavier. There is no one, and nothing, I will not go through to get her back. I am in no mood for your devious games or your manipulations."

Xavier didn't cower before him, but Braith sensed the vampire's trepidation.

"*What* do you know?" Braith demanded.

"I don't *know* anything."

Braith's hand slammed into the tree. Xavier's followers would be irate if he killed him; they may leave, they may even turn on him, but he was getting to the point where he would willingly take it to assuage some of his fury.

He didn't think he could survive much longer like this. Like a bowstring wound too tight, he was going to break. He didn't know what was going to happen when he did, or how many he would take with him.

"There are some things I *suspect* though," Xavier continued calmly.

"Xavier, not now."

It took all his patience to deal with Xavier's roundabout way of explaining things. Xavier seemed to sense this as he grasped his arm. "You have to keep it together, Braith; there are far more lives at stake here than hers."

"Why do you think I'm still here? Why do you think I haven't gone after her yet? But you have to tell me what you *suspect*."

Xavier bowed his head. "Keep in mind that I know nothing for sure. I would like to speak with her father."

"Fine, but what is it..."

Braith broke off as something else caught his attention. He released the tree he'd been so desperately grasping as he moved toward the edge of the hill. Below him, the forest spread out in a blur of dark shapes and mounds. Amongst the solid objects, shadows moved and coalesced as they glided through the trees.

He heard the approach of the others, but he didn't have to turn to know Gideon was in the lead. His step was somewhat louder than Ashby's slighter frame and Jack's more experienced movements. William, Daniel, and David barely made any noise as they approached; it was their scents he picked up instead of their sounds.

"They're coming," Gideon stated flatly.

"They are," Braith agreed.

"We should retreat to the caves until they move past."

Braith folded his arms over his chest as he leaned back. The shadows moved through his blood red haze; he could barely see them slinking through the trees as they climbed steadily up the hill. Jack stood behind him, while Gideon moved to the front.

"There are at least fifty of them," Gideon remarked.

"We're here to start a war," Braith reminded him. "Do you propose we retreat every time there is a threat?"

"We do not want to confirm our presence in these woods."

"He knows we're here anyway, why else do you think fifty some-odd soldiers are creeping through the woods right now?"

"I don't understand why there are so many," William muttered. "They only saw four of us in the town."

"Perhaps Aria told him there were more here," Gideon remarked.

"She'd never do that!" William retorted.

"You don't know what goes on in the palace or what the king is capable of."

"No!" Max stormed forward. He thrust his finger into Gideon's chest, startling the older vampire into taking a step back. "*You* don't know what goes on in there, and you don't know Aria. She wouldn't tell them anything; she'd die before she ever put any of us in jeopardy!"

Gideon grasped Max's finger and thrust it away. "Don't touch me!"

"Enough," Braith barked as he stepped between them. "It's my blood in her that has drawn them out and alerted the king to *my* presence in these woods. He suspects we are here for a reason, but has no way of knowing how many are with us. Send most of the humans to the caves; they can decide who amongst them remains outside. I want most of our troops to remain hidden. If any of the king's men survive, I do not want them to be able to report the extent of our force back to the king."

"And if we lose some of our own?" Gideon wasn't as much of a shadow as the soldiers creeping through the forest, but Braith couldn't make out his features.

"It's a war, Gideon, we *will* lose some of our own," he snarled. "Get the humans into the caves. You can come back," he added before William could protest.

William nodded and rushed into the woods. "What about you, Braith?"

"What about me?" he demanded of Ashby.

"Your vision—"

"Is fine."

"Your vision?" Xavier shouldered his way through Jack and Ashby. "What about your vision?"

"Its fine," Braith insisted.

Xavier seized Braith's arm when he went to turn away. "Is it tied to her?" Xavier demanded. Braith ripped his arm free of Xavier's grasp. "I assumed your eyes had finally healed over the years, but her blood brought your vision back, didn't it?"

"Xavier—"

"Answer me, Braith!" Xavier's voice was high, and the tone bordered not on consternation, but disbelief, or maybe even enthusiasm.

"No, it wasn't her blood."

"Oh."

Xavier seemed to deflate before him, but something about the vampire's reaction piqued Braith's curiosity and made him decide to reveal more. Besides, what difference did it make anymore? Most everyone standing here already knew his vision was linked to Aria, the ones who perhaps didn't were her family.

"It was because of her though," Braith said.

The bodies shifted and, judging by the smell, Max stepped forward.

"What do you mean?" Xavier demanded.

"Her presence was what brought it back. She was dirty and disheveled, but she was the most beautiful thing I'd seen in a hundred years as she stood there waiting to be auctioned."

David inhaled sharply, Xavier muttered something that sounded like a prayer, and Max stepped closer to him.

"When Jack took her from the palace, I lost my vision again."

"But you can still see now?" Xavier pressed. "As well as when she is around?"

Braith's jaw clenched and unclenched. "No, I cannot. I only see shadows and blurs. It's more than I could see before I encountered her but far less than when she is with me."

When Xavier grasped his arm again, his fingers dug into Braith's flesh. He could sense Xavier's intense scrutiny as he tried to search past the glasses. Xavier's hand grabbed the frames, but Braith jerked his arm free and knocked Xavier's arm aside when he tried to tug off the glasses. Xavier was thrown slightly off balance, but he caught himself and straightened to look at Braith again.

"Don't," Braith growled.

"*Both* of you don't," Jack inserted. "In case you've forgotten, we have company."

Though Braith knew he should be concerned about the men in the woods, his attention remained focused on Xavier as he strained to bring the vampire into view. It was frustrating not to be able to read the subtle nuances of Xavier's face. He desperately needed to know what Xavier *suspected*.

But Jack was right, they did have company and Braith was itching for a fight. He was itching for blood. He wanted to take his fury and frustration out on someone, and the king's soldiers were a good start. Slipping soundlessly through the trees with the others, he kept an eye on the shifting shadows as he homed in on his prey.

He thought he should be apprehensive about the excitement and bloodlust coursing through him, but he wasn't. No matter what it took, or what he *became*, he would do whatever was necessary to get Aria back. He didn't care who he had to destroy to do it.

Crouching behind a tree, he closed his eyes against the distracting shadows. He drew on the senses he'd honed during his hundred years of blindness to get a clearer picture of what was going on around him instead of using his broken eyes.

His ears alerted him to the approach of the men; his nose picked up their scent long before they reached the crest of the hill. He remained still as stone as he listened and waited for the soldiers to move closer.

Then, as the men rounded the top of the hill, and all he knew was the darkness the world had become without Aria, he slipped from behind the tree and descended on the men like an avenging demon. Something he feared he might become. He felt hate-filled enough to have come straight from the depths of Hell. Even before he grabbed the first soldier, he knew there would be no survivors.

As he drove the first soldier onto the ground, he realized he hadn't slipped into the darkness a demon would possess. He'd slid into the darkness the *king* possessed. What was inside him now was what he'd often seen reflected in the eyes of his father.

The worst part, he knew as he destroyed first one vampire and then another, was he didn't care. He welcomed it, embraced it, and relished in the death around him as it briefly calmed his tormented spirit.

CHAPTER FIVE

"Aria?"

Aria roused herself from the dirt floor. It was filthy in here in ways that even the caves weren't dirty. Her nose wrinkled, she tried to block out the scents around her, but it was impossible.

She had lived in some pretty hideous places, been cramped and filthy and foul more times than she could count, but the smells here were some of the worst she'd ever encountered. The air was ripe with mildew, the copper tang of blood, body odor, human excrement, and fear.

The smell of fear hung the heaviest in the cramped dungeons beneath the palace. She shoved herself into a sitting position as she strained to see the source of the voice through the darkness.

"Aria?"

Aria's legs shook as she climbed to her feet; her muscles were cramped from blood loss and being curled in on herself. Her hands were raised cautiously before her as she moved toward the bars trapping her within the small four by four prison.

"Who's there?" she asked softly.

There was a small exhalation, almost of relief. "It *is* you."

Yes, it was her, or what was left of her anyway. Blood trickled from Caleb's vicious bite marks, but she didn't attempt to wipe the blood from her body. What had been such an intimate bonding experience with Braith was twisted into something repugnant and cruel, and she couldn't bring herself to touch the reminders of that.

The taste of the king's foul blood had burned into her throat and seared onto her tongue. She believed Braith would come for her; she just wasn't sure what he would find when he arrived. Caleb and the king were only getting started, she was sure of it.

She grasped the bars as she fought against the overwhelming urge to curl into a ball and let it all go. Her middle finger protested the movement, but the king's blood was already having a healing effect upon it.

"It's Mary," the voice responded.

Aria's mind spun as she tried to place the woman, and then she recalled her. "Mary," she breathed. She was amazed the woman was still alive as they were captured together; it was Mary's son Aria allowed herself to be caught in place of what felt like so long ago.

"Yes. Yes, it's me," Mary said eagerly.

Through the darkness, she heard others moving about. She'd had only a brief glimpse of the other cells when she was pulled down here. She had no idea how many people were trapped with her, or who they were.

"What are you doing here? The prince..."

Mary's voice trailed off; there was a little muttering amid the darkness and whispers floated over her.

"We assumed he'd killed you," another said.

"No, Caleb will wait—"

"Not that prince, the other one, the one who bought you."

She was astounded by the insinuation. "Braith? Braith would never hurt me."

"He hurt the others," someone else whispered.

Aria shuddered as she rested her head against the bars. These people had seen Braith at his worst. They witnessed his plunge into depravity and violence. She rubbed her chest over the place where her heart throbbed. What was he like now?

"Was it true then Aria, did you escape?"

"Yes," she breathed.

There was a collective inhalation. "How?" A man asked hopefully.

"It's a long story."

"We have nothing but time in here."

Aria released a humorless laugh. It was true; there was nowhere for any of them to go right now. She told them Jack was the king's son who chose the rebel cause over the king, and how Jack had taken her from here the first time, but she didn't reveal to them it was her absence that had sent Braith spiraling out of control.

"Will Jack come for you again?" Mary inquired hopefully.

Aria hesitated for a moment. "Braith will." There was a collective inhalation as she continued to speak. "He's not a monster."

"Maybe he's not as bad as his brother, but he *is* a monster."

"He's not a monster," Aria insisted. "I know what he has done in the past, but—"

"You don't know what he's done," Mary interrupted abruptly. "You weren't here."

"He told me what he did, and he *is* a good man."

"He's not a man, Aria."

No, he isn't a man, she thought to herself. Braith's a vampire, and he's wild, powerful, lethal, and he *would* come for her. She just wasn't sure how much destruction he would wreak in the process.

"He's good, Mary."

"He sure didn't act like it when he was pulling women from here."

She didn't like to think about what her absence had driven him to, but she had to acknowledge it. She'd had good reason to leave him. Her life was in jeopardy, and he'd never told her about his fiancé, but she hadn't spoken to him about going before making the decision. Her sudden disappearance had driven him to do things he'd never done before.

"Many didn't return," Mary pressed.

Aria wanted to tell her to shut up; she didn't want to hear any more. She wasn't a coward though, she'd never backed down from anything before, and she wasn't about to start now. Braith had told her these things already, he'd tried to make her understand what he was capable of, but though she had acknowledged it, she'd never truly realized what it entailed until now. He couldn't go there again.

Dread trickled through her; she fought the urge to kick and scream and beg to be let out; she needed to get back to him before something terrible happened. She remained immobile though, her hands clenching around the bars as sweat trickled down her back. Humiliating herself down here wouldn't do her any good. She'd plotted with Jack and Gideon to leave him, to move on when the war was over in the hopes he would be able to keep control, but what if he didn't?

Aria thought he might let her go if she asked him to; Braith would do anything he could to make her happy, but if she up and left again with his brother, or if she died, he would lose it.

His father had just forced his foul-tasting blood into her, and yet she still felt the soul-deep bond she shared with Braith. He was inside her, intrinsically ingrained into each of her cells and the very fabric of her being. The king's blood, though inside her, was not a part of her. She could feel her body rejecting it as her cells struggled against the aberration in her system.

Braith was a part of her; he always would be. She was a fool and an idiot. Even if she left him, even if he succeeded in controlling himself and ruling as he should, she would never be able to sever the bond between them no matter whose blood was forced into her system.

It took everything she had to keep breathing.

He was in her heart, in her soul, and there was no way she was going to abandon him again. She didn't know how Gideon and Jack would react to her new decision, and she honestly didn't care. They would have to find another way.

Braith would have to agree to try and change her, or perhaps she could live out her life with him, but not be acknowledged as his queen. It wasn't a pleasant notion, and Aria didn't think she would be able to accept such a life, but she wasn't going to be able to carry out what she'd plotted with Gideon and Jack.

"We've all made mistakes, Mary. Braith will lead us to a better life though."

"My mistakes didn't involve me murdering someone," another man sternly interjected.

Aria fought the urge to shy away from their resentment and condemnation, but if she survived any of this, then she was going to have to get used to antipathy from those around her. She gathered her strength as she pressed her forehead against the cold metal bars. She braced herself for their disapproval.

"His mistakes made Braith who he is. They have made him a leader, and they have made him strong. He will come here, and if he is successful, he will free us all."

"And do what with us?" another woman asked. "Drain us dry like he did the others?"

"No, he will give us freedom, *real* freedom. You can return home, or you can stay within the town, but no matter what you decide, it will be your choice to make."

There was a protracted moment of silence, of breaths held in hope and disbelief. Most everyone here had been a part of the rebellion. This was what they had been fighting and hoping for their entire lives.

"He'll do good, *real* good in this world," she insisted. "My father believes in him."

There was shifting, and then a hand seized hers. Aria jumped and bit back a cry as the large hand wrapped around hers. It was a man's hand, calloused and roughened from dirt and labor.

"David trusts this creature?" the man asked.

The creature comment irked her, but she didn't pursue it. Some battles weren't worth fighting.

"He does," she confirmed as the man's hand tightened around hers. "And so do I."

"He bought you," Mary whispered.

"He *saved* me," Aria corrected.

"He didn't save the others."

"But he *will* save the ones he can, now. I wouldn't lie to you about this; I wouldn't steer you down the wrong path, he is our future, our *hope*; you must trust me on this. How many are down here?"

"There were fifty-two of us, but Walt hasn't returned since they pulled him up yesterday. There will soon be another auction; they usually run at least once a month, sometimes more depending on the number of raids. There will probably be around another fifty people in here with us after that," Mary said.

Aria's skin crawled, it was awful enough down here now, never mind cramming another fifty people into these cells.

"Have you seen my son, Aria? Have you seen John?"

The hope in Mary's voice pierced Aria's morose thoughts.

She would like to give Mary the answer she sought, but she couldn't. "I'm sorry, Mary, I haven't."

Aria's hand was still wrapped within the man's as she listened to Mary's faint sobs.

"I'll find him," Mary whispered. "If I somehow get out of this, I'll find him."

Aria tried to free her hand from the man, but he held on. "What of you, Aria?" he inquired.

"What of me?" She was growing annoyed he wouldn't give her hand back to her.

"You really trust this creature?"

Aria frowned, his voice was familiar, but she couldn't place where she'd heard it before. Then she recalled her capture and her time in the holding pen before she'd been brought on stage to be auctioned off. A man had told her to be strong, and though she hadn't seen him or known who he was, she recognized the voice now and knew it was the same man.

"Completely," she stated.

"It can't be any worse than it is now," the man murmured as he squeezed her hand and released her.

Aria didn't respond. She absently rubbed her injured finger as she strained to see. She wished she could part the shadows and rid the world of the shadows concealing it, but it was impossible. The darkness was absolute.

BRAITH GLIDED through the trees before kneeling at the edge of the wood's line; his eyes closed as he opened his ears to listen to the sounds of the day. David and Daniel knelt beside him. Daniel unraveled the designs he'd illustrated and laid them out.

Though Braith didn't open his eyes to see the dark shadows of the drawings, he knew the boy was talented; he'd seen some of his other work. Daniel outlined the attack plan for the town with the ease and knowledge of someone far older than his twenty-one years.

"This area here is large enough for us to move everyone into the town without becoming hindered by the forest," Daniel said.

Braith kept his eyes closed as he felt the open space Daniel described. The wind moved freely through the area as it was less crowded with trees and obstacles.

"Setting fire as we go will confuse them and drive them from any hiding spots they may have," Daniel continued. "They won't know what to expect from us."

"So this is where we will split off from?" Xavier inquired.

"Yes, from what Braith described the entrance to the tunnel is in this area of the woods." Daniel's fingers skimming over the drawings caused the papers to rustle. "If you split off from here, you'll be hidden within the forest until you reach the mountainside."

"Are you sure the king doesn't know about this tunnel?" Ashby inquired.

"I created it as an escape route from the man in case it became necessary. No one knows about the tunnel except for me," Braith told him.

"Must have taken a while," William muttered.

Braith's fingers and muscles clenched at the mere thought of the king. "You do what is necessary, no matter what the cost," he said bitterly. "I'll take twenty in with me when we first enter."

"You can't go into the palace so unprotected," Gideon protested.

"If I take more it will be impossible to move them through undetected."

"The tunnel is our best advantage to get more men inside without being seen," Gideon insisted.

"If they know we are inside they will make sure they have Aria with them," Braith growled.

"Braith—"

"No!" he barked. "No more arguments, Gideon. This right here, *this*, is not a democracy! Not when it comes to her. I will go in there with only twenty. We will have one hour before others may follow, but I *will* have that hour to try and locate her first. When the others enter, they can make their way to the main gate, but I will remain inside until I find her."

"Can we take all of the troops through the tunnel?" Frank inquired.

"No, there's not enough room to maneuver that many men through undetected. They would discover us, and we would be trapped, pinned down by the king's men if we try to move everyone inside the palace that way. It will be hard enough for the three hundred who enter behind us, but it will be doable."

They uneasily shuffled around him. "It's a solid plan," Ashby finally agreed.

Braith listened as Daniel rolled the designs back up and tucked them into his shirt. "Of course it is," Daniel said.

Braith normally would have felt some amusement over Daniel's self-assured response, but he was incapable of feeling such a thing right now. He rose to his feet and stretched his aching shoulders as he tried to ease some of the tension within them.

"When will we be ready?" he asked.

"Tomorrow, two days at the most. If we wait until nightfall there will be even less resistance," Daniel answered hesitatingly.

Braith's teeth clenched; his jaw throbbed from the pressure on it. Two days, it was far more time than he had expected. Two more days of Aria trapped in that palace and at the mercy of his father and brother. Taking down his father's soldiers had assuaged some of his bloodlust and craving for death, but it was coming back tenfold right now. It thrummed in his temples and pulsed through his body with every passing second.

"Two days it is," he grated.

They exhaled a collective breath of relief. Braith turned away from them and moved deeper into the woods. He had to get away from them. Rage burned his chest, surged up his throat, and strangled him with its intensity. Moving through the trees Aria loved so much, he took refuge in the forest she cherished as he climbed the hill. He could almost feel her here, laughing as she jumped from tree to tree and limb to limb.

He was thankful most of their troops were still in the caves; he couldn't deal with anyone else right now. Arriving at the top of the hill, he turned back toward the town and the palace. The shadows shifted and blurred before him, but he could make out the silhouette of the king's home.

Anger didn't tear through him now, but a sense of loss so profound it nearly drove him to his knees. He couldn't think about what was happening to her or what she was going through because of him.

It had been a simple mission, and he'd lost her. He'd let her down. He'd vowed to keep her safe, and he failed miserably. Even if he did get her back, Braith didn't know if he would ever be able to make up for the torture she was enduring. He shuddered as his hands fisted.

"Focus," he told himself firmly.

The only problem was, there was little to focus on besides her. It was why he'd come here. He couldn't see the boards scattered about him, but he knew they were there. William, Daniel, David, Max, and Jack had helped him to carry the wood here. Even Ashby, Gideon, and Xavier had wandered to the clearing to see what Braith had in mind for all the lumber.

"You can have mine," Ashby offered when Braith stated he planned to build a tree house.

Braith didn't want the memories that came with Ashby's though. He wanted something untainted by his father, something entirely for Aria, and he would build it for her. It was the only thing he could think of to do, the only thing helping to ease some of the pent-up rage inside him besides killing. It would be hers alone when he finally had her back.

He felt another presence before he heard or smelled anything. His head dropped; he searched the shadows the best that he could. Then something stepped out from behind the tree, and he caught the scent of it.

"Keegan," he murmured.

He couldn't clearly see the wolf, but he heard the faint padding of his paws as he made his way toward Braith. Braith had assumed the wolf found his own pack in the woods and he'd never see him again.

He dropped to his knees, finding some solace as his fingers slid into Keegan's thick coat. Pulling Keegan close, he buried his face in Keegan's fur and embraced his lost friend. Keegan's tongue was rough as it lapped at Braith's face. From behind the tree, another wolf appeared, followed by four small blurs rolling over the top of one another.

"Seems you've been busy also."

Braith turned at the breaking of a stick; Keegan lowered himself, and a low growl rose in his throat. Xavier emerged from the shadows with his dark head bent as he moved closer. Braith recognized David's scent and nimble gate as he picked his way around the boards behind Xavier.

"We must speak," Xavier murmured.

Braith had been waiting to speak to Xavier, but he wasn't sure he could take much more right now. If he didn't like what Xavier had to say, he feared he'd lose it.

"Aria?" He barely got her name out.

"Yes."

"What about her?"

Xavier's hands fell to his sides. He moved closer until he almost touched Braith as he lowered his voice. "I believe she is not what she appears to be. There is more going on here than what you, or I, know." He turned toward David. "Her father has some interesting information that perhaps you knew, but I did not. If I *had* known, all this would have made a lot more sense to me a while ago, and perhaps it would have made things easier."

CHAPTER SIX

ARIA WAS DRAINED OF ENERGY, blood, and life. She could barely move, it was almost impossible to pry herself up from the swirling gray marble floor. The king stood over her with her blood staining his mouth.

"Delicious," he muttered as he absently wiped his mouth.

He made a small slit in his wrist. Fresh energy flooded Aria when his blood quivered on the edge of his arm. She tried to shove herself up and away from him, but he grabbed her hair, yanked her back, and shoved his wrist into her mouth.

Much to her utter disgrace, and shame, tears slid free and rolled steadily down her cheeks. She hated herself for the show of weakness, hated him even more for pushing her to such a level. She simply couldn't take the taste of his blood in her mouth anymore or the volatile response her body had to it.

She gagged, choked, sputtered and finally retched, but nothing came up as he released her. She managed to restrain her tears, though they still burned her eyes as she wiped at her mouth.

The king bent before her; his eyes were level with hers as he studied her. "I see now what it is my son saw in you; you are a delicious little treat." His gaze raked disdainfully over her. "I never thought it was because he desired your body, a fact we both know to be true, right my scrumptious?"

Aria couldn't bring herself to think about the time she'd spent with Braith when he'd held her, kissed her, loved her, and fed on her. She couldn't think about the bond his father was maliciously trying to soil.

Her blood wasn't the reason, she told herself. That is *not* why Braith kept her around, and it was not why he would come for her. No matter what this man said, her blood wasn't the only reason Braith loved her.

Her entire body throbbed as blood seeped over her arms and legs. Though he had concentrated on mainly biting her in the areas Braith had, he'd left far more marks on her than Braith. At one time, he'd even struck up and down her arm much like someone eating an ear of corn.

Always, just when she was about to pass out from loss of blood and torture, he forced more of his blood into her to revive her, heal her, and bring her back for more. She didn't know if she could take much more of this; her skin felt as if someone had taken sandpaper and rubbed it over every inch of her. The mere thought of being touched made her want to scream. No matter what he did to her though, she would never tell him the answers he sought.

His finger slid under her chin, and he turned her head toward him. She itched to smack the smile off his face as he peered intently at her. Aria recoiled when his hand enclosed her breast and squeezed. He laughed cruelly when a small gasp of pain escaped her.

"What fun we'll have together when he gets here," the king murmured.

She almost yelled at him not to touch her, but she knew what he truly craved was a reaction from her, and she refused to give it to him. She would like to believe she would *never* give him the satisfaction, but this was merely the beginning of what he planned on doing to her and Braith.

She thought she could get through almost all of what he would do to her, but could she handle what he would do to Braith if he were caught? Could she watch Braith turned into a dried-up husk of a vampire like the ones crowding this appalling room?

And that might very well be the kindest thing his father did to him. What would she do if Braith was caught and forced to watch as this man and his revolting son violated her over and over again? It would destroy them both, far more than being bled dry and used as ornaments would.

Biting her bottom lip, Aria was able to suppress a small moan of torment as he lifted her hand and turned her wrist over. She was raw everywhere. His fingers ran up, and down the tender marks, he had left on the inside of her arm. He stopped and wiggled his fingers over the mark on the inside of her elbow. His eyes gleamed with amusement as he pressed down on the bite, causing her to wince as he continued to torture her.

He chuckled as he repeatedly pressed up and down her arm. She wasn't sure how but she managed to keep her face impassive. The less reaction she had though, the crueler he became until he was pinching her skin. Bruises appeared almost instantly as he spitefully twisted the flesh around each of the bite marks he'd placed on her. She was unable to suppress a low whimper when he poked and prodded with ruthless glee. His merriment faded at her cry, and he thrust her arm away in disgust.

"Take her back to the dungeons," the king commanded.

"Wait, father," Caleb protested as two of the king's men came forward. They clasped her arms and lifted her roughly to her feet.

"You can play with her later, Caleb. There are things we must discuss now."

58

She found no relief at this short reprieve; she'd prefer to get it over with rather than having it go on endlessly. The guards hauled her from the room and down a set of steep, winding steps.

She struggled to keep up with them, but her feet wouldn't cooperate with her mind. She tripped, fell, and was dragged before she was able to gain her feet once more. It did little good as she was unable to stay on her feet by the time they arrived at the stairs to the dungeon.

Her toes agonizingly bounced off the steps, and her teeth chattered as she was propelled downward. They arrived at the bottom and were pulling her forward when something caught her attention. Fresh life streamed into her; a strangled cry escaped as she found the strength to jerk back from the guards. One guard's hold momentarily slipped from her as she lunged forward and seized the bars of a cell.

"You bitch!" she spat. Lauren cowered further into the back of the cell as she watched Aria like a mouse watched a cat. "Was it worth it?" Aria demanded. "Was it?" The guards tugged at her, but she clung to the bars. "You better hope I get a chance to kill you before Braith does!"

The guards finally succeeded in prying her free; one of them chuckled as he hauled her past the rest of the cells. "Those are some pretty idle threats little girl, considering you're in here too."

"Maybe we can set up a fight between them," the other one pondered.

Their eyes lit with the possibility. "I think the notion would tempt Caleb."

Aria jerked her arm free when they walked her into her cell. She glared at them as they slammed the door into place.

"My money's on that one; she seems a little feral."

"Aren't they all feral in the woods?"

"Go to hell!" Aria snapped.

"Blondie wouldn't have a shot."

They both laughed as they made their way back out of the dungeon, taking the only source of illumination with them as they went. Aria turned before the light was gone entirely, and using her blood, she marked the wall.

She'd been here for three days now, or at least as far as she knew it had only been three days. She may have lost a day somewhere between the pain and blood loss, but she'd been conscious for at least three days in this cell.

Darkness descended over the dungeon. She rested her hands against the back wall and inhaled small, shuddery breaths. Now that the astonishment over seeing Lauren was starting to wear off, the weakness and fright were creeping back in.

She couldn't let herself think about being trapped within this tiny cell. Aria was afraid she would lose her mind if she did, afraid she would become the shriveling, begging mess the king was trying to turn her into if she focused on the walls surrounding her.

She had survived three days already; she'd be able to survive for as long as it took Braith to come for her. He would come; she knew it, just as she knew he wouldn't be the same as when she saw him last.

The Braith out there now was not the Braith she'd left in this palace months ago. He was more in control, more aware, just as she'd hoped he would be without her. Even though he hadn't come charging in here like a crazed demon, she didn't doubt his love for her.

Being in here, tortured and tormented, wasn't going to change her belief in him. She knew he was going crazy without her and beating himself up over what happened. He was probably impossible to be around, but he'd finally accepted that she couldn't always be first to him.

He would lead after the war; he wouldn't turn away from it

anymore. She may still have to leave him, but she wouldn't do it behind his back, not again.

Aria wished there was a way for her to escape before she became a liability. She paced restlessly around the cell. She'd spent three days here, knew every square inch of it, but still, Aria searched for something she might have missed.

After an hour of searching through the darkness, she came up with nothing like she always did. Frustration filled her as her hands fisted. When they removed her from here, two guards would take her to be scrubbed clean before bringing her to the king.

Though the guards didn't watch as she was cleaned, two vampire women stayed with her while the servants cleaned her. From the washroom, she was taken straight to the king.

It wasn't a lot to work with, there weren't many opportunities to escape, but if she bided her time and played meek, maybe they would present a chance for her to break free. The helpless act hadn't worked on Braith, but she had a feeling his father thought a lot less of her than Braith did, and that would be the king's downfall.

Braith would come for her, but she'd give him a hand in helping to free her. First chance she had, she was going to fight for her freedom.

Her forehead fell against the cool wall. For a moment, when she closed her eyes, she could almost feel the outside, almost smell the woods, and almost taste fresh air within her lungs. She could almost feel *him*. The gentle caress of his fingers against her face, the strength of his body when it enveloped her, the sweet taste of his blood when it filled her were all right there, almost within her grasp. She trembled with her need for him.

She hoped she'd get the chance to see him again and that they both weren't killed before it happened.

CHAPTER SEVEN

BRAITH HELD the torch Jack handed him as he waited for his brother to ignite it. Gathered on the hill, were thousands of men and women, vampire and human, working together for the same cause. Braith never thought he'd see the day, let alone that he would be the one leading the charge to defeat the king, but life was never what he expected it to be and all the surprises were what made the pain all the better. As long as he got Aria back.

"Will Melinda know we're coming?" he asked Ashby.

"I'm sure the flames will tip her off," Ashby muttered.

"Let's hope so."

The heat from the torch licked against his skin and warmed the side of his face. With a flick of his wrist, he tossed it into the stack of wood they had gathered at the top of the hill. They were nearly to the edge of town when the scent of smoke began to fill the air, and the first shout went up.

His vision improved a little the closer they moved toward the palace. He lit another torch and tossed it into a stack of crates next to the bar, the only building still showing signs of life at this late hour. Jack and Gideon lit two more torches and tossed them into the hay piled near a store. Fire licked up the buildings; sparks shot high into the sky as more screams and shouts of warning filled the air.

People blinked against the sleep clinging to them as they emerged from their houses. The glow of the fire lit their glossy-eyed and slack-jawed features as they gazed around them. Others scurried frantically around the street as they tried to get their bearings in the pandemonium.

He spotted some of his father's soldiers amongst the growing fire, but they were too flustered by the flames and trying to put them out to worry about what or who started them. Braith turned away from the town and slid back into the serenity of the woods.

He rejoined David, Frank, and the remaining humans. Saul, Calista, and Barnaby were already leading the first wave of humans and vampires to the main gate. David, Frank, Jack, and Ashby would lead the second group to the palace gates shortly. It would take a lot of force to get the gates open, but Braith was hoping they could take them down swiftly from within once he found Aria.

If they could get to the king quickly, many lives would be saved. The king's soldiers would fall apart if their leader were brought down. Their numbers weren't as strong as his father's, but they had the element of surprise and determination on their side.

He clasped hands with Jack and patted him briefly on the back as he wished him luck. David embraced his sons; the three of them huddled together, talking in subdued tones as they hugged each other again. David had wanted to go inside after Aria, but he agreed it was best for him to lead the rebel humans that were still a little uncertain about the truce with the vampires.

Though all he wanted was to be inside the palace, Braith waited while they said their goodbyes. Aria would kill him if she knew he rushed this moment when it could be their last together.

When they were ready, Daniel and William followed him as they split off from the others and headed into the lower lying woodland with the soldiers in tow. He'd chosen vampires from the outer towns for this mission. They knew the woods better, and were far more adept at moving through them quietly, than the occupants of The Barrens. Keegan plodded soundlessly at his side, he'd tried to get the wolf to stay in the woods, with his newfound life, but his old companion stuck to him like a tenacious burr.

William and Daniel stayed at his side, as silent and fleet as their sister as they moved through the woods. But then, if Xavier's suspicions were right, they would be. They had also all been raised in the woods, Braith reminded himself as he slid down the side of a small hill. They were at home in the forest, comfortable and assured in their environment; at one with it.

He'd yet to see either of them exhibit quite the same abilities as their sister, but then again not many people wanted to run and jump through trees as Aria did. He also hadn't spent anywhere near the same amount of time with her brothers as with her.

The closer they got to the palace, the more acute his vision became. His skin tingled with excitement, with need; they were getting closer to *her*. Though he could see better, it still wasn't his sharpest sense.

Closing his eyes, he tuned his other senses into the world around him. All the smells and scents drifting over him were familiar. He sensed nothing around him other than the usual creatures stirring in the night.

He heard the river moments before the fresh scent of water washed over him. The muted croak of frogs filled the air, and a small splash alerted him that the fish were jumping after the bugs. He slid down another hill, but this one was the river embankment. Holding up a hand, he waited as the soldiers gathered around him. He listened to the sounds of the night before continuing onward.

The frogs continued to croak, but a few jumped into the water as he waded into the shallows of the river. Keeping his feet planted firmly on the river bottom, he moved unerringly through the cold water as it reached his waist. The men followed behind him, and what little sounds they made Braith was confident could be passed off as fish and frogs.

There was a dip in the river most wouldn't have noticed, but Braith took it as a sign to climb back out. He didn't require his eyes to know they had reached the mountain the palace was carved into a hundred years before the war even started. It had been risky to undertake such a massive project, but his father refused to be swayed from his decision to create a home fit for a king, even if he hadn't been one at the time. Braith realized belatedly that his father built it to have more security for the war.

He climbed over three rocks before arriving at a large boulder set against the side of the mountain. Grasping the stone, his shoulders bunched and heaved as he started to lift the ten-foot-tall and six-foot-wide rock out of the way. It creaked and groaned as it slid to the side, revealing the small tunnel he had carved into the mountainside.

Braith hadn't created the tunnel because he thought one day he would attempt to take down the king, but because he expected the king to try and kill him after being blinded. Just to be on the safe side, Braith spent almost two months carving this tunnel from his apartment to the river flowing from the palace's interior. He was sure the other tunnels within the palace would be guarded or blocked now, but he didn't think this one would have been detected.

He wiped the sweat from his brow as he set the boulder down and took a step back.

William let out a low whistle. "Remind me not to piss you off."

"You already have a time or two."

William quirked an eyebrow as he chuckled. "Runs in the family, I'm told."

"That it does," Braith agreed.

His eyes picked up details of the tunnel from the little bit of light filtering in behind him as the soldiers followed him into the dark and dank cavern. He turned sideways through the twists created within the easiest areas for him to carve through.

At seventy-two paces, he knew it was time to start crawling. He pulled his glasses off and tossed them aside; they would only get in his way from here on out. Keegan went in front of him as he eased onto his knees and worked his way into the confining tunnel.

Using his fingers and toes, he pulled himself up through the rock tunnel as he pushed Keegan before him. The faint drip of water reached him; the cool walls dampened his thin clothing and caused it to cling to his skin. The passageway became more challenging to navigate as it grew steadily steeper in its upward slope.

Stones that were knocked lose clattered against the tunnel sides as they fell away. The men behind him were not as quiet as they had been in the river, but he hadn't expected them to be, not in here. Thankfully though, their grunts and scrapes were muffled by the rock of the mountain.

At the count of three hundred and two, the tunnel gave way. He placed his hands on each side of the opening and pulled himself into the wider space. The air flow was better here, and a slight breeze cooled his sweat-slicked body. His body began to pulse with the anticipation of seeing her as he moved quickly down the passageway.

After another sixty-seven steps, he arrived at the wall. Taking a moment to steady himself, he gathered full control of his senses as he tried to rein in the excitement tearing through him. He placed his hands against the wall and pressed an ear to it. Most of the other tunnels had small eyeholes to look out of, but there had been no reason to create one here.

He strained to hear, strained to sense if there was anything out there. His body stilled, for a moment there was nothing around him as he opened himself to the world beyond and tried to absorb the details of it. There was no way to know for sure, but he didn't pick up the presence of anything other than the bodies surrounding him.

Stepping back, he pulled down the lever he'd created. The back of the bookcase gave way with a small groan that set his teeth on edge. He was prepared for a fight as he stepped into the ruined library that used to be his. When his vision flooded back to him, it was nearly as acute as if Aria were standing beside him again.

"How FAR CAN you shoot that thing?" Jack inquired.

David's smile was grim, but his green eyes sparkled. "How far do you need me to shoot it?"

"Over the top of that wall." Jack lit the rag tied around the tip of the arrow and took a step back.

"I didn't know you planned to burn the palace down."

"I don't, but I do intend for them to open those gates and smoking them out seems like a good way to start the process. Fire when ready."

David leaned back on his heel, raised the bow and fired the arrow. It soared high into the air and hovered for a moment before falling into the abyss beyond.

"Another!" Jack called as exhilaration filled him.

More cloth was brought forth to wrap the tips of the arrows in. Jack eagerly lit them as David and five of his followers began to fire them rapidly over the wall.

The flames sparked as the arrows became a dazzling source of illumination against the night sky. The sparks reminded him of the flickering glow of fireflies on a hot summer day. The association seemed out of place amidst the death and mayhem surrounding them, but he couldn't shake the hope it brought with it.

Shouts rang out from inside the palace walls; more soldiers disappeared from the walls to handle the spreading fires leaping up the other side. Ten vampires ran past him, the trunk of one of the large trees they had chopped down was hefted between them. They were at full speed when they smashed into the solid gates of the palace with the tree.

They fell back beneath the force of the blow, and another group raced past to batter the entrance with another massive tree. More yells rang out from within the fortress, and the mass outside was forced to give way to the onslaught of deadly arrows raining from the sky.

They'd tried to gather as much armor as they could before attacking, but metal was scarce. Most vampires were bare, and the humans weren't in much better shape. Cries erupted from the group as humans and vampires were brought down by the projectiles. The copper tang of blood mixed with the smoke and ash swirling about them.

Behind him, the flames of the town caused sweat to bead on his neck and wet his shirt. People raced about, screaming and shouting as they tried to make sense of the chaos engulfing their town. The soldiers guarding the town were beginning to regroup as they prepared to launch an attack from the back, but the fire had cut off any chance the soldiers would have of escaping or trying to lay a trap for them if they were forced to retreat.

He'd always suspected Daniel was a genius; now he was sure of it as the flames continued to spread and cause chaos.

"Ashby, we need men behind us!" he called.

Ashby glanced at him from around a wave of arrows raised to fire another round. Ashby stepped back from setting them on fire to peer down at the town below. He nodded briskly before gesturing toward Calista and Barnaby. They took some of the militia with them as they pushed toward the back of the group, preparing to take on the soldiers gathering at the bottom of the hill.

Jack didn't like that their attention was now divided, but they'd known the guards in the town wouldn't be distracted by the fires forever. He could only hope they'd bought Braith enough time to have entered the palace already and that the other soldiers would soon be making their way inside after him. Jack was distracted by an echoing shout, and a loud bang as another tree rammed into the gates.

"Fire!" Jack shouted.

Another wave of arrows rained down from above as answering flames soared into the air. Jack jumped to the side in time to barely avoid being taken out by one. David grunted beside him and fell back as an arrow pierced through his shoulder. Jack grabbed for him, but his hand was knocked aside when an arrow shot through the center of it.

A hiss escaped him; his teeth clenched together as he snatched the shaft and ripped it from his hand in one sharp, jerking motion. He had no time to the blood flowing from it as he grabbed David and pushed him back from the onslaught of fresh arrows.

David's face twisted as his lip curled, but he managed to reach up and break off the tail end of the arrow. "I'm fine!" he yelled at Jack over the rising noise of the battle. "It's just bone."

Jack nodded but took the bow from him. Even if it wasn't a

mortal wound, there was no way David was going to be able to fire anything over the top of the wall. Jack took up the stance David had taught him and placed an arrow against the bow. With a trembling hand, David ignited the cloth for him.

Raising it, he aimed the arrow over the wall but failed as it bounced off the top of the battlements and spiraled back to the ground. He cursed as David shook his head and lit another arrow for him.

"Put some of that vamp strength behind this one, Wimpy," David told him.

Jack scowled, but he leaned back and fired the arrow with a lot more force. This time it cleared the high walls and sailed into the courtyard of the palace.

"Back away!" someone shouted as a sudden influx of soldiers lined the walls.

The troops outside the gates fell back as a fresh wave of arrows cascaded down upon them. A shout rose from the back. Jack had to strain to see over the sea of heads surrounding him as he turned to look behind him.

More soldiers had filtered out from the alleys and homes not on fire within the town. Jack suspected that, much like the tunnel only Braith knew about, there were also a few only the king did, and he had used one of them to establish more of his troops secretly within the town.

From the back, his father's soldiers released a loud battle cry as they charged up the hill. With a sinking feeling in his stomach, Jack realized they were pinned in between the soldiers behind and above as more arrows released on them.

CHAPTER EIGHT

MUFFLED shouts echoed from above as the sound of running feet pounded over the stone ceiling above her. Aria's head followed the sounds; her heart did an odd little skip in her chest as her throat went dry.

Moving to the front of the cell, Aria's hands curled around the bars as she strained to hear what was going on. She'd never hated the bars more; Aria wished she could rip them from the wall or bend them out of her way so she could crawl free of this awful place. She had to fight the urge to stomp her feet and scream like a two-year-old.

"What's going on?" the disembodied voice floated through the darkness from the cell to her right.

"It's Braith," she whispered.

Saying the words aloud made them real. Saying the words aloud confirmed the bubble of hope building inside her at the same time apprehension swelled within her. He was *here*, he was in danger, and she was trapped, unable to break free, and of no use to him. If she was there, she could help him.

"I'm sure you want that to be so child—"

"I'm not a child!" she snapped. "I *know* it's so. He's come; he's here."

"Do you really think so, Aria?" Mary whispered.

"Yes."

There was a collective inhalation of breaths, and then Lauren began to sob. Aria thought she should feel some pity; instead, all she felt was the hard rock of resentment festering inside her every time she thought of the girl.

Aria moved away from the bars; she peered up at the dark roof as she followed the running as far as she could. She felt like a caged animal as she paced within the small confines of the cell. If he were in the palace already, he would find her soon.

Though they had hoped the influx of another vampire's blood in her system would dilute Braith's ability to track her, she knew they'd been wrong. His blood was alive and well within her, it pulsed and surged with every beat of her heart. Even if the king could track her now too, the king's blood hadn't diluted Braith's blood; no ones could.

Aria flew back to the bars as the door at the top of the stairs creaked open. Anticipation hammered through her, she longed for it to be Braith. She ached to touch him, to feel him, to have him erase the hideous taste of the king and ease the awfulness of these past days. She needed him nearly as badly as she needed air at the moment. She clung to the bars and tried to peer up the stairs as a torch was brought forth.

Slowly her hope dissipated. This vampire was all wrong. She knew it before the glow of the torch hit the bottom of the well-tailored pants, knew it before the firelight played off his chest and face. It wasn't Braith who had come for her first.

Caleb lifted the torch higher as Aria fought the urge to slink into the shadows and hide in the back of her cell. She had nowhere to hide, and her self-respect refused to let her cower from him.

He'd never brought her down here, never pulled her from the filthy depths; he didn't know what cell she was in, but it wasn't going to be difficult to find her. She didn't shrink away from the bars, but she also wasn't going to call out, 'Right here, here I am!'

Caleb thrust the flame forward as he peered into each of the cells. He paused outside of Lauren's cell and his mouth twisted into a cruel grin. "How do you like being back in the palace, dear?"

Bitterness erupted through Aria. She didn't like Lauren, but she despised Caleb's cruelty more. He didn't wait for an answer as he continued onward before stopping in front of her. The fire played over the planes of his face as he studied her with a malicious gleam in his eyes. She tilted her chin up and glared at him as his smile widened.

His eyes roved leisurely over her body as he licked his lips. "Hello, kitten," he purred. "It seems as if big brother has arrived, and our time together is going to become truly pleasurable. I'm sure Braith is going to love watching."

There was a loud inhalation from the cell beside her as the man's hands appeared on the bars. Keys jingled as Caleb pulled them from his pocket. Aria gulped. They had already enjoyed tormenting her, but now was when they would begin to torture her to punish Braith.

Though she tried to fight it, a small tremor crept through her body. Her gaze darted frantically over the cell once more. Even with the illumination, she was aware there was still nothing she could use as a weapon outside of herself.

Caleb pulled open the door. "I'm going to enjoy this. Big brother won't, but I am going to enjoy every second of what I do to you." Aria did not doubt it. "Don't make me come in there after you."

"I wasn't going to."

Drudging up every bit of courage she had, Aria stepped from

the cell. Caleb put the torch into a sconce and extended his fisted hands toward her. Her eyebrows knitted in confusion as he continued to grin at her.

"Pick one," he said.

She'd played this game as a child, with her father and brothers, but she most certainly didn't want to play it with Caleb.

"Pick one!" he commanded when she didn't immediately move.

"What happened to you?"

The question popped out of her mouth. She hadn't meant to ask it, didn't think there was an answer for someone like him, but the words hung heavily in the air between them. She felt his rising impatience as he stepped closer, forcing her back as one of his fists pushed into her ribcage.

"Pick a hand, or I'll break both of yours," he snarled.

Aria felt like disobeying him just to show him she wasn't intimidated, but if she was to have any chance of defending herself against him she required her hands. Plus, she *was* scared of him, it was impossible not to be, the guy was nuttier than an oak tree. She hit his right hand as scarcely as she could.

He laughed as he shook his head and opened his empty right hand. "Wrong guess, kitten. Try again."

Aria somehow managed to keep her chin raised defiantly. The thought of touching him again caused her stomach to somersault, but concern for her life outweighed her revulsion as she brushed his other fist. His hand unfurled.

Aria was too horrified to breathe. In Caleb's hand, glimmering and bright, was a simple golden chain. The kind of chain blood slaves were forced to wear when they went into public, a chain Braith had put on her a couple of times. At least then, she'd known Braith would take it off her. There was no guarantee Caleb would do the same.

He watched her with a calculated malice that made her

realize he had no intention of ever removing the chain from her. His father's blood was inside her, but Braith's blood would always be stronger, and if the king died she would be free again. She didn't know if the chain came free if the owner died, or if it remained there permanently, but she wasn't going to take the chance she would have to wear it for the rest of her life. She'd rather die than have that constant reminder of Caleb.

There would be no waiting for the opportune time; there would be no trying to get her hands on a weapon. It had become apparent *now* was the only time she would have to try and escape.

He dangled it before her like someone teasing a cat with a string, and she suddenly understood his newfound, irritating, kitten reference. Caleb's eyes gleamed; the torchlight caught his teeth, highlighting the canines extended into fangs.

No, Aria thought savagely. There was no way she was going to let this sadistic son of a bitch think he had broken her, or allow him to put that *thing* on her.

Aria dropped her head to hide the rage sizzling through her.

"Give me your hand," Caleb commanded.

Aria stuck out her right arm, trying to appear limp and weak as she kept her shoulders hunched and her knees loose. He was reaching for her, the golden chain dangling by his feet when she seized his arm. He hadn't expected the movement, nor had he expected her to jerk him forward roughly.

While he was off balance, Aria lifted her knee and drove it into his groin with as much force as she could muster. She was glad her brothers had taught her how to fight dirty as Caleb released a low grunt of pain, instinctively grabbed himself and hunched forward. Before he could recover, she fisted her hands and slammed them into his back. A hollow echo resounded through the dungeon room as he fell to his knees.

She wasn't going to give him a moment to recover as she

leaned back and delivered a solid roundhouse kick to his face. His head snapped to the side with a loud crack. Aria didn't hesitate as she turned and fled down the aisle of the filthy dungeon.

"Run, Aria!" Mary screamed, the hysteria in her voice alerting her to the fact Caleb was already starting to recover.

Aria took the stairs two at a time as she ascended rapidly. She was dismayed to realize she was already breathing heavily and her heart lumbered from the effort. The loss of blood, lack of food, and brutality she'd endured had taken far more of a toll on her than she'd realized. A toll she was going to have to do her best to ignore if she were to have any chance of surviving this.

If Caleb got his hands on her now...

She shuddered at the thought and broke it off. Reaching the top of the stairs, Aria grabbed the knob on the heavy metal door at the top and swung it shut. Even though Caleb had the keys, and for all she knew he could get through the door without the key, she was still reassured by the loud click of the lock as she slid it into place and spun away from the door.

"Bitch!" Caleb snarled.

A small gasp escaped her when a hand snagged in her hair. She hadn't realized there was a hole at the top of the door. Caleb's hand cruelly fisted in her hair; she clawed at it and jerked roughly to the side as she tried to force him to release her by pinning his arm awkwardly against the door.

Frustration filled her; her eyes burned as he pulled her head back and bent her neck at an unnatural angle. He may not mean to do it, it would ruin all his plans, but she was becoming increasingly fearful he would accidentally break her neck.

She threw herself forward. Stars burst before her eyes; she could feel the hair ripping from her scalp as she kept her weight shifted forward. Losing her hair was far preferable to losing her life.

A clump of her hair gave way with a wrenching tear that

caused her eyes to burn. She fell forward; her knees and palms stung as they slapped on the floor. Scrambling to her feet, she didn't look back as she bolted down a lengthy corridor. She was completely unaware of where she was going as she fled into the bowels of the palace.

His rooms were much as he'd left them. Trashed. He recalled the last conversation he had with Caleb in these rooms; he'd been getting fitted for his wedding when Caleb came to him. The tailor had been terrified of him, *everyone* had feared him, even Caleb, and rightly so as he'd been an out of control, bloodthirsty monster after Aria left him.

But that conversation with Caleb had pushed him over the edge. Aria had been spotted, in a cave, with another man. He now knew the other man was William, but at the time Caleb's revelation had sent him into another frenzy.

He'd already destroyed his apartment once after discovering her gone, but this time he'd ripped it to shreds. Braith knew the damage he'd done, he'd been there for it, but this was the first time he witnessed it.

He'd gone to the dungeons after with the goal of sating the beast within him, but he never made it there. He'd finally given up his pride, vowed to hunt her down, and make her pay for turning him into this insatiable monster. Instead, she'd quenched the savagery within him.

Now he was standing here, back in the rooms where it all started, and he could feel the rising bloodlust pulsing through him. This time though, only death would satisfy him.

William let out a low whistle as he stepped over some broken furniture. "Your father has a temper," he muttered.

"I did this."

William's mouth dropped. "Why would you... Aria."

"Yes."

Braith nodded to the soldiers and picked his way carefully through the debris littering the floor. He could see, but he still relied on his other senses the most right now. He would hear and smell the enemy before he saw them.

The sitting room was in much the same condition as the living room, and he knew without having to see it that the room Aria spent the majority of her time in was the most devastated. He'd tried to destroy anything with her exquisite scent on it, anything she may have touched, but he hadn't been able to bring himself to ruin it all.

"Wow," Max breathed.

He didn't look back at them. Braith was not proud of what he was then; he had despised the lack of control consuming him and the death and misery he rained down on the innocent. He couldn't take it back though, and right now he welcomed the thrumming power that came with letting the darkness creep in to retake control.

He stepped into the room that was Aria's when she first arrived. He wasn't at all surprised to find the tunnel near the bed barricaded. He suspected at least part of the tunnel was demolished. He refused to look at the nightgown spread out on the bed as he turned on his heel and left the room. Keegan remained at his side as he made his way into the central living area.

At the door of the suite, he pressed his hands to the wood and his eye to the peephole. He saw nothing out there and sensed no one as his hand rested on the knob. He turned it bit by bit and stepped into the hallway. There was no one about, but he could hear running footsteps in the massive foyer below and shouts echoed off the cavernous walls.

Some walls broke the openness of the hallway before him, but for the most part, it was an open balcony to the main entryway below. They would be far too visible to the soldiers and people beneath them. Unfortunately, it was also the fastest way to the dungeons.

He turned and went the other way, disappearing deeper into the palace as he moved toward the servant's corridor. It would take longer, but this part of the hall was hidden in shadow and sheltered from view by massive walls. He had to turn sideways to make it down the stairs at the far back of the hall.

It didn't become any more comfortable as he finally stepped out of the stairwell and into the hallway the servants used to transport supplies and where they had their rooms. A man, stepping from his room, spotted them.

His mouth dropped as recognition lit his eyes. "Intru—"

Braith snagged him and snapped his neck before the man could finish his shout of warning. Daniel let out a low curse as William made a strangled sound. He turned back toward them. Max had his bow raised; to Braith's surprise the arrow wasn't aimed at his heart, but at the human he'd destroyed.

They stared at each other before Max grinned at him and lowered the bow. He didn't know when it occurred, but Max seemed to have started to put some trust in him. Or if not trust, Max had at least decided Braith would be the one to get Aria back.

Braith stepped negligently over the servant's body as he continued down the hall. The further they moved down the hall, the more candles started to cast shadows on the dark rock wall. Though the palace had electricity, his father had never installed it in these lower areas as a way to exert his control and torment the servants forced to reside in the dark.

The hallway opened as they stepped into a room filled with tables and a large stone fire pit at the end. Burnt logs were still in the pit, heat radiated from it but no servants were lingering around it. Everything seemed to be going to plan, but he couldn't shake the sinking sensation in the pit of his stomach.

He had to find Aria; he'd be able to think better and be less on edge if he could see and hold her right now.

He moved faster as they accessed another small hallway and the staircase leading to the lowest bowels of the palace, the dungeons. Even as he took the stairs, he knew something was wrong. He knew before he saw the ruined dungeon door Aria wasn't within the dark cells below. A low growl escaped him; his hands trembled as he pulled the heavy metal gate away from where it had fallen across the bottom of the doorway.

A snarl curled his upper lip as he bypassed the steps and leapt into the depths of the dungeons below. The smell hit him first. He had been here before, had drawn people from here, but he'd never truly noticed the smell until now. He hadn't even noticed it on his victims; he'd been too lost in the madness consuming him at the time.

It engulfed him now with its desolation and dread. Even though he was struck by the sharp scent, beneath it all, he could smell Aria's delicious aroma. She had been here, trapped and ensconced in this awful gloom. This place was everything her woods weren't, everything *she* wasn't. The clamoring madness inside him was briefly pushed aside as a lump formed in his throat.

Sharp gasps accompanied his sudden arrival. People scurried like cockroaches from the light to the backs of their cells. He deserved their terror, there may even be some women still within he'd fed from, but he didn't have time for it.

When he stopped before an open cell door, his hand twisted around the metal frame. He couldn't move as her scent overwhelmed him. He'd known what they would do to her, the abuse she would endure, but the strong scent of her blood slapped him in the face with the harsh *reality* of it.

He ripped the door from the wall with a violent wrench that did little to soothe him. He managed to restrain himself from heaving it at the back wall as it fell with a clattering ring at his feet.

He stepped away from the filthy cell and turned to the man standing in the middle of the one next to Aria's.

"What happened here?" he demanded. The man simply stared at him with a gaping mouth and bug eyes. "Where *is* she?"

Determined to get answers from the man, Braith seized the cell door. He was about to yank it free when a faint whisper pierced the air.

"Max?" Braith's head shot around at the name. "William? Daniel?"

The three of them had crept to the bottom of the stairs; the radiance of a single torch flickered over their horrified expressions as they took in the dungeon. Braith stormed down the hall toward them and the voice coming from their right. Snatching the torch from them, he thrust it forward which caused the woman within the cell to shrink back.

He didn't know if she was one of the women he'd fed from, he hadn't been able to see them, and they'd been a blur of blood that hadn't been nearly good enough. However, the wary expression of the woman made him think she might have been one of his victims.

"Mary." Max was staring at the woman in disbelief as he stepped closer to the bars. "I didn't think you would still be alive."

Her gaze darted to Braith, and her lower lip began to tremble. He might have felt bad, he was sure he *would* feel bad once his panic and wrath abated, but right now all he felt was irritated and incensed.

"Neither did I," she whispered.

"What happened here?" Braith grated.

The woman stared at him with large, frightened eyes. Braith

took a step toward the bars, causing the woman to shrink back further. Max shot him a look as he elbowed Braith out of the way. Braith's jaw clenched, and his hand tightened around the torch; he thought he might have preferred it when Max hated him and went out of his way to avoid him. This side of Max was a little too brazen for his liking right now.

"Mary, was Aria here?" Max asked.

"I *know* she was here," Braith retorted.

William and Daniel shook their heads as they stepped forward. Mary continued to study Braith like he was a hairy spider.

"You really trust him?" she inquired doubtfully.

"Yes. Please, Mary, was Aria here?" Max pressed.

"She was here," she answered after a moment of hesitation.

"What happened?" Braith thrust the torch at one of the soldiers as he grabbed the bars of the cell. "Who took her from here?"

"No one took her." The voice came from the man in the cell next to Aria's empty one. "Your *brother*," the word was spat at him. "*Came* for her."

"Caleb came into the dungeons?" Braith asked in disbelief.

"He did." Mary moved hesitatingly toward the bars. "He attempted to put the chain on her."

A cold chill flitted down the back of Braith's neck as beads of sweat began to coat him. Knowing his brother, Caleb may very well keep it on her until the day she died.

"She got away though." There was amusement in the man's voice, and a few chuckles emerged from the cells surrounding them. "Kicked his ass actually."

Braith didn't know if he was more proud or terrified. He did know he couldn't let Caleb get his hands on her again.

CHAPTER NINE

"CONCENTRATE on the ones behind us; we can take them!" Jack yelled above the twang of arrows and the growing shout of voices erupting from the crowd.

He pushed his way through the horde, heading toward the group that had turned to focus on the enemy approaching from the back. He grabbed Ashby and pointed to the top of the battlements.

"We need to get some men up there," he commanded.

Ashby stared at him as if he'd sprouted a horn from the middle of his forehead. "Jack—"

"Do it, Ashby!" he barked. "We have to keep them occupied if Braith is going to have any chance of slipping in from behind."

Ashby was unmoving before he visibly paled and rushed into the crowd of bodies. Jack could hear him calling for vampires and humans to follow him as he ran toward the wall. David appeared at his side and reclaimed his bow and arrow. He turned and slipped away toward the soldiers encroaching on their backside.

A loud shout rose from both armies as they collided with a loud crash of bodies and metal. Jack grabbed one of his father's soldiers and flipped him over his back. Slamming his foot down on the man's throat, he drove his wooden spear through the man's ribcage and into his heart. The man thrashed for a few moments before going still.

Jack ripped the spear free and turned in time to face the next threat barreling down on him. He spotted Calista within the crowd; blood already coated her dark skin and faded clothing. Calista grinned savagely; thoroughly enjoying the mayhem as she stepped back and heaved her spear at a soldier who made the mistake of thinking she was more vulnerable because she was a woman.

Two of their vampires fell around him, but the tide was turning in their favor as the militia battled through the soldiers with ferocious glee. They wanted this more than his father's men did, Jack didn't think that alone was enough for them to win, but it was enough for them to fight harder.

Assured Calista and the others had this under control, Jack broke into a run as he hurried toward the pack still concentrating on the wall. He snagged a bow and arrows from a fallen human and took up a stance beside the scattered line of archers.

Ashby and the men he'd gathered had managed to distract the attention of the guards on the wall. He hadn't expected Ashby to go up there himself, but he was climbing with a swift and deadly purpose. Someone shouted as one of their men fell from the wall, an arrow embedded at a downward angle through his shoulder. Even before he hit the ground, Jack knew the man was dead.

Another fell seconds later, and then others began to topple off as the king's soldiers turned their attention to the new threat scaling the wall toward them. They weren't going to be overpowered from behind, but unless Braith managed to get his group inside, Jack knew they weren't going to make it into the palace either.

Jack leaned back on his heel, but this time he didn't aim for over the palace walls, but at the soldiers gathered on top. He focused on one about to fire at Ashby and released the arrow. The guard's arrow went astray as Jack caught him in the shoulder.

Hurry, he thought frantically as more of their men fell from the wall and the growing heat of the flames from the town pressed against his back.

UNLIKE BRAITH AND THE KING, Caleb couldn't track her through her blood, but with her pounding heart and noisy breathing, it wouldn't be difficult for him to find her. She longed to pause to catch her breath, and calm her pulse, but she didn't dare stop for even a moment. She had a head start on Caleb, but not much of one, and he was much faster than she was.

His strange humming filled the air as he strolled through the dark halls, relentlessly and unerringly pursuing her. She fell against the wall, wheezing as her legs trembled and shook from exhaustion. She knew she was louder than usual, but she didn't understand how he managed to stay on her trail so easily.

Lifting her arm to wipe the sweat from her forehead, she froze as a small groan escaped her. His blood may not be inside her, but her blood was seeping from the multiple bites inflicted on her. Though most of them had stopped bleeding, there were a few of them still open and raw enough to leave a blood trail behind her. She was ringing the dinner bell, and Caleb was answering it.

He was taking his sweet time because he knew no matter what she did, she wouldn't be able to escape him. Tears burned her eyes; a knot lodged in her throat as she shoved away from the wall. Her teeth grated as she forced her legs to move. She would not go down this way; she would *not*.

"Here, kitty, kitty, kitty." Caleb's taunting voice drifted down the hall.

Aria had never wanted to punch someone more than she wanted to hit him. Rushing down the hall, determined to escape, she wasn't prepared for when the walls suddenly gave out, and she staggered into a sitting room. She stopped, momentarily confused by the sudden appearance of the room within the dark and twisted passages.

"I'm just going to catch you," Caleb called.

She glanced over her shoulder; she could tell by the clarity of his voice Caleb was gaining on her, but she still couldn't see him. Aria bolted across the room, looking for something, anything she could use to defend herself with but there were only three couches and a small table in the center of the room. She wanted to linger longer in the hope she would find something, but there was no time to waste.

Aria hurried past the room and plunged back into another hallway. She was unable to see her hand before her as she rushed onward. She didn't know where she was going, where any of these hallways led, and she didn't care.

She had to stay free of Caleb long enough to find a weapon of some sort or Braith. The sizzling energy in her veins made her think he was also close.

She was deep into the new passageway when she heard voices. She froze as shouts echoed through the narrow halls. She strained to pinpoint the location of the noise, but it was impossible as the shouting vibrated the walls around her.

She stepped forward, and the hand she had braced against the wall fell into nothing. It took her a moment to realize she had come to a crossroads. She was motionless as she tried to decipher which way to go.

Grimacing, she clamped her teeth together as she dug her fingers into the tender bite marks on her inner wrist. Fresh blood welled up and trickled down her wrist to her hand. She moved into the hallway on the right and wiped her wrist along the stones for the first five feet.

She stuck her wrist into her mouth, sucking on it to staunch the flow as she hurried back to the hallway that branched to the left. Aria didn't know if she was making the right choice, but she felt a stronger instinctual pull to the left tunnel, and she couldn't stand there until Caleb found her.

She hoped the fresh blood would draw Caleb away from her, but she didn't count on him being fooled for long. Eventually, he would realize her scent didn't go all the way down the hall. She just hoped she'd bought herself enough time to make some stand against the monster hunting her.

"GIDEON, collect all the soldiers that have emerged from the tunnel by now and take them to the palace gates."

Gideon did a double take at Braith's command. "Braith we should stay with the plan."

"I *am* staying with the plan. The snake needs to be destroyed, and Caleb is the tail."

"But—"

"I am not leaving this palace without her, Gideon, I made that clear before we stepped foot in here. Retrieve the soldiers from my apartment and lead them to the main gate. We must get the outside forces in here, and you will need the group waiting in the tunnel to do so. I will have an easier time surprising my father if I go in with a smaller force. If something happens to me, you should still be able to reach the main gate with the larger force."

Gideon started to protest, but light blazed at the top of the stairs seconds before Melinda plunged into the depths of the dungeons. The torch she held highlighted the planes of her face and her ashen complexion. Her gray eyes fell on Braith, and for a moment color returned to her skin as her shoulders slumped.

"You made it," she whispered.

"What are you doing here, Melinda?"

"I came." Her gaze flitted over the cells before landing on the broken door behind him. "I thought I would try to get to Aria while they were distracted."

"She's gone."

"Ashby." She took a step toward him, the yearning on her face nearly palpable. "Where is he?"

"Outside the gates."

Her face paled; her hand trembled on the torch as her lips compressed. "They're flanked out there, Braith; father had troops moved into the town. They're trapped."

He was still as his mind churned rapidly. He wouldn't be able to take any troops with him to find Aria. Every man and vampire would be needed if they were to succeed in getting those gates open and saving his brother and Aria's father.

It would weaken his chances of getting them both out of here alive, but if they were going to win it was what had to be done. It was not the choice he wanted to make, it was not the choice he would have made a week ago, but it was the choice he had to make now.

"You will take all of the men and go to the gates, Gideon; it's the only element of surprise we have and the only chance we have of succeeding." Braith had expected an argument, but Gideon simply bowed his head in acquiescence. "Melinda, go with them, Xavier—"

"I am staying with you," Xavier stated flatly. "I assume the humans will also insist upon going with you, and you ought to have another vampire at your back." The three humans glared at Xavier but nodded their agreement. "Getting those gates open is important, but keeping you alive is also a necessity. Besides, if we don't survive this, I would like a chance to see the girl and her brothers in action."

"What does *that* mean?" William demanded fiercely.

Xavier chose to ignore him, as did Braith.

"Fine," Braith relented. "We have to go."

"Braith, you... ah, you need to be prepared," Melinda's hesitant words froze his approach toward the stairs.

"Prepared for what?" he growled.

Melinda swallowed nervously as she glanced at Gideon and Xavier, but they remained mute.

"I don't know everything that has been done to her," Melinda said.

William stepped closer to Braith; his eyes narrowed, and his hands fisted as he studied Melinda.

"But she has suffered abuse, and it's very apparent," Melinda gushed out.

He was afraid to move for fear he would rip the entire place down as Melinda's words echoed in his head. He could barely get words out of his constricted throat. "I have to get to her."

"What about us?" the man demanded from the shadows when Braith spun on his heel.

"We'll come back for you," Braith responded impatiently.

"Wait, you can't leave us here!"

He was already moving down the aisle when Max grabbed his arm. Braith almost ripped Max's arm off in his rush to get to Aria.

"Braith, if we lose they'll be trapped here," Max said. "We have to let them out now. This may be the only chance they have."

"We can help you fight them," Mary said eagerly.

"We can't leave them here like this," Max pushed.

He pulled his arm free of Max's grasp and seized the bars of the woman's cell. With a brutal jerk, he snapped the lock on it and pulled the cell open. The woman stood for a moment, her mouth parted as she waited hesitatingly in the shadows.

"Free the others," he commanded gruffly.

He was almost to the steps when he froze, his nostrils flared, and his head turned when he caught a familiar scent. Lauren was cowering in the back of the cell, pressed flat against the wall as she stared at him. She whimpered when he took a step toward her.

"Please don't hurt me," she pleaded.

Braith's gaze traveled over her filthy, trembling body. "Except her; this bitch stays here," he snarled.

William and Daniel glared furiously at the girl, while Max didn't bother to look at her as he led the freed prisoners up the stairs.

"Wait! Please don't leave me here!" Braith turned away as Lauren took a hesitant step toward the door. "I just wanted back in! Please don't leave me here!"

William moved closer to the bars. "If he doesn't come back for you, I will," he assured her.

"I'll be coming back for her," Braith promised.

The feral, fleeting smile William flashed reminded him that her brothers were a lot more ruthless than Aria. Braith climbed the steps to the servant's hall and paused as he opened himself up to the flow of his blood within Aria's veins. Though it wasn't as strong as it had been, he could feel the rhythm of it within her as it pulsed through her veins.

He turned back the way they had come from.

"The scent of her blood goes the other way," Xavier pointed out.

"I can get to her quicker this way."

He maneuvered through the hallways, steadily climbing as rising horror began to pulse through him. Aria didn't know where she was heading, but he did. He was running, not paying any attention to the people he sensed still following him as he burst out of the servants quarters. The kitchens stood before him; startled servants stepped back from the group they'd huddled in.

"Your Highness," a woman blurted as she stumbled into one of the counters. "But... oh."

There had been no avoiding this; the kitchens were the fastest way to get to their destination. He couldn't kill all the servants within the massive room, and truth be told, he didn't want to. It was too late anyway. Aria was on a one-way path straight into the lion's den, and there was nothing he could do to stop it. He could only hope to get there first.

One of the women fell to her knees. Another man knelt, but the rest seemed too astonished by his sudden appearance to do anything other than stand and stare in amazement.

"Do we kill them to silence them?" Max inquired flatly.

One of the servants let out a startled cry as they stumbled into a workstation loaded with more pots and pans.

"It's too late for that," Braith informed him.

"What do you mean?" William demanded. "Does the king already know we're here?"

"No, but we can't remain hidden for much longer."

"Why not?"

"Because Aria is heading straight for the king's throne room."

William tripped and nearly fell as he gaped at Braith. "And that's where we're going?"

"It is."

He strode out of the kitchen, breaking into a brisk jog as his body thrummed with anticipation and bloodlust. She was so close; he could feel her there, just beyond his grasp. Fire licked over his skin with his driving urge to see and touch her once more. He needed it more than he needed blood to survive. He burst into the palace foyer, startling the ten guards stationed outside the throne room.

The guards leapt into action as they jumped forward to try and block him from the room. Braith grabbed one, shoving him back against the door as he drove a fist into the side of another guard's cheek. The man grunted as he fell back beneath the blow.

Another guard shouted as he called for more of his brethren. Braith seized his neck and ruthlessly tore the guard's throat out before he could raise too much of an alarm. An arrow whistled over his shoulder and pierced another guard in the forehead.

Xavier was suddenly beside him as a soldier grabbed Braith's shoulder and tried to pull him back. Braith drove his elbow harshly into the man's chin and snapped his head back. The dull thud of arrows hitting their targets filled the hall, and the shouts died away as Braith took down the last standing guard.

Rising to his feet, he wiped the blood from his face with the back of his arm. He doubted he got it all, but Braith didn't want to be completely drenched in blood when he saw her again. Braith grabbed the handles and flung the massive wooden doors open on the hideous room his father cherished.

The king sat at the end of the vast room, lounging on his throne, and seemingly unaffected by Braith's intention of killing him. He didn't appear at all concerned about the fact his soldiers had just been dispatched of with relative ease as he grinned at Braith and gave a small wave of his fingers. Braith's jaw clenched as he nodded a brief greeting in return.

Even with the light from the massive chandelier, his father had always insisted upon having torches lit across the walls to highlight every gruesome, emaciated, and unwilling occupant of his trophy room. William inhaled sharply, Max's step faltered, while Daniel studied the room with disgust. Keegan growled as he crouched at Braith's side.

"Awful," William breathed.

Braith hadn't seen the room with his own eyes in over a century, but it was as hideous as he remembered. In fact, it was worse. There were even more vampire, and human remains preserved within the room now. He also saw the reason for his father's nonchalant demeanor as guards slipped from the alcoves within the room. They moved noiselessly forward to protect the man they served.

"I was wondering when you'd join us!" his father called to him. "Come closer, son, I think *our* girl will be joining us soon. I sent Caleb to retrieve her for *us*."

Braith's gaze moved over the guards gathered within the room. There were at least thirty of them, and he wouldn't be surprised to learn more were hidden throughout the room. He felt no concern over being outnumbered; he had no fear anymore. He only had the burning urge to have Aria back and the vampire before him dead. He'd kill all these men if that were what it took.

"Is that Xavier with you?" the king asked.

The king leisurely rose to his feet and straightened the rich, voluminous maroon robe he wore. He scanned Xavier from head to toe as his eyebrow quirked, and a smile flitted across his mouth.

"You've sunk even lower than I thought, Braith, if this is the pitiful company you've started keeping. You thought you could beat me with *this* pathetic excuse for a vampire," his father sneered.

Braith refused to rise to his father's baiting. Xavier stepped forward with his hands encased in the sleeves of his robe, and his shoulders were thrust back as he stared wordlessly at the king. Max and William were beside him, but Daniel had moved a little bit away; he seemed oddly fascinated by the withered vampires. Braith had to restrain himself from grabbing the kid and forcing him to stay near them.

"What exactly was your plan here, Braith?"

Aria was close; he could feel she was almost within his grasp. He just wasn't sure which passageway door she would come through as he knew of at least three within the throne room.

"Did you honestly believe you could come in here and what, overthrow me? Kill me? With *this* sad assortment? They're not even all vampires. What were you planning on doing with these humans, distracting me with them as a snack?"

He didn't know what the plan was; he only knew he had to get her out of here, alive, if at all possible.

"They're still alive," Daniel muttered as he hastily stepped away from one of the desiccated remains.

"The vampires are," Xavier confirmed. "The king has always liked his trophies."

Daniel's eyes were huge as his hand twitched on his bow. Braith moved to the side, to step partially in front of Daniel. Daniel was usually stable, analytical, and rational to the bone, but this room seemed to have rattled his restraint completely. Braith was fearful Daniel would do something irrational before they had a chance to get Aria back.

"Where is your poor excuse for a brother?" the king inquired.

"Caleb is chasing down the *human* who escaped him," Braith answered, knowing full well that was not the brother the king meant.

A small flicker of a muscle in his cheek was the only reaction the king had to this revelation.

"Ah, the human," the king purred as he licked his lips. "She is quite the tasty little treat, Braith. I'm amazed by your astoundingly good taste, or should I say *her* taste and your restraint with her. I was unable to be so restrained with such a morsel."

"Easy, Braith," Xavier urged as Max stepped in front of him.

It took all he had not to launch across the hundred feet separating them and pound the smile from his father's hideous face. His vision clouded with red again, and his hands fisted. Father, or not, he was going to enjoy ripping his heart out and stomping on it.

"Yes, Braith, easy. We don't need you getting all worked up

before our girl is here to enjoy it. Oh, the fun we three will have."
The king rocked on his heels as he smirked at them and rubbed
his fingers together before him. "I assume since he isn't here,
Jericho is amongst the group being decimated outside the palace
walls right now."

Daniel and William exchanged an uneasy look.

"I have no idea where Jericho is, and he goes by Jack now,"
Braith managed to grate out.

Braith strained to hear something, anything, outside of this
room. Then he caught a muted scraping of feet and a muffled
heartbeat coming from within the walls. Unfortunately, she was
closer to the king than him.

But even worse was that behind the soft sounds of Aria,
Braith heard the relentless pursuit of someone else.

CHAPTER TEN

JACK STEPPED toward the gate as Ashby breached the top of the wall. Ashby, loveable, affable, carefree Ashby grabbed one of the soldiers and ripped him over the edge without one moment of hesitation. Apparently, there was a darker side to Ashby than Jack had ever suspected as he remorselessly tossed aside more soldiers.

David suddenly appeared beside him again. The blood from his seeping puncture was vibrant as it spread across his torn shirt, but it didn't seem to be slowing him down yet. Another group of vampires ran past and slammed another giant tree into the massive gates.

Though they were solid metal, and at least a foot thick, a wrenching noise alerted Jack to the fact the doors were starting to give way beneath the repeated force of the blows. For the first time, hope flowed through him. They were going to get inside; they were going to do this.

Running across the top of the battlement, Ashby moved swiftly through the soldiers trying to stop him. Ever whistling Ashby continued to toss them aside like discarded peanut shells.

Realization settled over him as Jack finally understood what caused Ashby to become so ruthless. Melinda.

She must be somewhere nearby, perhaps even in peril, and Ashby was going to do everything he could to get to her. With the way Ashby was moving, Jack thought they should have just used an army of vampires who had found their bloodlinks and thrown them into the fray. He suspected they might have won already if that was the case.

Ashby disappeared as he leapt from the top of the wall. The guards stationed on the battlements turned, their attention was divided as they sought to face the new threat from within the palace. Braith had arrived; Jack was certain of it. They'd made it into the palace and succeeded in reaching the front gates.

A hush descended over the battlefield as, for a poignant moment, they waited to see what would happen. A loud shout erupted from within, a few of the guards on the walls broke ranks and ran away; others renewed the fight with fresh vigor as arrows began to fire speedily down on both sides of the walls.

David took a step toward the gates, the look of longing on his face tugged at Jack's heart. Another loud shout echoed from within, flames and sparks leapt higher as something far larger caught fire. A few more guards slipped away from the wall and vanished over the side as a loud groan filled the air.

Jack stilled as the groaning grew louder. He had no idea what to expect and was half certain a mass of soldiers would burst forth to overpower them. The gates, bent and battered from the repeated blows they had sustained, moved agonizingly slow as they were pushed open.

Ashby was grinning from ear to ear as he stepped forward. His arm was wrapped possessively around Melinda. Ashby's gaze skipped over the group before settling on Jack.

"Well come on, you lazy bastard, there's still more of them in here to play with!" Ashby announced jovially.

Jack grasped his sister and kissed her forcefully on the cheek. "Good to see you, sis."

"You too." Though she was smiling, sadness resonated in her eyes.

"Where's Braith?"

Gideon's face was drawn and tired as he stepped forward. Blood coated him, but he didn't seem to be relishing the battle; instead, he looked far more reserved than Jack expected.

"He took a few soldiers with him and went after your father, and Aria," Gideon said.

Jack swallowed the hard lump in his throat as he turned to inspect the group surrounding him. He was acutely aware of the few people who were missing from it, and so was David as he inhaled sharply. They were all damaged and tired, but there was still far more they had to accomplish.

"We need to get to them," David said forcefully.

"Yes," Gideon agreed. "Before they're all killed."

Gideon didn't sound any more convinced it was possible than Jack felt.

ARIA HAD no idea where she was within the convoluted mess of passageways that made up the inner workings of the vast palace. Her shoulders and legs brushed against the walls as she hesitatingly felt her way forward. She longed to move faster, but she was worried about running face first into a wall.

Her fingers brushed against the solid walls surrounding her as she fumbled to find an escape. Caleb must have tracked her into the other tunnel before realizing she'd fooled him as she didn't hear his cheery humming anymore, and he didn't taunt her with calls of 'here kitty.'

She sensed he was behind her again though, back on the right trail, and like a dog on the scent he was homing in on her.

She stopped as her fingers brushed against a wall in front of her. She was unable to understand why it was there; unable to grasp she was now trapped between the wall and Caleb.

"I smell fear on the kitty," Caleb ridiculed.

Taking a deep breath, Aria forced herself to calm down. There had to be a way out, she was sure of it. She recalled Jack finding the secret lever to reveal the hidden passage in the room she'd slept in as a blood slave, and she knew well the intricate traps and unknown releases Daniel designed in the caves. Just as there was always a way out of those places, there was a way out of here; she only had to find it.

She bit back a scream of frustration as her fingers frantically skimmed over the smooth walls surrounding her as she searched for a lever or switch. It wouldn't be so hidden that the servants couldn't find it, so why couldn't she locate the damn thing?

Then her fingers caught on the small lever set at chest height; she pulled down on it and stepped back as the door swung inward. Light descended on her, and for a moment she couldn't see again, but her eyes quickly adjusted to this sudden influx. She was about to step forward when she saw what the open door revealed.

Her mouth was suddenly as dry as The Barrens; her heart lumbered as she stared at the atrocious throne room the king cherished so much. With sinking dismay, she realized she'd leapt out of the frying pan and into the fire.

"Boo."

She cried out as she jumped. She'd been too startled by the realization of where she was to hear Caleb's approach. His word, whispered near her ear, sent a fresh flood of adrenaline crashing through her, and with her hands fisted, she spun to face him. He was better prepared for her this time, but even so, she got in a glancing blow to his chin. He danced back before coming at her again.

With an infuriated cry, she kicked him in the knee with enough force to knock his leg back and pushed herself off him as hard as she could. She was fast, but she wasn't faster than a vampire. She was hoping to give herself a little bit of a head start as she turned and bolted out of the passageway. The king had to be somewhere nearby; she had a feeling he spent most of his time in this throne/trophy/monstrosity room he created for himself.

She bolted into the room, nearly tripping over her own feet as the king's soldiers spun toward her. She froze, her eyes widened, and her mouth dropped when the king turned to look at her. There was a malicious smile on his face as he leered at her with far too much amusement for her liking. Then, over the sea of heads and across the massive hall, she saw *him*.

Her heart lodged in her throat; tears burned her eyes as her gaze clashed with Braith's. The soldiers lifted their spears and moved to block him when he stepped toward her.

Braith's vivid gray eyes became the color of glistening rubies as his fangs extended past his lower lip. Though there were far more soldiers than him, judging by the look on his face he might plow his way through them to get to her.

Arms wrapped around her waist and lifted her up before flinging her to the floor. She cried out when her body bounced off the marble, and her teeth clamped down on the inside of her bottom lip. She had forgotten about Caleb in her astonishment over seeing Braith, but he hadn't forgotten about her.

She scrambled back and tried to regain her feet as Caleb came at her. Braith's ferocious bellow ripped across the room when Caleb seized her arms and yanked her to her feet.

CHAPTER ELEVEN

LEADING the way through the streets, Jack fought off the soldiers coming at them while he tried to avoid the unsuspecting souls scrambling to get out of the way. The only ones he genuinely cared about not killing were the children.

Though some of the king's noblemen resided within the palace itself, most had residences within the large town and bailey outside of it. Jack targeted those residences. He was sure most of the nobles had fled toward the palace when the attack started, but some would have stubbornly remained in their homes.

Wood cracked and popped as flames licked at the stores and homes. The stage where the slaves were auctioned was already fully engulfed. Screams echoed over the cobblestone and down the roads of the town as vampires and humans attempted to flee the devastation.

He wanted to be repulsed by the death, but a part of him was thrilled by the brutality of it. He was surprised most of their vampires were doing so well, especially the starving masses from the outlying towns. There were few here who wanted to win more than the broken masses the king had created though.

Drops of David's blood plopped onto the streets as he fought close at Jack's side. Though Jack had his baser instincts under control, the past few days had been a trying time, and David's blood seemed more distinct than the humans around him. Jack realized he'd never smelled it before. In all their adventures and trials together, David's blood had never spilled before tonight. The man was too quick for that most of the time.

David lifted his bow and fired at a soldier who emerged from the smoke and fire. The arrow pierced deep into the soldier's heart and knocked him back as he kicked and groaned in the final seconds of his life. Though David's jaw was locked, and determination radiated from his eyes, his arm trembled as he dropped it back to his side.

"It is essential you take care of your wound," Jack informed him.

"I'm fine."

"You're not fine."

David shot him a look as he lifted his bow and fired another arrow into a cluster of soldiers. Jack ignored the furious glare his friend gave him as he seized the bow from David.

"Do something about it before you bleed to death," he commanded gruffly. "Your children will kick my ass if something happens to you."

David glowered at Jack as he reached out and grabbed Jack's shirt. Jack wasn't expecting it when David brandished a knife to cut a large piece of cloth from the last shirt Jack had.

Clothing was hard to come by in the woods. Over the years, Jack had become accustomed to the lightweight tunics and baggy pants woven out of flax for the summer, and the heavy woolen articles created for the winter.

David's eyes sparkled as he deftly tied the shirt around his injury and used his teeth to pull the knot tight.

"I liked this shirt," Jack grumbled as he handed the bow back.

"It *was* nice," David agreed.

Jack's attention was diverted from the blood soaking through his friend's bandage when a shout of victory rang throughout the street. He turned to discover that Victor, one of his father's right-hand men, and one of the cruelest vampires Jack ever had the displeasure of meeting, had been taken prisoner.

Victor was beaten and bloody as a group of soldiers, led by Saul and Barnaby, propelled him down the street. Saul stepped back and pointed toward one of the growing fires, and the soldiers pushed Victor into the inferno. Jack didn't feel an ounce of remorse as Victor's agonized shrieks pierced the night.

Rounding a bend in the road, the palace came into view. It loomed over them, ominous and imposing as it stretched high into the night sky. Illumination from the leaping flames of the town shimmered off the pale palace walls as they approached.

Almost there, they were almost there. He could only hope his brother hadn't managed to get himself killed as the massive gold doors of the palace swung open and a new horde of the king's soldiers spilled out to challenge them.

BRAITH COULD BARELY BELIEVE what he was seeing as Aria burst free of the servant's tunnel. Seeming to sense his presence, she turned toward him. Hope and terror radiated from her brilliant blue eyes as she gazed at him. Even filthy, with her hair tangled around her dirt-streaked, porcelain skin, she was still the most beautiful thing he'd ever seen.

Beneath the dirt, he saw the bites, bruises, and blood covering her arms and the column of her throat. He couldn't bring himself to think about where else she might have bite marks, where else they might have touched her, and what else they might have done to her. All he longed for was to get his hands on her again and to get her out of here alive.

If at all possible.

She stepped toward him as Caleb emerged from the servant's quarters right behind her. Wrapping his arms around her waist, he lifted her up and threw her to the floor. Braith's vision became a shade of crimson as a bellow tore from him. He lunged forward, shoving through the guards closest to him as he felt the beast within taking over and all his control slip away.

He was consumed with bloodlust as he jerked a man forward and seized the spear from him. Turning it in his grasp, he twisted it under his arm and plunged it into the vampire's chest. Tearing it free, he drove it into the hearts of two more soldiers closing in on him.

Aria's frightened cry drove him heedlessly onward. All he cared about was getting to her and destroying anyone who dared to touch her. He didn't feel the spear piercing his back and tearing through his shoulder. He didn't know he'd been stabbed until the pointed tip shot out the other side of him.

He tore the spear free as he spun on the two guards staring at him with huge, frightened eyes. He was about to cross that line again, about to completely relinquish himself to the darkness, and he didn't care as he seized them both. He killed the one quickly, almost mercifully, as he grabbed him, slammed his fist into his ribcage and tore his heart out.

The other was not so lucky as Braith spun him around and used him to deflect the four soldiers rushing at him. The man screamed and howled as multiple spears and arrows pierced him. He squirmed within Braith's grasp, but Braith felt no compunction over continuing to use the man as a shield as he battered his way through the crowd.

He lost sight of her as soldiers engulfed him. Something else pierced through his calf, driving him briefly to his left knee. Pain lanced through him, but he forced himself to his feet as the guard he held heaved one final groan and went still in his grasp. Braith used his body to beat back two more soldiers as they lurched at him. He threw the limp body of the dead guard at three more of the king's men and knocked them over.

The soldiers fell back; the crowd parted giving him a brief glimpse of Aria as she tussled against his brother's hold. He grunted as another arrow tore through flesh and bone, ripped through sinew, and clipped part of his heart.

Driven to his knees, Braith felt the rush of blood from the damaged organ as it seeped into his chest. It wasn't a fatal blow, not at his age, not if he could feed soon, but it would weaken him. The guards approached with far more confidence than they had before, and on top of his other wounds...

"No!" Aria's scream was frenzied and raw with terror. "Don't! Stop it; you're killing him!"

Caleb tried to grab her again when she spun on him.

CHAPTER TWELVE

Panic tore through Aria as she watched Braith go down on the marble floor. A scream of anguish ripped from her; she'd never seen so much blood. They were killing him, and he kept trying to get up and reach her. It was becoming devastatingly apparent there were too many of them; the soldiers swarming him outnumbered him.

Caleb grinned maliciously as he grabbed her. Reacting on instinct and rushing adrenaline, she tried to drive her knee into his tender groin region again, but he was better prepared this time. He slapped her fist away from its trajectory toward his face when Aria tried to change tactics. She lunged at him, throwing him a little off balance as she shoved her weight against him.

Every dirty trick her brothers had taught her sprang to mind as she sought to free herself from him. Caleb was expecting her to go for his groin again, and she made a feigning attempt at it. His hands dropped, leaving his face, and her intended area of attack, exposed. Feeling like a crazed woman, she hooked her fingers and went straight for his eyes.

Caleb howled as she drove her fingers into his eye sockets. Aria tried not to think about what she felt beneath her fingers; she simply clawed as ferociously as she could until he threw his arms up and knocked her away from him.

The jarring impact caused her arms to go numb as she stumbled backward. His hands flew to his face, she had not blinded him, but she'd injured him enough that blood pooled from his battered right eye. Aria was not fooled into thinking it would distract him for long.

She clasped both hands into a fist, and with the full force of her weight, she twisted as she swung them upward. She caught him beneath his chin and knocked his head back with a loud crack that gave her a spurt of satisfaction.

Blood exploded from his mouth as he staggered back. Before this, he would have played with and tormented her, but now if he got his hands on her again, he would kill her in the vilest way possible.

She would have to make sure he didn't catch her again.

Aria turned and darted away from him. Her heart hammered as she spotted Braith somehow finding the power to rise to his feet once more and take down two more guards. Pulling one of them forward, he yanked the vampires head back and sank his teeth deep into its neck.

No, Aria moaned silently. *No, no, no.*

She may be too late, she realized. She may have already lost Braith to the monster he could become.

She threw herself forward, rolling across the ground as she avoided the searching grasp of one of the guards. Grasping a spear, Aria staggered back to her feet as she ran for Braith; adrenaline and terror gave her a speed and strength she didn't know she'd possessed until this moment.

She didn't know if it was the king's blood, or her driving need to reach Braith, but all her other injuries and exhaustion were forgotten as a strength she never knew she could possess surged through her.

Toward the back of the room, she spotted her brothers, Max, and Xavier. They had already been taken down; bloodied and beaten they were on their knees, surrounded by guards, close to the elongated tableful of the king's horrible "guests." Her chest constricted as she realized she was about to lose almost *everyone* she loved today.

Keegan raced around Braith, biting and snarling as he forced some of the guards back while dodging the weapons thrust at him. Braith tossed aside the guard as he rose to his feet and lurched toward her.

A soldier, who had the misfortune of getting in his way, was easily disposed of as Braith broke his neck and tore out his heart. Aria heaved the spear at another guard, driving it deep into his chest. The man's eyes bulged as he clutched at the wooden pole protruding from him.

She ripped the spear free as Braith went down again, an arrow protruding from his torso. She was dimly aware the soldiers must have orders to take them alive; otherwise, they would all be dead by now. Braith was powerful, and the bodies of the soldiers he'd destroyed littered the floor, but ultimately he was outnumbered. She was quick, she had caught Caleb off guard, but she was still human.

But then none of it mattered as she was almost *there*. She could practically feel him again. She barely spotted the guard who stepped in front of her even as she heaved the spear at him. It was off the mark as it pierced his throat, but it still knocked him away as he fell back against two of his cohorts.

She fell to her knees; tears burned her throat as she flung herself into Braith's open arms. A sob tore from her; she'd never felt anything as magnificent as his body molded perfectly against hers. Her fingers clutched at his back as his love enveloped her.

He bent over her, clasping her tightly as he cradled the base of her head against his chest and buried his face in her hair. She couldn't get enough of the feel of him.

"Arianna," he groaned, his lips were warm against her ear.

The relief and pleasure in his voice almost undid her as her hands rapidly fluttered over him. They were going to die, but at least they would have this moment, this one last time, and she so desperately needed it as she clung to him.

She wished she'd never listened to Jack, Ashby, and Gideon and tried to distance herself from him. She'd been foolish to think she ever could have let him go, or that he would be able to do the same.

Holding him now was the best thing she'd ever felt. She'd never thought to experience love in the first place, never mind *this* kind of love, with him, a vampire who had taught her there was far more to life, and the world, than she'd ever imagined.

She was in love with this beautiful creature who had taught her not everything was black and white, good and evil. There were shades of gray, there were in-betweens, and there were colors she'd never dreamed of. Colors that Braith had shown her in the garden, worlds, and experiences he'd opened to her when he taught her to read, love he'd given to her freely over and over again with his understanding, patience, and countless sacrifices he'd made for her.

Now they were here, back where it all started, and where it would finally end one way or another.

"You shouldn't have come." She buried her face in his neck; she couldn't get close enough to him.

"I will always come for you," he vowed.

Yes, he would. No matter what Gideon and the others

thought, he would always come for her, and she would always welcome him. Aria would have pretended she didn't want him to find her and would have stayed strong because she believed she was doing the right thing. However, she continuously would have hoped for him to find her, and she would have been waiting for him.

"You shouldn't have brought them," she said.

"I could no more have stopped them than I could have stopped you if the roles were reversed."

A harsh laugh escaped her at the truth of his words. "My father is okay?" she asked worriedly, though she knew he would have had to lead the humans into battle.

"He was fine the last time I saw him."

From the corner of her eye, she saw the soldiers narrowing in with their weapons raised with deadly intent. Her fingers trembled; she should pull away, but she couldn't bring herself to let him go. Not yet, she wasn't ready to say goodbye.

"Hold."

She was dimly aware it was the king who spoke the word, but she didn't care about the reason why he had chosen to give them this reprieve. She was sure he had some ulterior motive, but the king didn't matter, the men surrounding them didn't matter, not anymore.

Warm wetness pressed against her skin. She didn't have to pull back to know Braith's blood was soaking through his clothes and into hers. Another small sob escaped her; she clutched more frantically at him.

"Don't leave me," she whispered.

"Never," he groaned against her ear. "No matter what happens I will always be with you, Arianna. Always."

His shirt collar was growing wet with her tears.

"Always," she breathed.

His lips pressed against her ear, her cheek, and then his

mouth was on hers. It was meant to only be a chaste, loving kiss, one of goodbye, but the minute his lips touched hers, her body reacted as if lightning had stricken it.

She flattened against him as waves of passion and love cascaded through her, leaving her boneless and limp. She clutched at him, torn between wanting to scream from the injustice of it all and wanting to rip this room apart with her bare hands.

Unfair, it was all unfair. But life was unfair; she'd always known that, but she'd hoped this once it would work in their favor.

No matter what happened after, she would have the memory of this kiss and the taste of him. She would always have these few short moments and their love to help get her through it. She'd be strong no matter what they did to her. The king and Caleb would never break her; never beat her into the weak little human they thought her to be.

Braith broke away; he was shaking as his hands cradled her face. She lifted her eyes to his, relieved to see the beautiful gray and blue color she cherished so much. He pressed another tender kiss briefly against her quivering lips.

"I love you," he whispered.

More tears spilled free as she pressed her cheek against his and delighted in the feel of his stubble roughened cheek. The sweet scent of his blood swirled up to fill her nostrils. Horror filled her as she looked down. He was dying; she was certain of it as the stain of his blood spread across his solid chest and torso. Her large, powerful, magnificent vampire was gradually dying before her eyes. He seized her hands when she fumbled to try and staunch the flow of blood.

"I'll be okay love, don't worry about me."

"No," she whimpered, knowing he lied. "There's so much."

"The guard's blood helped some."

Her hands shook in his; she couldn't unclench her fingers from his to hug him once more. His gaze scanned her face, neck, and arms as his eyes faded back to a ruby shade. When he let himself go he was more destructive, more powerful; he could feed on his kind and be a monster like his father.

If he gave himself over to the darkness within he may even be able to get them all out of here, but at what cost? Would she ever get him back? She'd rather die than lose him to such a fate, to see him become as twisted and broken as his father and brother.

"Stay with me," she whispered. "Don't go there, Braith, don't let me lose you that way."

His eyes came back to hers. They shifted from that awful ruby color to a shade partially red and partially blue. That beautiful blue band around his iris surrounded by a murderous scarlet was disconcerting, but she could at least see *him* beneath it now.

She leaned toward him and pressed her lips to his as she slid her hands free of his grasp. She moved her lips unhurriedly over his as she realized what she had to do. She recalled Ashby's words from the tree house when he'd spoken of his bond with Melinda; we are stronger because we drink from each other. She traced the much-loved planes of his magnificent face.

"Love me, Braith; stay with me."

"Always," he vowed again.

Gently pressing her lips to his one more time, she turned her head to the side and guided his head to her neck. "I can make you stronger."

He hesitated; she felt his desire to recoil as clearly as she felt his hunger for her blood. He didn't hesitate because he was repulsed by the marks on her or the flow of the king's blood within her veins, but because he was frightened she couldn't handle any more blood loss.

He could become a monster to try and get them out of here,

or he could accept the gift of life she was offering him as freely as she offered him her love.

"It's okay; I can handle this. I know I can; *you* know I can," she said.

His hand cradled the back of her head as the other flattened against her back. His mouth pressed against her skin; a soft breath escaped her as his lips pulled back and she felt the hard press of his fangs.

Her raw skin caused her to wince as he bit deep, but the pain was fleeting, and the pleasure of finally joining with him again swirled inside of her. She fell into him as she was lost in this exquisite moment, perhaps their last.

Heat flooded her extremities; it pooled through her body and moved out from her heart as his love consumed her. The intensity of the emotion left her trembling, and shaken, but also stronger.

Awareness began to grow in her. Ashby had said he didn't know why the bloodlink between vampires made them stronger, but Aria understood it now.

It wasn't only the sharing of blood between such mighty beings, though she knew the strength of their blood was part of it, it was also the love and trust so freely given amongst creatures who seldom allowed themselves to be vulnerable to someone else. She wasn't a vampire, but she made Braith more powerful simply by loving him, by accepting his love in return, and by nourishing him with the blood he craved most.

She also understood something else; she wouldn't lose Braith. He wouldn't be overcome by the darkness and anger rolling through him. Anger he'd always harbored toward his cruel and heartless bastard of a father; a darkness that broke free of him every time he felt her life was in jeopardy.

He could lose himself, but he wouldn't, not with her here to help pull him back. Even now, in the middle of this whole mess, there was still hope, and a growing understanding of who she was, of who he was, and what they were together.

She knew because she knew him, that whatever happened from this point on, he wouldn't be driven by fury and hatred, but by love. And love was by far the stronger motivator. It was something his father would never understand, and it was their most powerful asset.

CHAPTER THIRTEEN

BRAITH EMBRACED her as her blood flowed freely into his mouth. She smelled of the dungeon, but beneath the stench of that hideous place he detected her natural, sweet essence as it flooded his senses and invaded his body. He could taste his father within her blood, and though he knew he should be infuriated by it, all he could find was relief, pleasure, and all-encompassing love that left him shaken.

He'd thought he'd lost her, and yet she was here, in his arms, holding him as she offered herself with the ease only she could. He heard the steady thump of her heart, felt the tears wetting his neck as she pressed her face against him, and tasted the power of her blood as it infused him. The knick in his heart sluggishly repaired as her blood worked to heal him.

He unhurriedly pulled away from her and nuzzled her neck before leaning back from her. Her tears had left streaks through the dirt marring her delicate cheeks. Her eyes fluttered open; their crystalline sapphire depths shimmered with unshed tears.

The love in her gaze humbled him and made him stronger as it radiated like a brilliant ray of sunlight. For her, he could do anything; even retain control when he was so close to losing it. If this were to be their last moment together, he would make sure she never saw the monster inside him again.

"Impressive, son," his father said.

He grasped her cheeks when she moved to face the king. He didn't want her to see the bastard again, not right now. "Look at me. Focus on me, Aria."

"I won't let them take me alive," she whispered.

"They won't take either of us alive."

She swallowed heavily and closed her eyes as she nodded briefly. He savored the sight of her before turning toward the king, the man who had fathered him but failed to turn him into the son he'd wanted him to be.

"Very impressive. I am actually proud of you for the first time," the king murmured.

The king spread his hands out to indicate the bodies littering the floor around Braith. He had managed to take down a good fifteen soldiers before Aria reached him. Caleb stood before the dais and his father; his forehead furrowed as he stared at them with glowing red eyes. Blood still stained his cheek, but the gouges Aria inflicted had healed. No, there was no way he would allow Caleb to get his hands on her again.

"I never knew you had it in you. It is her, isn't it? *She* is what makes you stronger?"

Braith held Aria's head still when she tried to look at his father again.

"Her blood is what makes you like this. I think there's a *link*." The word hissed out of the king as he stepped forward. "After what I've witnessed, I think I'll keep you both alive and use her to keep you under my thumb. You would be my greatest weapon to control and use as I saw fit, even against the forces trying to take me down now."

So that was why the king told his troops to hold, Braith realized. He'd wanted to know the lengths Braith would go to for her. He had needed to see how much he could control Braith by controlling her, and Braith had played right into his hands. He'd shown his father exactly what he was looking for and hoped to learn.

"I bet you'd even kill Jericho if it meant keeping her alive," the king said.

Aria inhaled sharply, her tears wet his fingers as he held her still.

"I'll make her watch as you destroy everyone and everything she loves, for her."

Braith would destroy himself first. "That will never happen."

The king grinned at him as he gave a brief nod of his head. "I want them alive."

The soldiers started moving in to shatter their moment of solitude in this brutal place. He turned his attention back to Aria. "Stay behind me."

The wild grin she shot him made him realize she would do no such thing, not his Aria. He grabbed her and wrapped her in his embrace as he launched to his feet. Her blood had renewed his strength and revitalized him in ways the guard's blood never could.

He hadn't taken enough to impair her, but even so, he bit into his wrist and offered it to her as he spun her away from the onrushing guards. She seized it and pressed it firmly to her mouth with an enthusiasm that surprised him.

She eagerly swallowed before releasing him. He reluctantly let her go to face the soldiers rushing at him. From the corner of his eye, he saw Aria leaping forward with the grace of a deer as she dashed to a spear discarded on the ground.

Snagging it off the floor, she spun with an eerie elegance toward the soldier charging at her. Her throw would have been lethal if the guard hadn't sidestepped the weapon at the last second.

Braith grabbed the two closing in on him. He snapped the neck of one with a brutal jerk before ripping the spear from his twitching hands. The man wasn't dead, but Braith didn't have time to finish the job as he drove the spear deep into the other guard's heart and pulled it free.

Aria ducked beneath the grasping hands of the guard. She moved so quickly even Braith didn't notice the broken end of the spear she'd managed to plunge into the man's chest until the guard fell back.

She ran toward her brothers and Max. Braith kept an eye on the guards encircling them as he deliberately moved back with her. Three more guards launched themselves at him; he fended them off as he fell back, determined to keep his body between her and the king. It would be Aria his father went for first, Braith was sure of it. Keegan leapt before him, growling and snapping as he forced one of the guards away.

Max, William, and Daniel launched forward suddenly. They shoved their shoulders into two of the guards watching over them as Xavier jumped to his feet. A guard grabbed William by the neck of his shirt and plunged a spear into his right leg. William shouted before his scream broke off and he grasped his thigh. Sweat beaded his forehead and upper lip, his face went deathly pale as he tried to rip the spear free.

Fury darkened Aria's features. She switched directions as she raced toward the man who maimed her brother.

"Aria!"

The shout came from Max as he managed to grab a bow and a quiver of arrows. He tossed them toward her before being beaten back by a blow that echoed throughout the room and probably knocked more than a few teeth loose.

Aria slid across the floor on her knees; she snagged the bow and arrow before leaping to her feet. Braith had no idea where she was going, or what she had in mind until she jumped onto the lap of one of his father's trophies, climbed onto the table, and launched herself at the massive, dark wood beams running across the rounded cathedral ceiling. She hung for a moment before swinging her legs up and catching the beam. Pulling herself up, she sat briefly on top of the beam before leaping to her feet.

She was back in her trees, Braith realized as she dashed across the wood.

Braith wasn't surprised some of the soldiers had stopped to stare at her as she leapt from beam to beam toward her brother, Max, and Xavier. Even the king was watching her with assessing, shrewd eyes.

Braith met Xavier's gaze over the crowd of soldiers. Xavier's dark eyes closed as he bowed his head to Braith and gave a brief nod. Braith didn't know if relief or anguish filled him at Xavier's confirmation of what he suspected about Aria.

But he did know they had to survive this before anything could be discussed or decided.

Braith shoved another guard out of his way as he struggled to get to the others. Aria jumped to another beam, leaned back on her heel and fired two arrows at the guard who stabbed her brother. He fell back as another guard snagged Daniel and hauled him to his feet.

Xavier was a man of books and histories, but even so, as the guard jerked Daniel up, Xavier grabbed him and slit his throat with deadly ruthlessness. Xavier pulled Daniel free and finished the guard with a killing blow to his chest. Pushing Daniel behind him, Xavier seized Max as the three of them were forced back beneath the crushing wave of the king's men.

Daniel tried to snag William, but the spear through his leg made it nearly impossible for him to move. Aria covered her twin by firing at any guard who dared approach him.

Braith leapt over the bodies of two fallen guards. Seizing William, he tried to lift him from the ground, but part of the spearhead was embedded in the marble. William released another shout which was eerily echoed by Aria, as Braith ripped him free with a merciless yank that tore muscle and bone.

William's fingers dug into his arm; his lip bled from biting into it, but he didn't offer a complaint as Braith shoved him at Max and Daniel. Something pointed and rigid pierced his shoulder; a ferocious growl escaped him as he spun back on the guard who shot him with an arrow. He leapt forward, looking to bring the man down, but an arrow pierced the man's chest before Braith could get to him.

Aria nodded as she smiled fleetingly at him. Turning to face the new wave of guards coming at him, he braced himself for their impending attack. An arrow whistled past his ear, and Daniel and Max jumped into the fray beside him as they attacked the soldiers with spears and arrows. Xavier hung back, protecting William as others poured forth to try and get at the injured human.

Keegan raced around the guards, barking and snarling as he forced them back from Xavier and William. A shrill yelp escaped the wolf as a guard managed to deliver a solid kick to his ribs that knocked him back a good five feet. The guard went after Keegan, but William had managed to retrieve a bow and fired an arrow through the guard's heart.

They were putting up a good fight, but Braith knew they would eventually be beaten down by the multitude swarming around them. Using his shoulder, Braith rammed back three more guards and dodged three arrows aimed at him. One clipped across his bicep, but it was only a flesh wound and would heal quickly. He managed to rip a spear and some arrows free from one of the men and threw the extra arrows up to Aria. She knelt down and snagged them out of the air.

Braith speared three more guards and released a series of punches on one of them that left his face battered beyond recognition. He ripped the spear free, falling back as more guards pressed against the five of them. Aria leapt to her feet; her eyes were riveted on the front of the room as she turned to face the throne. Braith fended off the guards, as he fell back toward the table to see what held her so enraptured and what had caused her to look like she'd seen a ghost.

Her eyes clashed with his as she gestured toward the front of the room. Braith leapt onto the top of the table in one bound. Staring over the raucous filled room, he watched in disbelief as Caleb, using the distraction of the battle had circled behind the king and was now closing in on him.

Braith stepped toward the dais as his brother sprang forward and shoved a spear through the king's back and straight into his heart. Blood pooled at the corners of the king's parted mouth as his eyes widened. His hands clawed at the spear; a strange guttural sound escaped him as his knees began to buckle. Caleb grinned at their father as he turned slowly toward the son who committed patricide with seemingly no remorse.

'It may be harder to take Caleb down now that he realizes he is the heir apparent.' The words, spoken so long ago by Melinda, floated across his mind.

As Braith watched his father fall he realized even in his death, his father was proudest of the offspring who had destroyed him than any of the other children he'd created.

Caleb ripped the spear from his father's chest and stepped forward to take his place before the throne he had just claimed as his own. He bent and pulled the royal ring from his father's lifeless hand and unhurriedly slid it onto his index finger. His eyes gleamed with pride; a malicious smile curved his mouth as he held his hand out before him and wiggled his fingers admiringly.

Braith had no love for his father, would have taken him down himself if it meant protecting Aria, but even so, loathing and vengeance flashed hotly through his belly. He would have slain his father, but he would have taken the man head on, he wouldn't have been as cowardly as Caleb had just been.

Caleb continued to bask in his moment as he lifted his head to survey the room that was now his. He smoothed the front of his black shirt and idly scanned the motionless crowd.

"Kill them." The command, almost nonchalant and flippant didn't immediately get the stunned soldiers moving again.

Their king had fallen, and a new king, one more ruthless and sadistic, had stepped forward to take his place. Even if they'd been trained their entire lives to one day follow Braith, Caleb's slaughter of their ruler had just earned him the throne.

"Except the girl, keep her alive if you can." Caleb lifted his head to survey Aria. "I have some truly magnificent plans for her."

A chill crept down Braith's spine as he met Aria's gaze. Her face was pale; her eyes shadowed and haunted as she stared back at him. She would never allow herself to be taken alive again. No matter what it took, he had to keep them all alive until Jack could get here, *if* Jack could get here, with the reinforcements.

The room erupted into violence again as the soldiers lurched forward to obey their new king's command.

CHAPTER FOURTEEN

ARIA FORCED herself to take a deep breath and steady her shaking hands as she pulled an arrow from the quiver. He'd murdered his father. Caleb had just killed the man who helped create him, who raised him and molded him in his image.

She shouldn't be surprised. She'd spent a fair amount of time in their company these past few days and knew there wasn't anything they weren't capable of, but she couldn't shake the disgust and horror ensnaring her.

The worst part was now *that* hideous spawn of the devil was the new king.

Struggling to keep her composure, her wounded middle finger gave a twinge she ignored as she placed the arrow against her bow and fired at a soldier narrowing in on William. She didn't think about William's suffering; she couldn't right now. Not when their death order had just been handed down. The arrow pierced through the vampire's back, driving straight through his heart as the man fell forward.

Max charged forward with a loud bellow and threw his shoulder into one of the soldiers closing in on William. Xavier grabbed the spear that was knocked free and used it to batter back three guards trying to get at Daniel as he hurriedly tended to William's wound. Keegan, seeming to sense William's extra need for protection, stayed close to his side.

Aria rapidly released a flurry of arrows on the soldiers focused on her brothers. She wished she could offer cover for Braith too, but he seemed to be handling the soldiers trying to get at him reasonably well from his elevated position on the table. Her brothers were unprotected, vulnerable, even with Max and Xavier trying to battle back the men bent on destroying them. Aria fired two more arrows; there were only five left in the quiver Braith had tossed her.

Her gaze ran rapidly over the hall; she *had* to find something else to use. A loud shout jerked her attention back to the battle below. Blood seeped from a deep cut on Max's cheek; his shirt had been torn open to reveal his firm chest and the blood welling from his flesh. Aria clenched her jaw and fired an arrow at the vamp closing in on him. The guard jerked forward before keeling over from the fatal blow.

Max nodded a brief thanks to her before turning his attention back to helping Xavier. Five soldiers surrounded Braith, she managed to take one of them out, but another one quickly replaced him. Terror tore through her; there were too many of them, it was only a matter of time before they were overwhelmed.

Caleb stepped casually over the body of his father as he climbed down the steps of the dais. Taking a steadying breath, the world around her went strangely silent as she focused her entire being on Caleb and fired an arrow straight at his already cold and deadened heart. At the last second one of the guards dove forward and threw themselves in between Caleb and the arrow.

Caleb's head tilted back, a wicked grin curved his mouth as his lips pulled back to reveal his elongated fangs. Aria met his gaze, refusing to back down, refusing to cower from the twisted perversion within his eyes. Then, ever so deliberately, he tilted his head and nodded toward where she had last seen Braith.

Braith was being pushed back by the wave of soldiers pressing against him. She fired three more arrows in rapid succession, killing two guards and knocking another one away from Braith. There were only two arrows left; she'd have to make them count.

Adrenaline pounded through her as Braith was maneuvered toward where Max and Xavier stood before Daniel and William. They were going to die. She was about to watch the people she loved most be slaughtered right in front of her. Caleb passed beneath her beam as a grunt of pain escaped from Braith. Heart hammering, panic drove her as she scurried across the beams toward a flag hanging above the king's throne.

She knelt on the beam and stretched out as her fingers fumbled for the tip of the flagpole. She nearly tumbled from the beam as she lurched forward, but managed to catch herself by locking her ankles around the solid wood at the last second.

Her hand snagged the pole, and she jerked it free of the wall. She barely glimpsed the king's coat of arms, with a red dragon on it, as she fell forward, spinning around the beam to dangle by her ankles for a heart-stopping moment.

Taking a deep breath, she used the pole to help shimmy herself back around. The wooden flag handle was solid and reassuring in her grasp. She longed to sit for a moment and steady her shaking muscles, but there was no time. Her legs trembled as she pushed herself back to her feet and hopped her way back toward the fray gathered around Braith and the others.

Soldiers parted from around Caleb, stepping back to allow him access to the people they had herded into the back corner of the room.

They were going to die; Caleb was going to kill them all.

Desperation drove her as she lifted the pole up and smashed it as forcefully as she could against the massive beam. The force jolted her arms and hands but the pole splintered within her grasp. It wasn't much, but it was far better than nothing.

She placed it onto the beam, and drawing out her last two arrows, she fired them with deadly accuracy into the soldier closest to Daniel and the one nearest Xavier, as they were the two being most threatened right now.

She tossed the useless bow aside as Braith seized one of the guards by the throat. He drew him abruptly in, and for horrifying moment Aria thought he was going to lose himself in the darkness again, but he lifted the guard instead and threw him into the soldiers encircling them.

Xavier lurched forward, stabbing the spear deep into another soldier and forcefully thrusting him back. Daniel managed to get William onto his feet and had him propped against the wall behind Daniel and Max's back.

Their shoulders heaved, all of their faces were bruised and battered, their blood and the blood of others coated them, but they still looked prepared to continue the fight as they raised their meager weapons. Aria hefted the broken spear; she rotated it in her hands as she moved to the place where she had climbed onto the beam. Bending low, she was about to leap onto the table when the doors on the other side of the room burst open.

Aria gawked as Natasha burst through the doors with Jack, Aria's father, and the others hot on her heels. The aching tension in her muscles eased as she rose to take in the new melee erupting in the room.

King's soldiers and militia converged with a loud clash of metal and shouts of wrath and pain. Aria recoiled from the violence reverberating through the room and the blood so ruthlessly and methodically shed, but she welcomed the hope the new arrival brought with them.

The attention of Caleb's men was diverted as they were torn between pursuing Braith and trying to fend off the new threat pouring into the room. Calista surged to the forefront as Natasha attempted to flee the invading army. Calista grabbed the vampire woman and brought her down beneath her. Aria had never liked Natasha, but that didn't mean she wanted to witness her death either.

Aria turned away before Calista delivered the final blow. Daniel, Max, and Xavier leapt forward as the guards encircling them were distracted by the troops flooding the room. She was bracing herself for the leap down when Braith appeared beneath her.

His face was bloody, his plain forest clothes were torn and ragged. There was still a hole in his chest and stomach, but he appeared to be healing rapidly. Though she sensed violence in his set shoulders and locked jaw, his eyes were not red as they met hers.

"Stay up there!" he barked.

Aria bristled over his command. He didn't give her time to protest though as he began to push and fight his way toward Caleb. She was about to ignore him, about to jump down anyway, when she froze.

If her capture had taught her anything, it was that she had to think before acting, and she sensed this was one of those times when it was best for her to stay out of the way and not plunge into the fray. She would only be a distraction to her family and friends, and especially to Braith. Her rebellious nature struggled against her decision, but she managed to restrain herself.

Through the mob, Aria spotted her father by the doors of the massive throne room. There was a bloody bandage wrapped around his shoulder, but he appeared unhindered by the wound as he fired an arrow and killed a guard lurching at him. Relief filled her; tears burned her throat as he lifted his head and spotted her across the crowd. They exchanged a brief smile and a wave before the crush of people once again swallowed him.

Her attention was brought back to Caleb as he attempted to lose himself in the press of bodies while the two sides hacked and stabbed at each other with ruthless intent. Aria wasn't about to let him get away that easy though.

She followed him across the beams as Braith tracked him on the ground. The tide of the fight seemed to be turning in their direction, but it was still far from over as Caleb barked orders while retreating toward the table, and then onto it. Aria realized only too late what he was doing, what he intended. He'd never been fleeing but heading towards something.

"Braith watch out!" she screamed above the incessant din of the room as Caleb seized hold of a bow and arrow and took aim at Braith.

Braith twisted to the side, barely dodging the arrow Caleb shot at him. A loud roar escaped him as he finally broke free of the crush and bolted toward his brother in a blur of motion. Caleb fired another arrow that Braith snatched out of the air and tossed aside. Caleb threw the bow uselessly at Braith and braced himself for the impact.

Aria winced as they collided with a thunderous shout and the loud crack of at least one broken bone, though she didn't know who had suffered it. She didn't want to look, but she couldn't take her eyes away as they fell on top of the table, pummeling and tearing at each other with a ferociousness that rivaled two alpha wolves fighting for dominance.

All their hatred toward each other erupted in a violent battle that shattered the plates, crushed and bent the golden goblets, knocked the candle holders over, and toppled a few of the poor souls trapped within the chairs.

They rolled across the table as they punched and kicked and scrambled to stay on top, to remain in control, to destroy the other. The guttural, animalistic noises coming from them were unlike anything she'd ever heard and hoped never to hear again.

Braith healed fast but he was still impaired, and Caleb had been feeding better than he had. But even so, it appeared Braith was winning as he leveled Caleb with a brutal blow that caved his cheekbone. Caleb howled as he clawed at Braith's face, trying to tear at his eyes as he fought to escape Braith's devastating punches.

Nausea twisted in Aria's stomach. This is war, and it's brutal, she reminded herself. She'd done her fair share of killing today, but what was between them was something more than the war surrounding them. This violence had been building for centuries and was finally being released in a torrent of blood and loathing.

Caleb somehow managed to twist in Braith's grasp and dodge the next punch. Braith's fist slammed into the massive wood table; the harsh sound of cracking bone was distinct even over the raucous of the room.

Braith cursed loudly; he jerked his broken hand back as Caleb thrust his fingers into Braith's Adam's apple. Braith was thrown off enough by the switch in attack methods that Caleb was able to get his legs in between them and push Braith off. Braith fell back on the table as Caleb scrambled out from under him. Caleb staggered to his feet, nearly fell over, but somehow managed to keep his balance as he grabbed one of the torches in the sconces above him.

A cry of horror escaped her as Caleb thrust at Braith with the flame. Braith jerked back as the flames caught at the tail end of his shirt. He slapped at the fire, beating them out as Caleb launched at him again.

Knocking the torch aside, Braith seized Caleb's arm and jerked him forward. Caleb managed to dodge Braith's punch, he slammed his shoulder into the lower part of Braith's chest and propelled them both across the table.

They tumbled over, bouncing across the hard surface before spilling onto the floor beneath her feet. Braith seized Caleb's shirt, lifted him, and smashed him into the floor. Caleb was stunned for a moment, but then he rapidly kicked out at Braith as he was lifted high again. Aria had been so focused on the fight between them that she didn't notice the soldier coming up behind Braith until he smashed a club off Braith's back.

A cry of distress tore from her as Braith pitched forward beneath the force of the blow. Braith spun as the guard went back at him with the club raised high and a malicious gleam in his eyes. Grabbing the club, he ripped it from the man's hands and swung it across his face.

While he was distracted, Caleb threw himself at Braith's back. The knife he brandished gleamed in the light of the room. Braith knocked his hand aside, blocking Caleb from slitting his throat completely, but Caleb was still able to cut him. Blood spilled forth as Braith's sliced skin began to bleed profusely, and more guards encircled him.

She had relented and stayed aloft, but there was no way she could stand idly by and watch Braith be murdered in cold blood. Her gaze fell on the piece of broken flagpole she had left behind, and she scurried back to it. The ominous feeling she may already be too late gave her a burst of tremendous speed as she propelled herself back toward Braith.

Braith was struggling against two guards when Aria launched herself off the beam at Caleb. There was a moment when it almost felt as if she were flying, almost felt as if Braith would die while she was suspended like a feather in the air. And then, finally, she was falling.

Caleb staggered beneath her as she crashed onto his back and nearly drove him to his knees. He somehow managed to catch his balance as she wrapped her legs around his waist and clenched her thighs against his sides.

With a ferocious cry, she lifted the makeshift stake above her head and plunged it down. Caleb's skin and bone gave way with a loud crunch beneath the fractured wood as she drove it through with a strength born of terror and love. His legs gave out as the pole broke through his ribcage and pierced the other side. Even before she saw the angle of the pole, she knew it hadn't been a direct blow to his heart.

A howl escaped him as he jerked back and tried to throw her off, but Aria adhered to him like burdock to cloth. She bit back a cry of agony and frustration as he clawed at her over his back, tearing her arms open but not slicing as deep as the creatures from The Barrens. Caleb beat at her, catching the corner of her eye, and splitting her lip as she tried to keep her face shielded from him.

Suddenly Braith was before them. She'd never seen him look this feral and lethal, but with an air of control he'd never possessed when her life was threatened before. His eyes, as they met hers, were not rubies. Instead, they were a piercing gray that touched the very core of her soul with their beauty. She knew, without words, without a gesture or move, what he wanted her to do.

A final burst of energy poured through her as she leapt off Caleb's back. Braith lunged forward and grabbed her around her waist. Pulling her protectively against him, he slammed his right hand into Caleb's chest. An inhuman wail escaped Caleb; he reared back beneath Braith's assault as Braith yanked back with a mighty heave. Aria turned away and buried her face in Braith's neck as Caleb's wail increased in frequency before silencing completely.

She shook against him, clinging to his solid frame as he held her flush against his side with her feet dangling in the air. His hand trembled as he brushed the sweat-dampened strands of hair back from her face. She didn't even care he was touching her with the hand that had destroyed his brother as she lifted her gaze to meet his frantic eyes. She simply stared at him while she basked in the feel of him.

A small breath escaped her; he was the only thing she could see, the only thing she could feel as he kissed her firmly, bit into his wrist and offered his blood to her. She stared at it for a moment before snagging it and pressing it to her mouth.

She eagerly swallowed, pulling his blood into her body as she tried to rid herself of the awful taste of the king's blood staining her tongue and throat. The sweetness of his blood, the pureness of it flowed into her, healing her at the same time it helped to purge her system.

He kissed her forehead as he stepped back from the table and turned her into the shadows of an alcove. Aria gradually became aware of the hush around them, and she released Braith's arm. Her hand pressed into the hollow of his back as she leaned around him to survey the room.

The few soldiers continuing to fight were swiftly being taken down. It seemed that when Caleb died, most of the king's remaining soldiers had given up the fight. They were pushed against the opposite wall, their weapons on the ground at their feet and their arms raised in surrender.

There was a new King now.

"Are we safe?" she whispered.

Braith's lips were warm against her ear as he bent his head to hers. "Yes. You are safe now, Arianna."

Aria's heart hammered, and her hand clenched on his back, she didn't want to let him go, but she had to.

Her grip on him eased as he slid her to her feet. Bodies littered the ground; blood splattered the floor, walls, and fighters who remained. She somehow managed to keep from vomiting as she surveyed the carnage.

Jack momentarily came to the forefront; he gestured frantically for Braith to join him. Foreboding filled her as she took a step toward the large group. Braith seized her face, turning her away from the casualties strewn about the room and spilling into the hall beyond the massive doors.

"I have to help them." She managed a small nod as his eyes raked her face. "I need you to stay here, Aria. Please, do as I ask until everything is secure."

She should help, but the idea of plunging into that pile of dead bodies was more than she could tolerate right now. The thought of finding one of her loved ones amongst the dead caused her stomach to twist into knots.

It may be cowardice, but she couldn't face that possibility right now. They were all right; they had to be. She just couldn't see them right now through the crush of humans and vampires filling the room.

"I will," she said.

He kissed her before reluctantly releasing her; he grabbed a bow and a mostly empty quiver of arrows from the body of a dead guard. Aria accepted the blood splattered weapons. She took a step back as she watched Braith disappear into the swell of bodies. Though she didn't relish the thought of killing anyone else, she pulled an arrow from the quiver and rested it against the bow as she searched the crowd.

She finally spotted William leaning against the far wall with his bow and arrows. Aria tossed the bow over her shoulder, grabbed the quiver, and bolted to the top of the table. Some of her dread and queasiness eased as she moved further away from Caleb's body.

William glanced briefly at her before focusing on the group of soldiers being restrained by Braith and the others. Landing beside him, she took reassurance in his presence as her fingers entwined with his and he pulled her close for a hug. Aria fought back the tears as she embraced him.

"It's good to see you," he told her.

"You too."

He released her and fell back against the wall to turn a watchful eye back on the crowd. "Don't do that again."

"I'll try my hardest not to."

He smiled at her as he lifted an eyebrow. "You do have a habit of being vampire chow."

"Haha," she muttered. Her free hand fell to Keegan's head as she wordlessly thanked the wolf for watching over her brother. "Are you okay?" She warily eyed the bloodstained bandage Daniel had hastily wrapped around his thigh.

"I'll survive."

"That's reassuring," she told him.

"Are you okay?"

"Yes."

His eyes ran over her as he tried to judge the truth behind her answer. It seemed as if he was trying to see into her soul, trying to see what had been done to her, who she was now, and if she would ever be the same. Nothing would ever be the same, but some things would never change.

"I'm okay," she said.

His gaze raked over Caleb's ragged claw marks, and the raw bites covering her arms, collarbone, and neck.

"Really," she insisted.

His eyes, so similar to hers, met and held her own. "He deserved what he got, Aria."

He knew her so well, so unbelievably well. Caleb had deserved what he'd gotten. He would have done far worse things to her and Braith, but she couldn't rid herself of the feel of his body lurching beneath hers. Aria braced herself as she turned to survey the survivors. It was nearly over; she should feel more excited, she merely felt sick and desperate to see her family.

"Where are Daniel, Max, and Xavier?" she asked.

"They went to help in the fight."

"Have you..." She had to swallow before she could continue. "Have you seen them? Dad?"

His eyes closed as he gave a small shake of his head. She was finding it difficult to breathe as she blinked back the tears burning her eyes and focused on the group before her. Jack and Ashby had joined Braith in front of the remaining king's guard.

Most of the king's men had dropped to their knees at Braith's approach, but a few remained standing out of sheer defiance. For the first time, she noticed Melinda pressed against Ashby's side, she looked almost as shell-shocked as Aria felt as she leaned against him.

Over the sea of heads, she spotted more fighters on the other side of the massive doors opening into the hallway. Aria held her breath as she took a step forward. That was where they had to be, her dad had been near the doors, and the others must have fought their way out the doors and were now helping to oversee things in the hall.

Calista and Gideon appeared from the hall and encircled Braith and Jack. Calista gestured toward the doors as Gideon solemnly bowed his head. A frown creased her forehead as Jack turned and bolted toward the doors. Seizing her arm, William halted her as she took another step forward.

Dread curled through her stomach when Jack began frantically tossing aside fallen bodies. Braith was at his side in an instant; they shouted something to each other that Aria couldn't discern above the roar of blood pulsing through her ears.

Aria's gaze flew over the crowd; she spotted Saul and Frank, but where were her father and Daniel? Where were Max and Xavier?

Her heart hammered as her throat went dry. Something was clawing at her insides, something hideous and frightening; something that made it difficult to breathe as Jack tossed aside another crumpled body.

Jack froze; his hand stilled in midair as a look of despair crossed his and Braith's faces. Aria shook off William's weak grasp as she took another small step forward. She couldn't see what they were looking at; there were still too many people moving in and out of her line of sight.

Aria's hand moved slowly to her mouth; she couldn't breathe as the room lurched sickeningly. William leaned on a spear for support as he stepped beside her. Daniel burst free of the crowd in the hall, Max and Xavier were close on his heels while he shoved past some of the restrained guards.

A scream lodged in Aria's throat; her paralysis broke as she bolted forward. William lurched awkwardly after her, trying and failing to grasp her as she sprinted toward Braith and Jack.

Braith's head shot up as she heedlessly charged through the crowd. Braith jumped over the bodies scattered around him, rushing to meet her as she raced at them. His arms encircled her waist, and he lifted her high. The cry she'd been unable to release before finally ripped from her throat.

"Daddy!" she screamed as her heart shattered and tears of anguish burst free.

Her arms stretched out as she reached for the body Daniel had fallen beside. Braith's hand wrapped around her head, he pushed her face into the hollow of his neck as he clutched her. Braith refused to let her look again as she sobbed against him. It was too late, he was trying to protect her, but she'd already seen enough to know her father was gone.

CHAPTER FIFTEEN

BRAITH HAD ORIGINALLY TAKEN Aria to Melinda's apartments to get her away from the turmoil and her father's body. However, after the first day of mute silence scattered with intermittent weeping, she made her way out of the palace while he was preoccupied with trying to sort out things.

He found her in the stables with Max, tending to the wounded animals with stalwart care. The two of them seemed content away from the confusion of people and vampires, and he didn't have the heart to protest.

He couldn't dislike Max anymore and had come to respect him. The boy had gone through things Braith would never understand, he'd been damaged and tormented by them, but somewhere along the way he'd stopped being a boy and grown into a man. A man who had protected his back and unflinchingly followed him into the palace while knowing he would never have the one person he coveted most.

Max noticed him first in the doorway of the stable and nudged Aria to get her attention.

"I know," she murmured as she snipped off the thread she'd

used on a wounded lamb. "I'm not going back in there, Braith, you can't make me."

He couldn't help but smile as she glanced at him over her shoulder. Dark circles shadowed her haunted, reddened eyes. She hadn't slept last night, and she probably wouldn't sleep tonight, but her chin jutted in determination, and her gaze was defiant when it met his. She was damaged and partially broken, but her radiant spirit still flickered beneath the sorrow.

"Have I ever been able to *make* you do anything?" he asked.

Max chuckled as he lifted the lamb, nodded to Braith, and wandered down the aisle of the only stable that survived the fires. It had taken most of the day to extinguish the flames within the palace walls, and there were still a few houses burning in the outer town. There was a crew working on putting them out with water from the river, but hopefully, they would have them out by nightfall.

Aria wiped the blood from her hands with a dirty rag. "I suppose not," she admitted with a tremulous smile.

"How long have you been out here?"

"A couple of hours."

"You should have told me," he admonished.

"You were busy."

"I'm never too busy to make sure you're safe. There are still some out there who were loyal to my father, we haven't caught them all yet, and it's no secret what you mean to me anymore."

Her eyes flickered, and tears sprang forth, but she rapidly blinked them back. "Max has been with me, and I have my bow."

The slender curve of her neck drew his eyes as she glanced toward the barn doors. He winced at the myriad of bite marks and bruises from his brother and father, stark reminders of the brutality she'd endured and wouldn't talk about. He didn't know how to ease the air of desolation around her.

"At least have a vampire with you; I can't lose you again, Aria."

Her freedom was essential, but she *had* to stay alive. Something flickered in her eyes as she turned back to him, she looked about to say something more but nodded.

"Xavier has stepped aside as leader of his people," he said.

Her eyebrows drew together over her nose. "Why would he do that?"

"Xavier has always preferred his books and histories more so than his role as an aristocrat. He was never afforded the opportunity to step aside before, but now he has a chance to set his destiny. He has chosen to stay on as an advisor and sit in on important issues involving the people he represented when it's necessary, but he doesn't want to be involved in the daily running of the government, not anymore. We have all agreed to accept his decision. He said he would stay with you if that's okay?"

"Why would he want to stay with me when he just gained the freedom he desired?"

Now was not the time to give her the real answer, but he couldn't bring himself to lie to her either. "He's curious about how the rebellion worked. He won't push you, won't ask you anything, but if you're willing to talk with him, he is more than willing to listen."

"I see," she murmured. "That's fine."

"Aria—"

She held up a hand to forestall his words. "I don't mind if Xavier stays. I would just like to be out here, away from..."

Her words trailed off; her gaze darted toward the palace. Her father was one of the few who hadn't been buried yet. He'd been placed in the second hall on the main floor so his followers would have a chance to say goodbye. Barnaby, whose body had also been recovered, was lying in the room beside David's. His father, Caleb, and Natasha hadn't been awarded the same luxury and had already been buried in unmarked graves away from the palace.

"I have to be outside for a bit," she said.

"I understand."

Her attention was diverted as Max returned with a small piglet that was squealing in his arms and bleeding from a gash in his leg. "I have to get back to the animals."

He thought she was going to turn away from him and shut him out. After a moment's hesitation though she hurried over, wrapped her arms around his waist, and hugged him. He felt the wetness of her tears, but when she pulled away, she had already stopped shedding them. He brushed the hair back from her face as he kissed her softly and released her into the care of Xavier and Max.

Braith hated he couldn't be with her when she retreated to the stables for the following two days, but there was so much to repair and order to be re-established. Barnaby's followers were confused and scrambling. Calista and Gideon had taken over trying to organize them while Adam, Barnaby's second, was slowly working to assume command.

Xavier reported back to him every night, but it wasn't the same. He longed to be with her during the day, but he couldn't always have everything he wanted. Not anymore. He refused to leave her at night though, no matter what necessity might arise to draw his attention from her, he wouldn't leave her side. He'd placed Jack and Gideon in charge of any crisis that occurred at night.

For two nights, he held her as she lay awake. She remained mute as she stared unseeingly into the darkness, sometimes shedding silent tears that broke his heart. In all his years, he'd never felt more helpless, not even when Caleb had taken her from him.

At least then there had been a plan; there had been a mission and someone to destroy. There was nothing now; there was no one he could protect her from, no way for him to ease her deep heartache.

Braith didn't know how to handle grief, he couldn't beat it, he couldn't break it, and he couldn't kill it. All he could do was lay helplessly beside her and hold her as she suffered through the nights. It didn't help that she wouldn't talk about it, the mere mention of her father made her flinch; her face would become stony and impassive every time his father or Caleb was brought up.

Finally, last night, something had changed. Long after everyone retreated to sleep, she rose from his bed, grabbed a robe, and padded away noiselessly. His exhaustion clung to him as he followed behind her, uncertain of where she was going until she arrived on the first floor.

He'd held back, hovering in the doorway as she'd wandered to her father's side. She stood beside the casket hiding the injury he'd sustained to his shoulder and the spear hole through the heart that was his downfall. Braith was infinitely glad the wounds were hidden as she sat on the stool next to her father, placed her head on his chest and wept more openly than she had for the past three days.

Though he'd yearned to go to her, to hold her, or pull her away, he'd remained unmoving. He sensed she was instinctively seeking a way to heal and say goodbye on her own; he didn't belong here. He'd retreated from the doorway, leaving her within as he settled on the cold marble floor outside the room and waited for her to come back to him. She didn't emerge until the first rays of daylight broke over the horizon.

He'd carried her back to bed, where she fell into a fitful sleep for a few hours; it was far more than the mere minutes at a time that claimed her for the past three nights.

Now, on the fourth day, they were burying David. A man, who even he mourned the death of, and not just because of

Aria. David was a good man who had created a fantastic woman; he'd loved his children and accomplished so much in his short, mortal lifetime. They'd butted heads over Aria, but it had been because of their mutual love for her, and in the end, David revealed everything he knew. Though none of what David told them offered any certainty to the questions Xavier had presented.

Braith kept his arm around her waist; he wasn't holding her up, but he felt it was only a matter of time before he might have to. Her brothers stood beside her, as stalwart as she'd been over the past few days. They'd gone almost woodenly about their days as they helped to oversee the repairs to the worst of the destruction wrought and the reformation of the new government.

Aria's skin was unnaturally pale against the black enshrouding her. He kept the umbrella over her head, sheltering her from the steady rain as she pressed closer to his side. Her hair fell forward to hide her delicate features as she kept her head bowed.

Depression had taken its toll on her. Her collarbone, the bones in her chest, and the back of her hands stood out more. She hadn't eaten much over the past few days, but Xavier and Max made sure she ate breakfast and lunch, and he made sure she put some food in her stomach at dinner time. He was concerned about her, but beneath the choking sorrow, he knew she was still strong, vibrant, and very much determined to live.

At least he hoped she was.

The funeral was not like the other human funerals he'd witnessed over the years, or even like the more elaborate vampire funerals he'd attended. There was no preacher; instead, the people who felt like speaking each took a turn.

He'd lost count of the humans who stepped forward to speak of David, then Jack, and finally Daniel had assumed the spot at the head of the gravesite. Though they wouldn't be buried next to one another, Aria had asked for her mother's name to be added to the tombstone, and Braith had been more than willing to comply.

Though there were a few times Daniel's voice broke, he didn't cry, and he appeared every bit as strong as the leader he'd just become as he spoke of his father. Beside Aria, William's fingers twitched; the two of them briefly clasped hands before breaking contact. A single tear slid down her face as Daniel said a final goodbye and stepped away.

Aria's delicate fingers twirled around the single red rose she held. She stepped forward, momentarily exposed to the rain as she tossed the flower onto the coffin. She was shaking as she stepped back beside him. He ached for her so much that he felt her suffering almost as acutely as if it were his own.

He turned her away and walked with her amongst the crush of humans and vampires as they moved away from the woods and back toward the palace. He'd offered to bury their father in the royal cemetery, but they refused, stating he would be happier in the woods, and Braith knew they were right.

Once inside the palace, he led her toward the stairs. Gideon's brown hair was still damp from the rain as hurried to catch up with them.

"Later, Gideon," Braith informed him.

Gideon looked as if he was going to argue, but he closed his mouth as he met Aria's haunted gaze. "As soon as you are able, it is essential we speak."

"I'll be down again in a few hours."

Gideon nodded and bowed his head as he stepped away. Braith felt the eyes on his back as he led her up the stairs and to the new rooms he'd claimed for them until his old suite was restored. He didn't even know yet if Aria would be willing to stay in the palace, but he wasn't going to push her on the subject of their future now. They'd speak of it when she was ready.

Once inside the room, he slipped the damp black cloak from

her shoulders and tossed it aside. Her arms were chilled, and the small blue veins running through her pale skin were visible.

The marks his brother and father had inflicted on her were dark and vivid. His jaw clenched, he wished those marks would fade far quicker than they were. She stood, unmoving before him as his hands briefly traced over her bare shoulders.

"You have to start eating more, Aria."

Her eyes were dark and remote as she studied him. "I will."

He knew though she said the words she would do no more than pick at the food he'd ordered brought up for her. "A bath will help you warm up."

"Yes."

She stiffly moved with him to the bathroom. He unzipped the back of her simple black dress and slid it away from her as warm water filled the tub. Though she was bared to him, he felt nothing sexual as he helped to ease her into the water.

All he aspired to do was comfort her, to protect her, to ease this for her somehow, and he still didn't know the extent of the torture his father and brother had exerted over her. Her body was still covered with faded bruises and bite marks marring her fair skin.

He unhurriedly dipped a cloth into the water and ran it over her shoulders and down her back. Aria didn't shy away from his touch; she wasn't embarrassed by it like she had been when she first came to the palace.

She drew her knees against her chest, not to hide her nudity, but in a gesture of comfort as she wrapped her arms around her legs. She rested her cheek on her knee as she watched him. Unshed tears shimmered in her eyes as he rubbed the cloth over her lower back in small, soothing circles.

"Aria—"

"I'll be okay; I just hurt."

"I know you do."

"Please don't worry about me. I'll get through this. I need time. But time seems so long now, so... empty? Maybe not empty, but wrong somehow, and I don't know how to explain it. There's this hole inside me, and all I want is for it to be filled again, but that's impossible, and I have to learn to live with it because there are no other options. I have to figure out a way to patch the hole enough so I can breathe again without feeling as if the air is suffocating me."

His hand stilled on her back; it was the most she'd said to him in the past four days. "Tell me what to do to make it better."

She frowned and her hand slipped from her legs to entwine with his. "There is nothing you can *do* other than being here," she murmured. "Time will help, I suppose. I've heard it heals all wounds, but I don't think this one will ever completely heal. How could it?" Tears slipped down her face; he wiped them away with the pad of his thumb. "You being here makes it better, you being with me makes it better. *Together*. We won, Braith, and that is more than I dared to let myself hope for."

"We did."

And she'd been so immersed in her melancholy she didn't know she'd become a hero of sorts. Daniel had stepped forward to claim his father's place, and William and Max had become his seconds in command, but Aria was the one everyone talked about, the one they whispered about in awe. The human who helped take down the king, the ex-blood slave the new king cherished. Even the vampires admired her, even more so than they had before.

Her eyes closed as he washed her back and kneaded her skin as he sought to ease the knots in her muscles.

"I knew there was a good chance we would lose someone, I prepared myself for it," Aria said. "I know we're lucky more weren't lost, and lucky to be alive and free."

"But you still miss him."

"Yes." Her misery was palpable in that one word. "I never got to say goodbye." More tears slid down her cheeks, but he didn't brush these away; they were hers to shed. "I never had the chance to tell him I loved him again."

"He knew."

Her eyes appeared even brighter with the tears shimmering in them and the shadows outlining them. "I know, but before we separated in the past, we always said our goodbyes and exchanged our love. Caleb robbed me of that."

His hand stilled on her back, every muscle in his body froze. If his brother hadn't already been dead, he gladly would have killed him a thousand times over. He waited, unable to tear his eyes from hers as she finally spoke of his family.

"I'm mad at myself for going into the town, but I'd do it again. That's the person my father raised; it's who I am."

"It is," he agreed, still unable to bring himself to ask the questions lodged in his throat. He was desperate to know but terrified of the answers she would give him.

"I'm sorry for your losses also," she whispered.

"I suffered no losses."

"I know you weren't close with your father and brother, or Natasha, but they were still your family."

"*You* are my family. Jack and Melinda are my family, even Ashby has started to grow on me again, and somehow I've come to terms with the fact I've begun to like your brothers."

A small smile flickered across her lips; her eyes lit with amusement as she chuckled. The sound of her laugh warmed him and eased some of his fears.

"That surprises me, with William especially."

"He *is* the more annoying of the two," Braith agreed.

Her smile widened as her fingers danced over his. "My father always said one of us would have been bad enough, but two of us were a sign he was being punished for something in an ancestor's past."

Now would be the time to tell her, but he found he couldn't. Not when she was smiling again, not when there was happiness shimmering in her eyes instead of despair. Later, there would be time; they finally *had* time for each other, with each other.

"I'll take the punishment," he assured her.

"I hope so."

"Hell, I'll even take Max."

"I've noticed the two of you have been getting along better. I'm glad," she murmured.

"I'm glad you're glad."

A sigh escaped her, and the smile slipped away. "Would you tell me if you were bothered by the loss of your family?"

"They were my blood, but I'm not sorry they're dead. They were brutal creatures who never would have changed. If Caleb hadn't taken my father down when he did, things might have been far different, Aria. We may very well be dead. He was a powerful man and would have been far fiercer competition than Caleb. Thousands upon thousands of lives will be better because of their deaths. Including *ours*."

He lifted her arm gently, hoping to distract her from her thoughts as he rubbed the cloth over her ribcage. He didn't want her feeling any guilt over their deaths when he felt none. He was surprised to find her contemplating him when he placed the arm back down and took her other one.

"You must be hungry," she said.

He shook his head. There was enough for her to deal with right now without having to worry about his needs too. "Gideon brought me some blood yesterday; I'm fine."

"It's not as good."

He smiled wryly at her. "Nothing is as good as you."

He pressed a chaste kiss to the inside of her wrist, the one not as bruised and raw looking. He froze, his muscles bunched as he spotted her black-and-blue middle finger. Though the bone was healed, he knew what had been done to it. It took everything he had not to bellow in rage, but that was the last thing she needed right now.

"But it's enough," he managed to choke out.

Her fingers stroked his cheek before slipping under his chin to lift his head slightly. "I miss the bond it establishes between us."

"As do I, but not until you're better, Aria."

She turned her hand over in his and clasped his fingers. "What they did to me, Braith, you can see it all."

His hand clenched around the cloth; his shoulders stiffened as he froze. He'd tried not to think about the fact they may have taken more than her blood from her, tried not to think about the degradation she would have experienced.

It made him wish they were both alive so he could draw out their deaths in ways his father hadn't imagined possible. He'd love her no matter what; take her any way he could get her. No matter how much time it took, he'd be there to help her heal.

He swallowed as he leaned closer to her, almost afraid to hope. "What are you saying, Aria?"

She pressed her palm to his cheek. "They didn't rape me, Braith; they were waiting for you for that." She tilted her head as her thumb brushed briefly across his bottom lip. "I wouldn't have hated you if they had."

"I didn't come for you. The other things they did to you." His gaze focused on her finger and the lingering bites.

"You did when you could, and you came straight for me. Getting yourself, and everyone else killed for me, would have been foolish Braith. I'm glad you waited."

"I know you have nightmares." She recoiled, but he pressed her hand to his cheek before she could pull away completely. "I see the way you are now in the dark."

Her haunted eyes flitted away from him. "I didn't like being in the caves, and the dungeons..." she shuddered as she bit her lip. "They were awful. I'd like to say I'll get over it one day, but I don't know if I'll ever be able to be in enclosed spaces like that again. Maybe one day we can turn the bathroom light off though." She managed a tremulous smile as she dropped her cheek to her knee.

"The worst thing they did..." Her nose scrunched up, disgust filtered over her features as her mouth pursed. "The king forced his blood into me, to keep me alive. To punish me and try to break me, but he didn't. There may be lingering nightmares, but I'm sure I'll eventually stop having them. I'll learn to deal with my fear of entrapment and the dark, and time will eventually erase the taste."

He fought to keep his face impassive even as something malicious coiled through his gut. He hadn't realized the dark bothered her until now. She insisted he leave the bathroom light on at night, but he'd assumed it was because she no longer slept. The dungeons had left a lingering impression on her; one he suspected was more profound than his father or Caleb.

When she closed her eyes, she looked so young it took everything he had not to snatch her up and firmly declare she was never going to leave his arms again. It was a foolish thought, impossible, and one she would only resent.

"His blood was so different than yours. It was awful; I'd never tasted anything so vile." Then she was looking at him again, her eyes clear and questioning. "Why was it so different?"

"Because you belong with me." It was the most simple answer he could come up with.

"I do, don't I?"

"Yes." He hadn't meant it to, but the word came out as a low growl.

She smiled at him as her fingers flitted over his arm. "I could feel my body rebelling against his blood, fighting against its intrusion into my body. It's intrusion into *you*. Even my body knew only you belonged there."

She'd rendered him speechless. Emotion entwined so firmly in his chest he thought he might cry. He didn't think he'd ever done that in his life. Rage drove him, and an ardent need to keep her safe, as well as an overwhelming urge to possess her in every way.

This was different. He loved her, he'd die for her, but he realized now fear had mostly driven their relationship. Fear of her blood slave status, the fear that came of losing her, fear of failing in this war, and fear of Caleb and his father.

However, at the very center of everything they had accomplished was the two of them, and the simple miraculous gift of his love for her, and hers for him.

It had driven them both to do things they'd never imagined they could do, and in the end, they'd won. He didn't know what their future held, but no matter what, this gift had been worth every nightmare it brought them and every horror it may continue to produce.

He was astounded by the love that flared through him and pushed aside his enduring hatred toward his father and brother. They were his past, and sitting before him was a future more promising and beautiful than any he'd ever dared to hope for.

"Even if they had done more to me, I would still be glad you hadn't come. You did the right thing, Braith. It may have taken me time to heal, but they wouldn't have broken me. I'm not breakable; I may be shaken right now, but I'm not broken."

She was grieving and trying to come to terms with the abuse she suffered and the loss of her father, but she wasn't broken. "You'll make a remarkable queen, Arianna."

She became rigid; her eyes widened as she stared at him. "Braith, I'm aware they won't accept me as a human."

He pushed the long strands of her dark auburn hair behind

her ear. He relished in the silken feel of her skin beneath the palm of his hand as he lingered on her cheek.

"And I know you don't want to change me," she said.

"It's not that I don't want to change you, Aria, I would love nothing more than to spend eternity with you."

"But you're frightened I won't survive the change."

"There are some things we must discuss when you're feeling better."

Her forehead furrowed. "What things?"

"Later, Aria. For now, take some time to heal. We *have* time now, enjoy it."

"We do, don't we?" she replied with a small smile. "I miss him."

"I know."

"I wish he survived to see us succeed."

"He knew."

Her eyes drifted closed as she rested her cheek on her knees again. He continued to hold her until the water turned cold, and he helped her out. She stood; shivering as he dried her off with a towel and helped her into a robe. As they entered the sitting room, Aria took a sudden step back at the sight of Jack on the couch with his legs leisurely crossed at the ankles. Braith wasn't the least bit surprised to see his brother though.

"I brought the food."

Aria eyed Jack warily as she circled him to the tray of food he'd placed near the window. Keegan lifted his head to watch her for a moment before yawning and dropping his head back to his paws.

"Thank you," she muttered.

Braith was reminded that he'd suspected something off between them before she was abducted. He hadn't had time to think of it after, but the tension between them was evident as they stared at each other. His brother wasn't so foolish as to believe he could take her from this palace again without Braith destroying him, or was he?

"Why are you here, Jack?" Braith inquired brusquely.

"They would like to have a meeting tonight to decide what will be done with the remaining soldiers."

Aria placed the piece of bread she had been picking at down. "What do you mean what is to be done with them?"

"They worked for the king, Aria," Braith reminded her.

She shook her head as she glanced between the two of them. "I know, but are you going to kill them because of that?"

"That is not my decision to make."

"I know you expect to establish this democracy type of government, but to start with this type of slaughter is to create a government founded on blood. It started with a war, but what happens from here on out will shape the future."

"There are times when blood is necessary," Jack said.

The fire in her gaze hadn't been there for the past few days as she glared at his brother. "Death is not the answer here."

"Then what would you suggest?" Jack demanded. "We turn them loose to gather a rebellion against us? There are men loyal to my father who could easily instigate another war. Is that what you would like, even more death?"

The color drained from Aria's face; her hands fell limply into her lap. Braith took a step toward his brother as Jack threw up his hands and leapt to his feet. He cautiously edged away from Braith and toward the door.

"I didn't... I wasn't thinking; I'm sorry, Aria," Jack stammered. "You know how much your father meant to me too."

"Get out, Jack," Braith grated.

"Wait." Aria pushed aside the tray as she rose to her feet. "I know you didn't mean anything, Jack, and more death is the last thing I want, but there must be another option. The soldiers were just following orders; some of them *must* be worth saving."

"I'm sure some of them are," Jack agreed as his gaze shot warily to Braith. "But there are others who must be destroyed; you have to understand that, Aria."

"Does my opinion matter?"

"Your opinion has always mattered to me, and many admire and respect it also," Braith informed her. Her brow furrowed as she stared at him. "You helped to take down not only an aged, powerful vampire but also a king."

Her jaw clenched as she glanced away. "I don't like to be admired for death, no matter how awful Caleb was."

"I know that, Aria, but you're also admired for your bravery."

Her face colored; she looked uncomfortable with the notion as she shifted uneasily. "I understand the men and women most loyal to your father have to be put down. I know the way of the world, and the repercussions of war, but some of those guards had no other choice. Some of them were simply doing their jobs to take care of their families and survive. We've all done things we didn't want to do to stay alive; you can't punish them for doing the same."

"Would you like to come to the meeting to state your opinion?" Braith inquired.

"I would."

Jack's eyes darted worriedly toward him. "There is something else you must know first."

Aria quirked an eyebrow as she studied him. Braith didn't want to tell her this, but he couldn't hide it from her, and he wasn't about to lie to her.

"Gwendolyn is one of the prisoners," Jack said.

For a moment confusion marred her features and then her eyes widened as her mouth dropped. "Your fiancée?" she blurted.

"*Ex*," he growled.

She blinked as she shook her head. "Yes, ex, whatever. What is she doing there? *Here?*"

"She was an aristocrat, Aria; she resided in the town and was amongst those captured. Lauren will be there also."

Her nose wrinkled as her lip curled. Keegan rose and pressed against her legs as he sought to offer her comfort.

"I would still like for you to attend," he said.

Braith thought she might refuse and retreat into the world of despair that had clamped its teeth into her.

Instead, she turned toward him and nodded firmly. "So would I."

He couldn't help but smile at her as relief filled him, his Aria had never retreated from anything.

CHAPTER SIXTEEN

On the way down, Aria had been terrified the meeting would be held in the throne room. It was the king's room, after all, and the largest room in the palace. Braith's room now, she reminded herself, still marveling over the fact they had won, and the man walking so proudly at her side now presided over them. He was the man who would lead them into a new time, a new rule, a new form of government, and if anyone could make it work it would be Braith, she was sure of that.

She was relieved when Braith guided her in the opposite direction of the throne room though, and into a private solar off the main hall. Thankfully not the one her father had been kept in either.

It was nowhere near as big, or as elaborate as the throne room, but it was more than enough for what they required and didn't house anything threatening or cruel. It fit Braith far better than his father's monstrosity of a throne room would have.

Everyone had already gathered in the room; they rose as Braith entered, but she was aware of the eyes tracking her as she moved through the room. Daniel stood at the side of the table with William and Max behind him. They all smiled at her, but she sensed their surprise over her presence. William was still on crutches, his injured leg propped out before him as he gave her a thumbs up.

The massive chair at the head of the table was obviously Braith's, but as he strode toward it, he snagged another chair with one hand. He shoved the larger chair to the side and placed the smaller one next to it. He held it out for her, a look of defiance on his face as he raked the table with his steely gaze.

It was only then she realized he hadn't worn his glasses in a while. She studied his magnificent profile, and the short black hair falling about his forehead in waves. Holding his gaze, she had to fight back the tears of love and pride filling her eyes. He'd been born for this, he excelled at it, and he desired for her to be at his side, even if she couldn't be.

Swallowing heavily, Aria slid into the chair. She'd expected some condemnation, some irritation, or some form of protest against her sitting beside Braith, but she saw only curiosity and some sadness as she looked around the table at "The Council" as they had dubbed themselves. They'd officially relinquished the aristocratic titles they'd held in the past in favor of starting fresh and new.

"We are sorry about your father; he was a good fighter."

This statement from Calista caused another kind of lump to form in her throat. She struggled against the tears burning her eyes at the reminder of her father. She was taken aback by the kind words from a woman who had seemed nothing but distant before, and who ruthlessly slaughtered Braith's sister.

"Thank you," Aria managed to respond.

She started in surprise when Braith seized her hand. Aria tried to tug it free, but he held on as he gazed at her. She knew there was no denying their relationship now, but she was still apprehensive about being so blatant about it. Then, she realized, she didn't care. There was no hiding this anymore, and she didn't want to.

Aria watched as ten men and two women were led into the room; they were dirty and disheveled, but they didn't appear overly mistreated. They certainly weren't as abused as she had been. Resentment filled her as she recognized one of the women as the vampire who had owned Max.

Which meant the other one, the beautiful doll-like brunette staring hatefully back at her, was probably Gwendolyn. Though she knew Braith had never cared for the woman, she couldn't help the bolt of jealousy shooting through her. Braith held her hand steady as he stared at her, and she realized jealousy had no place here.

Besides, there was someone in this room reliving far worse memories than her. Max's chin was raised, his gaze unwavering as he met the other vampire woman's hostile stare. Aria had to fight the urge to jump up and throttle the hideous woman for everything she had done to Max. She remained unmoving though as everyone around her decided what would become of the women and their cohorts.

A lump formed in her throat as Max's eyes met hers. She had a better idea now of what he endured while in captivity, but she would never be able to understand the full depth of brutality that woman had put him through.

Aria listened as those at the table discussed their fates. These vampires had been the most treacherous and cruel of their kind. They had been the king's body, helped him keep power, and relished in the decisions the king made and the sadistic world he'd created.

Aria hoped every one of them fried, but it wasn't her decision to make. Braith also remained silent as he listened to them debate before coming to a unanimous decision they were all to be executed.

"It's agreed then?" questioned Braith.

"Yes," Gideon stated.

"Wait! You can't do this, Braith! We were to be married!"

Braith's hand tightened around hers as Gwendolyn's pleas fell on deaf ears and she was removed from the room.

Aria's heart ached at the reminder, but she managed to keep her face impassive as Daniel's and William's heads shot toward her.

"Bring the soldiers in," Braith commanded.

Aria braced herself; this was why she'd come. She understood the aristocrats had to be eliminated, but this was an entirely different matter. All the wind went out of her argument as Jack led Lauren into the room last.

Her mouth dropped, and the breath rushed out of her as she glanced at Braith. He'd told her she would be here, but Aria hadn't expected her to be grouped in with the soldiers. His eyes were unrelenting; his jaw locked as he stared back at her. She grasped his thigh and held tight to it as he soothingly massaged the back of her hand with his thumb.

She barely heard the talk going around the table, but this discussion was a lot more heated than the last one. Daniel and Ashby were for leniency. Calista, Frank, and Saul were entirely against it; Adam, Gideon, and Xavier remained mute as they listened to the arguments of the others.

Aria realized she had to speak up when it seemed like Ashby was starting to sway toward Calista, Frank, and Saul. "Can I say something?" she asked.

They all turned toward her, their faces twisted in various expressions of displeasure. Though she sensed their annoyance was due more to the fact they couldn't agree than with her interruption.

"Please do," Saul remarked dryly.

Aria felt somewhat uncomfortable as they all focused on her.

She glanced briefly at Daniel before taking a deep breath and plunging onward. "I understand the other deaths are necessary, if given a chance they would start a rebellion, and the pattern would never end. However, these men were simply doing what they were ordered to do. For years, death, torture, and intimidation ruled here. Don't start this new government the same way. If you slaughter them all, it will only show the people nothing has changed, and mercy is impossible. If these vampires swear fealty to you, and perhaps are even monitored for a while, I don't think they should be executed."

She couldn't believe those words had left her mouth. Just a few months ago she would have said kill them all because they were vampires. She would have said to kill Braith, and Ashby, Jack, and Melinda too, but she would have been wrong. They weren't all monsters, they were merely different and had different needs, but for the most part, they were kind, protective, and loving. There were bad apples among both human and vampire alike.

There was a moment of silence, and then they burst into conversation again. Xavier entered the debate for the first time on the side of Daniel, while Gideon and Adam continued to watch and listen.

Braith finally ended the argument by calling for a vote. Aria was unmoving as she waited breathlessly to see what they would decide. They had established a more civilized and kinder rule in The Barrens, and she hoped it would prevail here.

"I think we agree that if the soldiers are willing to swear fealty to us and consent to being monitored for whatever period we see fit, they may be allowed to live. If not, their lives are forfeit," Calista declared.

Saul and Frank didn't look overly pleased with this decision, but they didn't protest it either.

The shoulders of most of the soldiers slumped, some nodded

enthusiastically, but there were a few who didn't look at all pleased. Aria wondered if they would choose death over their new regime. If so, that was their choice to make, and she wouldn't interfere with it.

"And the girl?" Aria turned at Ashby's question.

"I think that should be Arianna's decision." She sensed a test behind Gideon's words as she met his gaze. "It is you who was harmed by her the most."

Aria focused on Lauren, but the girl wouldn't meet her gaze as she stared at the wall behind Braith's head. Braith's thumb stroked the back of her hand. Whatever she decided he would abide by it, they all would. Resentment twisted through her, she would like for Lauren to look at her, to give her some sign she regretted even a little of what she'd done. There was nothing.

"Let her go," she said.

As much as she wanted to, she couldn't exact revenge on Lauren. Though there was a time after her first capture her father wrongfully wanted revenge for her, for the most part, he hadn't believed in it and insisted everything they did was not for revenge, but to create a better world.

She couldn't throw that aside now; she couldn't let her father down because of her desire to punish Lauren. A small smile tugged at Gideon's mouth as he gave a brief bow of his head and sat back. She realized he'd been trying to discern if she would ask for leniency for others but punish those who wronged her.

"She isn't a threat to us," Aria said.

Aria hadn't expected to see relief nor had she expected to see gratitude, so she wasn't surprised by the hatred blazing from Lauren's eyes. Braith's jaw clenched; Aria was sure he would have preferred Lauren dead, and he would have been the one to do it.

"You may leave, but you're not to stay within these palace walls, the bailey, or the town beyond. I don't care where you go, but if I see you again, I can promise you will not be spared next time. If I were you, I would get as far from here as you possibly can, as fast as you can," he grated, and for the first time, fright trickled over Lauren's features. "Max, would you please escort her to the palace gates."

"With pleasure," Max responded with a tight smile as he strode toward the doors and pulled one open. He made a sweeping bow to Lauren who remained pale and slack-mouthed as she stared at him.

"That isn't the choice I would have made," Braith said so quietly only Aria heard him.

"I know."

"If I see her again, I will kill her, and I *will* enjoy it."

She turned toward him, not at all intimidated by the darkness simmering beneath his smooth exterior. "I know. She won't come back again, Braith, but if she does, I won't interfere."

He shook his head as he leaned closer to her. Stubble shadowed his square jaw; he hadn't had time to shave in the past few days between the new demands placed upon him, and staying by her side every free moment he had. Love swelled within her heart; there was such darkness inside him, yet such good and understanding. He released her hand, his arm wrapped around her waist as he pulled her closer to his side.

"Sometimes you are too forgiving," he whispered against her ear.

"And sometimes you're the same stubborn prince I first met; only now you're a king."

Something flickered in his gaze as sadness filtered across his features. He didn't have to tell her; she already knew he would stay king. It wasn't what he would have chosen, he'd done nothing but fight against it, but he'd finally come to realize this was where he was supposed to be. The only problem was, she didn't know what would become of her, and neither did he.

"I'm tired; if you don't mind, I'd like to return to the room."

His fingers gently stroked her cheek. "I'll take you."

"Stay. I know my way back."

"Are you sure?"

"Yes."

Though she still felt strange being so open about their relationship, she leaned forward and pressed a feathery kiss on his hard mouth. She had meant for it to be quick, but she lost herself in the pleasure and taste of his lips. For a moment, there was no despair, there was no war or uncertainty. There was only the two of them as the warmth of his lips heated her all the way to the tips of her toes.

She forced herself to pull away and smiled as she met his dazed gaze.

"Get going," he said gruffly.

She pecked his cheek before rising to her feet. "Excuse me, everyone." She gave a brief bow of her head before she hurried from the room.

Stepping into the hall, she was relieved to find it deserted. She hurried toward the stairs, but before she began her ascent, her gaze was drawn to the closed doors of the throne room. She stood, her hand resting on the newel post as she studied the doors with a mixture of dread and morbid curiosity.

Moving away from the staircase, she slowly approached the room. Her hand shook as she turned the handle and pushed open one of the doors. She braced herself for what lay within.

She peered inside as the door swung open, but she hadn't been expecting what was inside. Everything was spotless and bare, the massive table, chairs, and throne were gone. Even the hideous trophies of people and vampires the king had so proudly displayed had been removed. The blood had been scrubbed clean, and the gray marble floors gleamed in the light filtering through the upper windows.

Her gaze ran over the beautiful fixtures gracing the room as she stepped in further. The room was stunning, but it would never be anything but cold and hideous to her. Her eyes lingered on the beam she had been perched upon and finally the spot where her father's body had laid. There was nothing to mark the place, but she knew where it was.

Tears burned her eyes; she hastily wiped them away as she felt the presence of someone else in the room. She knew it wasn't Braith even before Jack stepped beside her. "I wish I could have done more to save him."

"I know." She was unable to stop the tear sliding down her face. "But there was nothing more you could have done, Jack. We all entered this battle knowing there would be losses."

The words were true, but they didn't give her any comfort. She rubbed her chest, but it did nothing to ease the knot in her heart.

He rested his hand on her shoulder. "It doesn't make it better."

"No, it doesn't. I'm not going to leave him, Jack." The words were blunter than she intended, but they had to have it out. There couldn't be any more subterfuge and plans between them.

"I know."

"I can't. I mean I could, if I thought it would do any good, but..."

"It won't," he finished for her when her voice trailed off. "I know that now, so does Gideon. You're the yin to his yang."

"The what to his what?" she asked in confusion, not sure if she should be insulted by the strange words.

Jack smiled, but it did little to ease the sad resolve in his eyes. "It's an old saying; you're the light to his darkness; the good to his bad. You temper each other, and though I believe you can be separated, it won't make either of you stronger to do so. After what happened, they may very well decide to accept you as a human. It will be your choice if you stay or not, even Braith knows that now. This isn't exactly the life you've prepared for, Aria, or one you ever wanted. For all its opulence, in some ways, it's more arduous than the one you will be leaving behind if you choose to stay."

That was for sure. "What will become of us?" she pondered.

"I don't know."

"I'm going to tell him, you know; what I was going to do."

Jack glanced at her sideways from under lowered lashes. His resemblance to Braith was more subtle than the king's but far more appealing. There was a carefree air to Jack that seldom showed in Braith, but on those infrequent occasions when Braith let his guard down, he resembled Jack the most.

"If you feel you must," Jack said.

"I don't know what will become of us, but no matter what, it has to be a fresh, open start. There can't be any secrets between us."

"I understand. You may be better off downplaying the part where you and Gideon had a secret agreement about your possible death."

Aria winced at the harsh tone of Jack's voice. "He told you?"

"Yes. He also told your brothers, Max, and your father."

She couldn't stop the small tremors racing through her. "My father, he didn't think I wanted to die, did he?" she managed to croak.

"He understood, Aria; believe me, he understood."

She couldn't stop the flood of tears pouring from her eyes. "I hope so."

Jack wrapped his arm around her shoulders and pulled her close to his side. "I know so. He was unbelievably proud of you and your brothers. He didn't like the course you chose, but he understood it, just as you must understand his death wasn't in vain. He also knew I wasn't going to let what you and Gideon agreed to do, happen. I would have taken you away to separate the two of you, but there is *no* way I would have agreed to your death."

"That's why I went to Gideon."

Exasperation flashed over his features; his steel gray eyes narrowed into a very Braith look. "It wouldn't have happened, Arianna, it was foolish of you to think it would. It was foolish of Gideon. It was bad enough I was going to take you away from him again, but ending your life never would have happened."

She bowed her head and pressed her face to Jack's chest as she strived to regain some control of her tears. After a while, she was finally able to take a steadying breath and pull away from him.

"The trophies," she choked on the word. "Where are they?"

His eyes hardened. "There are times when death is more merciful." She blinked in surprise. "There is no saving some souls no matter how much we would like to. They would have been strong allies, it was why they were tormented so, but they were too far gone. These poor souls had been trapped and starved for far more years than those creatures you encountered in The Barrens. Even a vampire cannot recover from that."

"Oh," she breathed. Her thoughts turned to the pitiful creature the king tormented with her blood. "How awful, what he did to them..." She shuddered as she broke off. "Why wasn't Ashby kept here?"

Jack gestured around the room. "It's beautiful in here; it's rich and fancy and elegant in a way Ashby appreciates and craves. Ashby was kept in a separate, stronger dungeon for vampires for a few months after the war, but the king thought it was a far worse fate to place him somewhere away from all the things he loved so much, and Melinda encouraged it. He could have left Ashby in the dungeons, but that wasn't as much fun for my father."

She was grateful for that. "Lucky for Ashby. Did Braith send you after me?"

"He's worried about you."

"I know, but I'm good."

Jack smiled wanly. "You always are, kid."

She rolled her eyes. "Ugh."

He grinned at her as he turned her away from the empty trophy room and led her toward the doors. They slipped back into the hall as Max reappeared. "I think we should have taken her into The Barrens and left her there." Max candidly informed her as he stopped before them.

"That would have been fitting," Jack agreed.

"This might not be any better," she told them.

"It is for her," Max muttered. "Are you going back to your rooms?"

"Yes."

"I'll take you."

Jack released her shoulders when she gave him a subtle pinch in the back. Max held his arm out to her, a gallant smile on his face as for the first time she saw genuine joy in his eyes again. Aria slipped her arm through his and smiled back at him.

These past few days she'd welcomed his presence in the stable with her, and the fact he knew when she felt like talking and when she didn't. She enjoyed the friendship that had become easy between them again.

She hesitated outside the rooms she once shared with Braith. Max tried to hold her back, but she pushed open the door. She gasped as she took in the destruction of the room. Releasing Max's arm, she stepped carefully over broken bits of furniture, paintings, books, and clothing as she made her way to the room that was once hers.

"The king must have been in a foul mood after Braith left," Max said from the doorway.

"That's not necessary, Max; I know it was Braith who did this."

The room was a mess, but there, in the center of the bed, was a nightgown she had worn. It was laid neatly out, set on the mattress, untouched by the violence surrounding it. Tears burned her eyes, and her throat hurt; she ached over the suffering she sensed here.

She turned back to Max, needing to escape from the reminder of the things that transpired here, and the events which led Braith to a breaking point. Leaving him again, without telling him, would have been the biggest mistake she ever could have made.

Max held his arm out to her again; she gratefully slid hers through it and grasped the lean, corded muscles standing out against the fabric of his shirt.

"Do you feel better now that she is going to die?" Aria inquired.

He didn't pretend not to know who the *she* was. "I'd thought I would, but I don't. I feel better now that this is over, and we now live in a world none of us ever *dreamed* possible. I thought revenge was the answer to it all, and I know she has to die, but no, it doesn't make me feel better. Her death is a necessary means to the end of a brutal regime. It's going to be better now, Aria, for all of us."

She smiled at him as she leaned against his side. "It is," she agreed.

And it would be good for all of *them*. She found that, for now, the idea was more than enough. Her future had always been uncertain; she supposed it didn't make a difference it still was.

"I'm sorry, Aria."

"There's nothing to be sorry for, Max."

"There is. I didn't believe you, I didn't believe in *him*, and it nearly cost me everything. I was angry, I was foolish, and I was stubbornly holding onto boyish dreams." She stared at him in surprise as color heated her cheeks. "I should have known to trust your instincts. You were right."

"I always am," she teased.

"Yeah well, I wouldn't go that far."

Aria laughed as she bumped his hip playfully. "You went through a lot more than I did Max; you had every right to be angry and disbelieving. I probably would have been too if I was treated as poorly as you. I didn't experience what you did, either time."

"Are you still having nightmares?"

Aria couldn't meet his gaze as she focused on the rug beneath her. She hated the images plaguing her at night and her lingering fear of the dark, but she couldn't shake them. She supposed it would get better with time, but she was still ashamed of the enduring impact she'd allowed the king and Caleb to have on her.

"Yes." She didn't like to admit her weakness, but she wasn't going to lie to Max about it. Out of everyone, he was the person who understood the most.

"It will get better."

She nodded as she squeezed his arm and stopped before the apartment Braith had claimed for them. "I know it will."

His gaze focused on the door behind her as he released her arm. "Braith is a good man, Aria, a better man than I thought he was, but even good men can be driven to do horrific things when they are pushed to it. I know you're aware of this, but please don't forget it."

She hesitated, her hand on the door handle as she turned toward him. "I don't plan to leave anymore, Max."

"Good. You deserve a happy ending too."

"There are times when a happy ending just isn't possible."

"Be optimistic, Aria; look at everything else that has happened."

He squeezed her arm briefly before she turned and slipped into the rooms. The tray of food was still there, heaped with fruits and bread. She wasn't sure how safe the cheese and meats were any more, but as her stomach rumbled, she was surprised to realize her appetite had returned.

CHAPTER SEVENTEEN

OVER THE NEXT THREE WEEKS, mourning weighed her down like a wet blanket threatening to suffocate her within its cloying folds. She spent most of her time in the stables. All the animals that could be saved were tended to, but she still sought out the comfort the building and animals offered her.

Some moments were tougher than others. At times, she could barely breathe through the sorrow constricting her chest. In those moments, it took all she had to gather the strength to breathe again and not lose herself to the tears and misery.

Gradually, over the days, though the grief didn't lessen, she became more accustomed to it. She was better able to deal with it as she accepted she would never see her father again. Never hear his laugh, or bask in his smile, or receive his crushing hugs that always made her feel cherished.

Slowly, she began to accept her life would have a constant hole in it, but it was a hole that one day wouldn't cripple her as it did in those first couple of weeks.

In the stables, she found peace and solace with the animals and her friends. She fed the horses, cleaned them, and sat with them. Xavier remained her constant shadow, but she was surprised to realize she didn't mind. She grew to enjoy his company. For the first few days they didn't speak at all, and then Max became tired of the quiet and began to strike up conversations with him.

There was so much Xavier knew, so much history he was eager to share with them. In those moments, when he was regaling them with stories of pyramids, vast seas, boats, sweeping buildings, flying airplanes, and distant green lands filled with people, she found an escape from her sadness.

Aria found herself enraptured by his stories and the beautiful tribal tattoos marking his dark skin. Sometimes, she and Max would sit in the middle of the aisle as Xavier told them everything he knew. It all sounded a little frightening and overwhelming, but amazing. She was glad Braith had chosen Xavier to be her guard, and she suspected a big part of that reason was Xavier's tales.

"What was it like here before the war?" Max asked.

Max didn't look up from the saddle he was polishing, but Aria paused in the middle of brushing a large bay stud. They'd never asked what it had been like around here. She hadn't wanted to know, and she'd assumed the same of Max, but apparently, she'd been wrong.

Xavier was thoughtful as his hands folded into the sleeves of his robe. "Peaceful. Braith's father had chosen this area because it was serene and secluded. He was able to build the palace away from the prying eyes of the higher populated human areas, and the location offered us great security. There were some outlying vampire establishments throughout the world, but some of them came here when it became clear there would be a war, and the ones who didn't..."

"Were destroyed," Aria whispered.

Xavier nodded. "It was a relatively good life here once."

"It will be again." Max lifted the saddle and tossed it onto a sawhorse. "Where is here? You've told us all these stories of far-off lands and countries, of kings and wars and mythologies, but you've never really told us about this land. *This* place. What was it called?"

"Pennsylvania. It was once called Pennsylvania, and it was at one time a part of the United States."

"Pennsylvania," Aria found she liked the strange word as she sounded it out. She'd read about the United States in a couple of books, but she'd never heard of Pennsylvania. "Tell us about it," she encouraged. "All of it."

Xavier smiled at her as he settled onto a bale of hay and started to regale them. Aria put the brush down as she found herself drawn forward. She sank onto the bale beside him as Max pulled down another saddle and began to polish it.

It never failed to amaze her how Xavier remembered all the things he did, and how astute he was at pointing out details she never would have noticed otherwise. She became so engrossed in his words that she didn't see the sun setting until Max pointed it out.

"We should head back, I'm starving," Max said.

Aria rose from the bale and wiped the hay from her pants. She followed them out of the stable, pleased by the number of changes already being rendered. Most of the smoke and fire damaged buildings had been torn down and removed, and there were already new homes and structures going up.

There were smiles and friendly waves from the people and vampires surrounding them, and though complete trust and amicability still hadn't been solidified, they were already making a good start on a world Aria had never dreamed of living in.

The massive palace gates, battered beyond repair, had been taken down. Though they would be replaced, they would also be left open as an invitation for everyone to move freely in and out of the palace town.

Most of the blood draining facilities were destroyed during the battle. The remaining ones were emptied of all devices used to bleed and torture humans and reopened as a donation center that seemed to be doing well. Or at least she hadn't heard of any problems with it, and a few people were standing outside waiting to go in as they passed it.

She stayed close to Xavier as they traversed the streets toward the looming palace. The sight of it still caused an uneasy pit to form in her stomach, but she was becoming better accustomed to the building. She was gradually finding her place within it, something she never would have thought possible even a week ago.

Tomorrow she'd stop hiding in the stables, she decided. Tomorrow she'd face what she'd been trying to hide from, a world without her father in it. She had to figure out a way to live again in this world without him. She had to figure out her place here; she couldn't avoid it anymore. She could be helpful; she *would* be helpful. It was what her father would expect of her, and she wasn't going to let him down.

Xavier and Max followed her up to her rooms. They usually ate dinner with her before retreating to their rooms or going about whatever it was they did at night. William was already waiting for them with a large tray of food when they arrived.

It was one of the few times during the day she had a chance to see her brother. He had taken to burying himself in rebuilding homes, even though he was still on crutches. She understood his desperate need not to think, she had the same feeling after all, but she missed him.

She hugged him before grabbing a plate and heaping it with food. She plopped onto the couch and began to eat with a gusto she hadn't experienced in a while. It felt good, for once she felt almost alive again, and she welcomed the sensation.

"Did you know this was once Pennsylvania?" Max asked.

"What is a Pennsylvania?" William demanded.

Xavier was more than happy to fill him in as Aria went back for seconds. She wondered if Braith would return to eat with them; most nights he and Daniel were here for dinner, but sometimes they didn't make it in time.

After dinner, she retreated to the bedroom with the newest book she'd been reading. She was used to Braith being curled around her before she fell asleep, holding her as she cried, and comforting her through her sorrow.

After she'd stuffed herself to near bursting though, sleep dragged her into its deep depths. Now, as the blankets were pulled back and the bedsprings creaked, she was awakened by the pressure of his weight on the mattress.

"Braith," she whispered.

"Go back to sleep, love."

His arms wrapped around her. She nestled closer to him, pressing her back against his solid chest as her hand stroked the hair on the corded muscles of his arms. She loved those arms, so different from hers, so protective and strong.

Her heart hammered, her mouth was dry as a new type of hunger stirred within her. Aria had shut herself down to him before the war, denied them both because she thought she would be leaving, but after her time in the dungeon, she knew she'd been wrong.

She didn't know what would happen in the future, and she didn't care, it didn't matter. All they were guaranteed was the present, and she was going to start living in it.

She could barely catch her breath as something coiled within her belly and spread leisurely through her limbs. She rolled over, turning to face him. The light coming from the slightly open door of the bathroom was dim, but even so, she could see the brightness of his gray eyes, the firm planes of his magnificent face and square jaw.

She was unmoving as his fingers traced over her cheeks,

pressed briefly against her lips before slipping back to brush her hair aside.

"You ate again," he said.

Over the three weeks, since she lost her father, she started to put weight back on. Even the bite marks had faded to dark smudges on her skin thanks to a daily dose of Braith's blood. Though he still stubbornly, and annoyingly, refused to feed on her.

"Yes."

She smiled as she rested her hand on his chest, pressing it flat against the solid wall of him. His flesh was warm and smooth beneath her palm as she slid it slowly down the length of him. His body stiffened, his muscles shifted and flexed subtly beneath her touch.

Her fingers slid unhurriedly back up his chest as she explored him. It fascinated her how different his body was than hers. From the wiry hair brushing against her fingers to the unyielding hardness of his body in areas where hers was supple and giving. He fascinated her in every imaginable way; she couldn't get enough of him as her fingers slid lower.

"Aria..."

She moved closer to him and pressed her breasts against his chest. Her skin prickled; even through her nightgown, she felt the warmth of his skin. She felt a strange urge to cry, but she fought it back. If she started to cry now, he wouldn't allow this to continue.

He would think it was out of grief she was seeking him out, and perhaps a part of it was grief, but mostly it was because she loved him. She wanted to have this experience with him, and for once she craved something for them. Not for anyone else, but just for *them*.

"I love you, Braith."

"I love you too."

Her lips were trembling as she pressed them briefly against

his mouth. His hand enveloped hers. He rested it over the place where his heart would have beat, but even though it remained still, she knew his heart belonged to her.

Then, he released her hand, slipped his hand into her hair, and kissed her with a tenderness that left her limp and desperate for so much more. His tongue slid into her mouth, and the faint hint of spices assailed her as it brushed over the roof her mouth.

He tasted her in long leisurely strokes that left her breathless. There were so many things out there she was scared and uncertain of, but here and now, she had no uncertainty as he held and kissed her with a reverence that awed her.

His mouth was heated against her skin; his hands tender as he slid the nightgown from her. Goosebumps covered her body. Electricity seemed to pulse through her as her nerve endings screamed for more.

She could scarcely think as her mind spun and her entire being became solely focused on him and the pleasure he elicited with each stroke and passionate kiss. She craved more, but she didn't know what she wanted. She only knew she couldn't seem to get close enough to him as her fingers curled into the carved muscles of his back.

Everything else fell away; she forgot about all the horrible events of the past month as every cell in her body became centered upon him. His hands slid over her skin in caressing strokes that left her trembling and weak. She tasted the salt of his sweat as she kissed his neck and jaw and savored in the press of his body against hers.

His hungry gaze slid over her, but unlike before, when she would have felt insecure about her body and her inexperience, she felt only love as fire lit his gaze, and his mouth came back to hers.

"Are you sure?" His voice was hoarse as his hand stilled on her thigh.

Though she sensed the tension in him and his passion for her, she knew he would stop if she asked him to. She knew he would accept her decision, and continue to wait patiently for her. It only made her want him more.

"I've never been more certain of anything in my life," she said.

A low groan escaped him before he reclaimed her mouth and gently pressed her into the mattress. She was trembling and aching, lost in sensation as his hands awakened her to pleasures she'd never known could exist until he touched her.

When she was certain she couldn't take anymore, sure she would scream from the unfamiliar tension curling through her body; he moved over the top of her. There was pain, but he eased it with soft kisses, and whispered words of love, as he waited for her to adjust to the new sensation of joining with him. He held her and stroked her with a reverence that made the pain ease and steadily rekindled her desire for him.

She could almost feel the bond encircling them, tightening around them and linking them together irrevocably. But it was more than the strange bloodlink vampires experienced; it was deeper and stronger. It was a love so pure and true she came to believe it could conquer anything. Even death.

Her body splintered apart as pleasure swamped her and she was swept into a realm of bliss she'd never known possible. His body trembled as he rolled to the side, pulling her against him as he encircled her within the steel band of his arms.

This was it; this was where she had always belonged. There was no past anymore, not for him and not for her. There was only the present, and she cherished every moment of it.

"I love you," he whispered against her ear.

"And I you."

His hands clasped her face, and he kissed her trembling lips.

The look on his face tore at her soul as he pressed his fingers against her lips. "I will love you until the end of days, Aria; never doubt that for a moment."

"I couldn't possibly." She traced the contours of his face before wrapping her hand around the back of his head and guiding it toward the hollow of her neck. "Please."

He hesitated before biting down. She sighed with pleasure as they were joined again.

CHAPTER EIGHTEEN

BRAITH FOUND her with her brother; their heads were bent close together and their shoulders touching as they sat on the bench before the fountain in the garden. Their hair, identical in color, shimmered a deep auburn in the radiance of the sun. Their words were hushed, their arms in front of them as they seemed to be pulling and pushing at each other.

It wasn't until he was closer that he realized they were holding hands, and attempting to pin each other's thumbs down as they tugged at each other. Though they were playing a game, they were also talking about their father, reminiscing and laughing. Heartache had weighed heavily on them, and they wore it similarly in their thinner frames, and halfhearted smiles.

William pinned her thumb down and grinned at her. "You're slipping, sis."

"You cheated," she accused as she pulled her thumb free and they battled again.

He was captivated by her, entranced by the laughter finally radiating from her again. How had he ever thought she wasn't beautiful? She may not be perfect in the classical sense, but her soul was glorious, and it shone from her like the sun. He'd sensed her spirit even before he could see it.

And he had no idea what was to become of her, of him, of them.

He took a step back, intending to return to the palace. She had so few moments of peace and tranquility; he wasn't about to intrude on this time with her brother. She turned suddenly, and her head tilted as she spotted him.

Her smile grew as her cheeks colored beautifully. William frowned at her before turning toward him. Their hands remained joined, but the game was forgotten as they stared at him questioningly.

Even from here, he could hear the increased beat of her heart and feel the joy suffusing her, along with the shy hesitance she'd experienced briefly this morning when they woke.

He'd hoped it would be gone by now, but he had a feeling it had more to do with her brother than being around him as she glanced nervously at William. Her brother looked between them; heat rose in his face as he released her and rose to his feet.

"You don't have to go," Braith informed him. He hated to break them up, especially for the reasons he had come.

"Yes." William glanced at Aria who offered him a small smile and nodded. Braith sensed there was more behind their look, but William was already turning back to him. "I do."

William squeezed Aria's shoulder before moving around the bench and leaving the gardens. Braith walked around the bench and sat beside her.

"Do you remember the first time you brought me here?" she inquired.

He stared at the fountain as he recalled that day. He hadn't known what to make of her then, hadn't known what to make of anything happening to him. She'd thrown him off balance, rattled him and confused him in a way he'd never been confused before.

She still did.

He didn't think he would ever get used to her or the way she made him feel; the way she could melt him, infuriate him, and drive him nearly to his knees all in the same moment.

"I do," he said.

"I was so uncertain of you before then."

"You sure didn't act like it," he muttered.

She released a velvety laugh as she leaned against his side. He loved the way she looked at him like that, from under lowered lashes, playful and joyful. It almost made him believe she wasn't still aching inside, but even through the smile, he saw the persistent torment in her eyes. It would be there for a long time to come.

He took her hand and pressed it gently between his as he placed it in his lap. "Well, I couldn't *let* you know I was a little scared of you; you'd take advantage of me then."

He couldn't stop a snort of laughter. "Oh, I'm sure, as you're so easy to take advantage of."

"Only with you."

Her cheeks colored more, and he couldn't help the increase of his laughter. It was so rare and fleeting to see her embarrassed or shy about anything.

"Even then you're like a thorn," he teased.

A burst of astonished laughter escaped her; she leaned over to kiss him. He knew she'd only meant it to be chaste, a small show of affection, but the minute her lips touched his, heat flashed through his body. He grabbed her shoulders to hold her in place as memories of the night and morning burst through him.

He was unable to control the powerful wave of desire that swamped him. He'd most certainly never loved another woman before, but he'd also never been this enthralled or rattled by one either. He'd thought possessing her would ease the need somewhat; he'd been wrong. It had only increased.

She was breathing rapidly; her face flushed with a different kind of heat when he regained enough control of himself to finally separate from her. Her eyes were wide with awe; her lips parted and swollen from the force of his kiss.

He craved nothing more than to take her back upstairs and forget about everything as he lost himself to her, but things had to be settled between them. There was only so long they could push away reality, and though he would have liked a few more days, he knew it would make things more difficult in the end.

"There is something I have to tell you, Aria."

Reality crashed over her as she straightened her shoulders and thrust her chin out. "There is something I have to tell you too."

"Does it have to do with what has been between you and Jack recently?"

She paled as she leaned away from him. "You knew?"

"I *suspected* something; I'm not a fool. You haven't been the same since The Swamplands. I'm aware you were trying to put some distance between us; I suspected it was because you were nervous one of us wouldn't survive, but I've come to believe it was more than that, wasn't it?"

"You're going to be mad."

He shifted uneasily, but he'd known he would be. "I don't doubt it for a minute."

"Just please try and control your temper."

His jaw clenched. "I'd never harm you."

"I know!" she cried. "But I do enjoy this garden and the fountain, and I'd like to keep it all in one piece."

He quirked an eyebrow at her. "It's that bad?"

She shrugged, but there was no casualness to the gesture. "Depends on your point of view."

"From my point of view?"

"You're probably going to feel like breaking something, but for me, please don't."

He didn't like the sound of that. "For you, Aria, I can do just about anything."

He wasn't going to promise her though, not when he didn't know what she was going to tell him. He didn't believe anything romantic passed between her and his brother, but other things might set off his temper.

She took a deep breath and blurted her words so fast he had a tough time trying to follow what she was saying. The quicker she spoke though, and the *more* she talked, the more anger and dread curled in his belly, through his chest, and into his outer extremities. He was struggling not to shake, trying hard not to clench down on the hand he held.

He'd suspected they were plotting something, he even suspected it might have been something like this, but it did nothing to ease the acid churning through his stomach. Nothing to reduce the sense of betrayal he felt building through him.

"I never meant to upset you, Braith."

"And leaving me again wouldn't upset me?" he grated through clenched teeth.

She looked as if he'd slapped her when she recoiled from him. "It's not what I wanted to do," she whispered.

He released her hand and rose abruptly. His muscles trembled as he struggled against the urge to lift the bench on the other side and smash it into the ground. He fought for control to keep his half promise to her.

"Jesus, Aria."

"I'm sorry, I truly am. But no matter how much I love you and believe me I *do* love you more than I ever thought possible, my happiness, *our* happiness is not as important as the thousands upon thousands of lives who depend on you. Because of that, I was willing to forfeit my happiness, my *life*..." She broke off abruptly, wincing as she seemed to realize she'd said too much.

"Your what?" he barked. "Jack was going to... no, not Jack. Jack wouldn't have the heart and neither would Ashby. Gideon," he stated with dawning realization.

Her gaze focused on something else within the garden. "They didn't know. Jack and Ashby didn't know, and Gideon, well I went to Gideon, he didn't come to me."

He wanted to scream at her and tear the garden apart. He had the urge to shake her until he rattled some sense into her thick skull, but even as all those urges slammed through him, he also felt a deflating of his spirit.

He'd driven her to this; he'd driven them *all* to this.

He'd been determined to believe he could walk away, and wouldn't be necessary here; he was so determined to bend the world and everyone in it to his will. He hadn't stopped to think of anyone other than himself, and her. He'd only meant to keep her safe and protected; he'd been insistent he would leave with her as soon as the war was over, but by doing so he pushed her and the others into trying to find a way to make him stay.

He didn't doubt she would have sacrificed herself to make him lead. He ran his hands through his hair as he dropped onto the bench beside her.

"You're angry with me," she whispered.

"I am. I'm also angry with myself."

"Know it was *never* what I wanted. I always wanted you. My heart." She pressed a hand to her chest. "Would always have been yours, no matter how far I went, or how long we were apart."

His head bowed, he folded his hands before him as he listened to the reassuring beat of her heart. "My blood is inside you, Aria, Jack knows that means I can track you anywhere."

"We were hoping if someone else's blood diluted it..."

He couldn't stop his low groan of anguish at the thought. It was a stab to his heart his father had done such a thing to her. He could no longer taste his father's blood in her, but if he'd still been alive he could find her anywhere she went.

"Perhaps it would lessen your ability to track me," she said.

"And if not, Gideon was the backup plan," he growled.

She managed a small nod as her lower lip quivered. "Yes."

"Aria," he moaned as regret filled him. Pulling her against him, he pressed a firm kiss against her forehead. "I would have found you, you know, diluted blood or not I would have found you. I'll always find you."

"I know." Her fingers curled into his shirt as she pressed her face against his neck. "I think I always knew."

"Gideon became your entire plan at one point."

"Yes."

"You should have come to me," he broke off as he shook his head. "You couldn't; I wouldn't listen. Why did you change your mind? Why have you decided to tell me this?"

She pulled slightly away. "Because I couldn't be that person anymore. I simply couldn't leave you a second time. I was trying to do what I felt was right by leaving now, but it was never going to be right, not in the end. It would have destroyed us; even if you found me things never would have been the same. No matter what, you would have brought me back here, and you would have resented me for the rest of my life for betraying you, even if you could have forgiven me. You've also come to realize we're not the most important thing, not anymore. While I was in that dungeon, I knew you'd become the king."

"I don't understand."

"The stubborn, determined, unwilling to bend Braith I knew would have stormed through those gates with no thought to reason and logic—"

"I came as soon as I could."

She smiled as she rested her forehead against his; her fingers were as delicate as a butterfly's wing against his face. "I know you did. But you restrained yourself, and you put the greater good ahead of me, and you."

"I would give my life for yours, Aria, never doubt that."

She tilted her head to study him. "I know that, but you're a king, Braith, so many depend on you, and I'm—"

"A queen if you agree to be."

She closed her eyes, and her hands stilled on his face. "I know they won't accept me as a human."

"They have agreed to it." Her eyes flew open as she leaned back. "They will accept you as a leader, as a human, and as a queen. They will recognize you."

"Because of Caleb."

"You may not want it for that reason, but you gained their respect and admiration for it. I think they would have eventually agreed even if you hadn't helped take down Caleb. They are beginning to realize if things are to be equal, this is one of the things that will have to change. They accepted and respected human leaders in The Barrens, and they'll accept them here as well. You make me stronger, Aria, and it will help gain the support of the humans if you are by my side. They will recognize you as my queen."

"You had a meeting about this?"

"Yes."

"And if we have children?"

His hand fell instinctively to her belly. "I will love our children no matter what, human or vampire. I never thought I'd say those words, never even thought I'd care for any progeny I had, but I will love our children as much as I love you."

Tears shimmered in her eyes. "I know that, Braith, but they will not be accepted if I stay human, will they?"

"They have agreed our oldest child will have a seat on the council, but if the child is human, he or she won't be accepted as my heir. It will have to be a vampire child of ours, and even if it doesn't sound like it, that is a huge concession for them. Though, I don't plan on stepping down for a very long time."

"Would others accept them?"

He hesitated. "It's going to be very difficult for a while, Aria. It's going to be a long time before our society operates the way we want it to."

"Probably not in my lifetime though," she muttered. "The life they will face..." Her voice trailed off as she turned toward the fountain. "We fought to make a better world, but our children will still know hardship and hostility—"

"No." He grasped her chin as he turned her head toward him. "No. *Our* children will know no such thing." But even as he said the words, he knew he was trying to make things bend to his will again. "Okay, yes, they may face some obstacles, but all children do, and things will be different for them. There will be prejudices, distrust, and hatred for a long time to come, but one day all of this will be just a memory, and the hatred will fade."

"Just as the memories of the old world have faded, I don't have that many years though, Braith."

"I know." This was it; the time had finally come to tell her. He was fairly certain of the choice she would make; he just wasn't sure *he* was ready for it. "Aria, there is something you must know."

She frowned at him. "What is it?"

He braced himself before continuing. "Xavier knows many things; more than both of us could ever learn, figure out, or understand over hundreds of years."

"I know, he's fascinating."

"That's one way to describe him, I suppose; most go with peculiar, but I guess fascinating works. He also sees deeper into people than anyone I've ever known, and he understands more about the way they work. He sees things in this world no one else would or could. Before you were captured, I noticed he'd taken a particular interest in you."

"What kind of interest?"

"That's what I was curious to know, and I confronted him about it."

"What did he say?" she prompted when he didn't speak for an extended moment.

He didn't want to say the words, as badly as he wanted to blurt them. "He believes you have vampire blood in your heritage."

She became as still as a stone; even her heart seemed to freeze before giving a forceful kick against the inside of her ribs. "That's not possible."

"I think it is."

"No." She shook her head so vehemently her hair fluttered around her face. "No, Braith. I'm human."

"Yes, you most certainly *are* human. However, I believe that one of your ancestors was the child of a vampire. Listen to me, Aria, it makes sense," he said when she continued to shake her head. "You're faster than most humans, and only Daniel and William move with the same sort of soundless grace you do." He didn't add in her father; this was difficult enough without that reminder.

"Max is quick and capable in the woods, but nowhere near as quick or as silent as the three of you. You're strong; you destroyed the vampire in The Barrens. The first time I ever saw you maneuver through the trees, even I thought the speed and grace with which you moved was extraordinary. I'd never seen anything like it. If I'd been thinking clearly at the time, maybe I would have picked up on it, but I don't think I've thought clearly since I met you."

"Same here," she muttered as she stopped shaking her head and frowned at the fountain.

"There's also the bloodlink."

"It's never been with a human before; Ashby and Melinda were so baffled by us."

"As were Xavier and Gideon. No vampire has found their bloodlink in a human; Xavier is certain of it."

"That might explain why I unreasonably felt like I could trust you from the beginning, and why I was strangely unafraid when I first met you. I was always so reckless and driven to find a piece of me I didn't know was missing until you kissed me and I found it. Maybe there is a little bit of vampire DNA in me that recognized something in you."

He quirked an eyebrow as she frowned at him. "You weren't fearful of me? I'm terrifying."

"Nowhere near as afraid of you as I was the other vamp who tried to claim me." He would have protested if she wasn't smiling at him so endearingly. "But what does it mean, Braith? What difference does it make if somewhere along the way there was a vampire in my family?"

"It didn't have to be a vampire; it could have been a human-vampire child banished from the palace, one who fled to avoid the abuse they received."

Dawning realization settled over her features. "My great-grandfather left the palace when he was a child. He later started the rebellion."

"I know, you told me that in The Barrens, but I didn't think anything of it at the time. When I spoke to your father—"

"My father knew of this? What did he say?" The yearning in her voice tore at his heart.

"He told us what you did. His grandfather left the palace at thirteen; he struggled to survive on the streets of the town before retreating into the woods. Once in the woods, he gathered a loyal following that, over time, became the rebellion. Your father didn't know much about his time in the palace, only that his grandfather left after his mother died and had a deep hatred of vampires.

"David assumed it was because of the abuse he sustained while in the palace. He admitted it could have been possible there was more to it. He said there were strange rumors about the man when David was a child, but they faded after his death and were chalked up to having been created to add an aura of mystery and power to the rebel leader."

"What kind of rumors?" Aria inquired.

"That he was faster than a human, stronger, could see and hear better than a hawk. Your father never really thought anything of it, and your great-grandfather was killed when your father was ten. He'd never spoken about it with his father as there had been no reason to question any of it—until Xavier."

"And did my father believe his grandfather could have been the child of a human and a vampire?"

The world became oddly still as every sense he had focused on her. He didn't miss that her hand was against her belly as she watched him. He rested his hand on hers and leaned closer as he pressed a kiss to her temple.

"He did believe it was a strong possibility once he thought over everything."

"I see," she murmured. "But what difference would it make if I do have some vampire in me?"

"Xavier believes it will make a difference on your chances for survival."

Her nostrils flared as she inhaled quickly. "Of surviving the change?"

He didn't want to desire this, he honestly didn't, but deep inside he did. He had to release her to grasp the bench with both hands. His arms locked; the stone of the bench bit into his palms as he tried to steady his emotions. He didn't know if he hoped for her to say yes or no, more.

"Yes," he said.

She sat in stunned silence before she started to laugh and flung herself at him. He barely felt the force of her slender weight as she wrapped her arms around him and settled in his lap. Anguish and ecstasy swamped him as he hugged her back.

"There's still a chance you won't survive. Xavier says the only survivors he knows of had vampire heritage of some sort, but we're still not entirely certain you do," he said.

"I'll survive."

"Aria—"

"I'll survive, Braith; I'm stronger than all of them, and I'd say all the evidence points toward a 'yes' about my heritage. I'd never thought I'd be happy to hear that, but I am. I feel it's *right* somehow."

He almost couldn't look at her. If she didn't survive, he would be the one who killed her. He shuddered at the thought, his hands clenched on her. But if she *survived*...

An eternity of promise unfurled before him; the hope was almost too much for him to bear.

"I don't want to be the one who kills you," he said.

"You won't be."

"Either way, I will, Aria. You can stay human; you can stay with me as a human." He had to make sure she thought over all her options.

"I will still die. I would love to have those years with you, Braith, truly I would, but I'd love to have many *many* more with you."

"Perhaps if we wait a few years—"

"We could do all of those things. I could grow old with you, and you could watch me die that way. We can live together now for a few years, and then we will come to this same crossroads, and it will be even more difficult to make the decision. Especially if there are children involved, I could never take the chance of leaving them. I'm not vain, but I don't want to push this off year after year until I'm dying from old age and there are no other options."

"You'd still be beautiful."

"To you, of course, but it would be weird, and you wouldn't desire me."

"It would be a little weird, but believe me there have been times when you've been the most unkempt and smelly thing I've ever come across, and I still desired you. I'd take you any way I could get you."

Her eyebrows lifted haughtily; her eyes sparkled with laughter. "You're depraved."

"I am what you made me."

She grinned at him as she wiggled in his lap.

He clenched his teeth as he tried to remain focused on the discussion at hand. "The last thing I want to do is die, and we've been waiting so long to start our lives together. I'd like to do so with the promise of eternity. I understand if you decide against doing this, I don't know how I'd handle this if the roles were reversed. I'd be terrified."

He rested his face in the hollow of her neck. He inhaled her sweet scent, savoring it as he allowed it to soothe some of the tension in him. He could smell his blood within her, but if he did this, if this were the step they took, his blood would fill her even more. *Their* blood would forever be mingled.

"I'll agree with whatever you decide, Aria; this is your life we're talking about here."

"I know. I was never sure I would live to this age to begin with."

A distant look settled over her face. He could almost see the reality sinking in with the knowledge she would die from this and possibly never reawaken.

"I wouldn't mind a few more years with each other; *perhaps* we could wait. Though there is only one way to guarantee we don't have children," she said.

He quirked an eyebrow at her; she smiled playfully in return and shifted mischievously in his lap again. "You're hilarious."

"I am." The smile slid away, and her expression became grave once more. "I think I'll survive, Braith, but if I don't what will become of you? What will happen to *you*?"

"That's not something you should be concerned about."

"Yes, it is. I saw your old rooms. I was in the dungeon with the survivors; I know what you are capable of when you lose control, and Ashby said bloodlinks cannot survive without each other."

"Ashby's an idiot."

"Braith—"

"I'll survive, Aria." His hands splayed across her back. "I promise you I *will* survive. I'll hate myself, and I'll hate this world if it doesn't have you in it, but I'll keep it together, and I'll go on *because* of you. It's the only thing I'll have left of you, to do what you would expect of me, to do what would make you proud. I won't destroy any humans; there won't be any other blood slaves. This is not the same as last time, I felt betrayed then, as did you," he added when her eyes darkened. "I was out of control, lost, and furious because I didn't know what was going on with me, with you, or why you left me so abruptly after claiming to love me. This will *not* be the same."

"Our bond is stronger after last night."

"Our bond was stronger before we slept together."

The words were far harder than he intended, but he'd seen the look of guilt flickering through her eyes. He wasn't going to let her have any regret over what happened between them.

"Sex was not going to solidify it even more, no matter what Ashby, Gideon, or any of those idiots believed. This—" he seized her hand and pressed it over his still heart— "there are times I can almost feel this beating for you. You have owned it since the moment I saw you. It may have taken me a while to come to the realization, but it's true, and *nothing* will change that. Not blood and not sex. You were made for me, Aria; you're my bloodlink, my soul mate.

"The bond between us has been stronger for a while now. When Jack helped you escape from the palace, I lost my vision completely. When you were taken this time, I never lost my vision at all. It wasn't the best vision, but I *could* still see, and that was long before last night, understand?"

She closed her eyes as a single tear slid free. "Yes."

When he brushed the tear away, his fingers slid over his fresh bite marks again as he ignored the rest of the fading marks on her body.

"So your eyes are healing?" she asked.

He shrugged. "I think your blood has helped them heal; you've made me stronger than I ever knew I could be."

"And if I'm gone?"

"I don't know; it may stay the way it was this time, or I may become blind again. I will get through whatever happens though. Don't concern yourself with that, Aria."

"I'd like for you to move on, to find someone else—"

"No," he interrupted as his fingers stilled. His entire being recoiled at the thought, revulsion twisted like a poisonous snake through his belly. "No."

"You will require an heir."

"There is Jack for that, or Ashby and Melinda."

"Braith—"

"No, Aria, no. I can promise you I'll keep on living, and I will stay in control of myself and lead justly. Those are promises I know I can keep, but I will *not* make that one. I will not be able to uphold it, and I won't lie to you."

"Maybe not now, but you have years ahead of you. You will need love, companionship."

"No!" he said forcefully. "*No.* There is no one after you. Five hundred years, another thousand years, hell forever is not going to change that. Don't push this, Aria; the answer will not change no matter how you try to spin it."

For a moment, he thought she was going to argue again, but she finally relented.

"Okay." She kissed his nose as her fingers traced over the faded scars surrounding his eyes. "I'm afraid, Braith. I never thought I'd live long, I never thought I'd have this kind of life, and I'm afraid to lose it. I wasn't afraid to die to be away from you, and I shouldn't be afraid to die to be *with* you—"

"Great way to put it," he muttered sardonically.

"But I am," she continued. "I'm afraid to lose the years we could have if something goes wrong, and though I know I'll survive, or at least I'm fairly certain I will..."

"I know; you don't have to explain it to me. I understand."

He closed his eyes; his fingers slid through her hair before stroking her shoulders. It was easy enough to jump all over this, to say yes to the promise of eternity, but to face the certainty of death was frightening, and the last thing he wanted was for her to be frightened. He wanted eternity, but he wanted her happiness more.

"It doesn't have to be now, Aria, you don't have to decide right now. We can wait and discuss it further once you've had time to think it over."

She nodded; her eyes became distant and thoughtful. "Yes, I think that would be for the best."

He was relieved she was going to think this through. Even so, he felt the sharp knife of disappointment in his gut.

"I'm not ready for children, Braith. No matter what happens, if I change soon or if we wait a few years, I'm not ready for children."

His arms clenched around her waist as he pulled her against his chest.

"I want them with you!" she gushed out. "But not right now. We just discovered this world of relative peace, and we're finally able to be together without having to hide our feelings. I'd like the time to enjoy it and you. Human or vampire, children are a lot of work."

"That they are," he murmured.

She peered up at him from under lowered lashes. "I'd like a brood one day though."

"A brood?"

"Well at least three."

He laughed as he rested his chin on her head and nestled her closer to him. "I can handle three, but there's only one way to guarantee we don't have children right now," he reminded her.

She shot him a disgruntled look. "Well, that's not going to happen."

He laughed as he rocked her a little. "Minx."

"My birthday's next week."

"I didn't know that."

She smiled as she shrugged. "William and I don't celebrate it; it's just another day in the woods and this year... well this year, with dad being gone, it seems like even less of a reason to celebrate. I never thought I'd make it to eighteen, especially after I was captured."

"I think we should celebrate it this year."

"Maybe it would be nice," she murmured though she didn't look convinced.

"Are you sure you can live with this life?"

She frowned at him as she leaned back.

He rose and placed her down as he gestured around the garden. "This isn't your world, Aria. I remember how unhappy you were in the palace, how much you missed your woods and your freedom. There will be many demands placed on us, lots of pressure, and even less freedom. Even if you choose to stay human, this is not the life you expected."

"Braith—"

"I mean to make sure you understand, Aria. I won't force you to stay. If you choose to leave because you won't be happy here, I won't make you stay. I'll abide by your wishes, but I can't, I simply can't go right now, maybe not ever." He choked on the words; it took all he had to get them out. "Sometimes love..."

"Isn't always enough," she whispered.

"It's always enough, but sometimes it's learning to put someone else's happiness ahead of your own. It's learning to let go, Aria, if it's necessary, and I will let you go if you ask me to. I'll set you free if that is what you require. It will destroy me to lose you, but I will not harm anyone, and I will let you live the rest of your life in peace. I will not take your freedom from you."

"I know." She rose to her feet and walked over to him. Her arms encircled his waist; her head tilted back to study him as tears slid down her cheeks. "I know you would let me go, but I don't want you to."

"You can't rush into this decision."

"I'm not rushing into this," she whispered. "And I can go into the woods once in a while, can't I?"

"As often as I can, I will take you into the woods," he vowed.

"Good. I think I can keep my sanity then," she grinned at him as she nudged his hip.

Braith groaned as he pulled her against him and stared at the sculpted figure of the couple in the fountain. The couple who was forever fated to look but never touch. He never wanted to let go of her, yet he may be the one who destroyed her if she decided to choose eternity.

CHAPTER NINETEEN

THE CELEBRATION WAS FAR LARGER than she'd expected. Before this day, she and William celebrated their birthdays by receiving larger slices of meat, usually a new bow and some arrows, and being serenaded with a silly song they hated.

Now they had more food than she'd ever seen in her life, a small band playing instruments, and a massive cake she couldn't tear her eyes away from. Her mouth watered every time she looked at the elaborately decorated thing, and all she craved was a giant piece of it.

"I think I'm jealous of the cake," Braith said.

"Huh?" Aria muttered as she tore her gaze away from the massive creation of sugary goodness in the middle of the table.

Braith laughed as he slid his arm around her waist. "I'm jealous of the cake; you can't take your eyes off it."

"I've never seen anything like it," she marveled. "It's amazing."

"Even more so than me?"

She waved her hand dismissively at him. "Of course not, but wow."

"Would you like a piece?"

"Aren't we supposed to eat first or sing or something?"

"It's your birthday; you can do whatever you like."

William shouldered in between them. He placed his crutch in front of her, blocking her path. He was perfectly willing to trip her if she even attempted to get a piece before him. "It's my birthday too, and as the older, wiser sibling I should get the first piece."

"I'll give you older, but you are most certainly not wiser," she retorted. "And as the younger, *female* sibling, I should get the first piece."

"As the still crippled and hobbling sibling, I beg to differ."

Aria snorted. "I could kick the crutch out from under you."

"You wouldn't dare."

"Try me."

"Why don't you each get a piece at the same time," Braith inserted reasonably.

Aria shot him a look.

"Reason doesn't apply to the twins, brother. They won't shut up until they're stuffing their faces," Jack informed him as he sauntered toward them.

William shrugged casually but nodded enthusiastically in agreement. "The man has a valid point."

Braith looked confused but shook his head and headed to the table. She watched Braith's deft hands as he slid the knife through the bottom of the cake, cutting off one pink rose and one red one.

She became more fascinated with those hands than with the cake. Those hands were strong and brutal when they had to be, yet so achingly tender and loving when they slid over her. Aria mentally shook herself from her thoughts before they wandered to things far from appropriate here.

He started back with two large pieces.

"Can I mess with him some more?" William asked.

"Sure," she replied.

Braith handed her a slice of cake before giving William his.

"Hers is bigger," William said.

"Excuse me?" Braith inquired in surprise.

"You gave her the bigger piece."

Jack burst into loud laughter as Braith stared incredulously at William. Aria bit her upper lip as she tried not to laugh.

"You two are just freaking hilarious," Braith muttered.

Aria couldn't stifle her laughter anymore, but her attention was diverted by the giant slice of cake in front of her.

William eagerly dove into his piece. "Delicious."

Aria eyed her brother with envy as she grabbed her fork. She still found utensils annoying, but at least she was getting better at using them. "Amazing," she agreed.

Braith watched her with a raised eyebrow and a small smile on his face. "Hopefully, you'll like our wedding cake as much."

She choked on her cake; William froze with his bite halfway to his mouth.

"Excuse me?" she managed to get out around Daniel's solid thumps on her back.

Braith grinned back at her in the same annoying way William had been smiling at him.

"You heard me," he said.

She glanced at her brothers, not sure she understood him right. Marriage wasn't something she'd ever really thought about before, but then how else did someone become a queen?

She realized she'd never put a whole lot of thought into it, but marriage would solidify her position. When Braith told her he wanted her as his queen, and they would accept her, he'd also been saying he planned to marry her. She felt like an idiot.

She couldn't think of anything better than being his wife for the rest of her life. A flood of childhood dreams came rushing back. There had been a time when she'd dreamt of a husband, children, and a marriage ceremony underneath the banquet tree. With her family surrounding her...

A hot rush of tears filled her eyes. She'd been doing well today, trying to stay upbeat; enjoying her time with her brothers and Braith, trying not to think about the fact their father wasn't here to celebrate it with them. The smile slipped from Braith's face as he watched her.

"I'll give you away, Aria," Daniel offered.

"We both will," William interjected forcefully.

"Easy there, hop along. She's not used to dresses, and between the two of you one of you would end up falling over." Jack smiled at them as he tried to ease the mood again.

"Especially if she's wearing heels," Braith added with a small wink.

Aria forced herself to shake off her melancholy. Braith was rarely lighthearted, and he was trying to be so now. She would be too.

"Oh, that must be like a fish out of water!" Max declared with a loud laugh. "I actually wouldn't mind seeing it!"

"I would kind of like to see it too," William said.

"It's not pretty," Aria admitted, and her smile didn't feel as forced.

William and Max laughed as they poked at each other and then snickered at her. She rolled her eyes at them as she fought the urge to kick William's crutch out from under him. Braith took the empty plate from her hand and slid his arm around her waist.

She was a little confused as she stared up at him. Had she just been proposed to, or was he only teasing her as she and William had been teasing him? She didn't have time to ponder it as he swept her off her feet and twirled her out to the dance floor.

Aria laughed as he eased her back down. "I don't know how to dance."

"I'll teach you."

She glanced around the room; though the party was elaborate, there were few people in the room she didn't know, a fact she was relieved about. They weren't staring at her and whispering behind their hands as some of the others in the palace did.

Though most of the attention she received seemed more curious than malicious, she was still a little troubled by it and happy she didn't have to deal with it today. Today was a celebration, and that was what she aimed to do. There would be no more sadness, she decided firmly. Not today.

He pulled her close against him, wrapping one arm around her waist as he took her hand and pressed it to his chest.

"Isn't there supposed to be some room between us?" she asked.

"That's what they say, but I don't agree," he told her.

"Good." She rested her head against his chest and closed her eyes as she savored the delicious scent of him and the sense of security enveloping her. "The people within the palace and the vampires who fought with us are curious about me."

"They are."

"They don't understand us."

"They don't," he confirmed. "But it doesn't matter. We do, and eventually, they will too. I have a surprise for you later."

She lifted her head to look up at him. "What is it?"

"It's not a surprise if I tell you."

"I'm not very good at waiting."

"I won't make you wait long, I promise."

She was going to hold him to that promise. "A bigger surprise than talk of wedding cakes?"

He lifted her and spun her around. A small gasp escaped her as for a moment she felt like she was flying.

"I meant it too," he informed her as he stopped spinning her but didn't place her on the ground. "I am going to marry you."

"Aren't you supposed to ask me first?" she inquired.

"I thought that would be redundant."

"So you just assumed I would say yes."

"Of course."

How the hell was she supposed to argue with that?

"You're arrogant," she said.

"Hmm." He shrugged as his hands stroked her back. "And you love it."

She shook her head as she rested her hand on his chest again. "When I was little, before I gave up thoughts of marriage, I always pictured being married under the banquet tree."

"The banquet tree?"

"It's a giant apple tree William and I discovered. We were the only two who knew its location."

"Then you'll have it; just tell me where to be," he murmured against her mouth.

She shivered as thrills of pleasure swept her spine. Her fingers curled around his solid biceps as he continued to dance with her feet off the ground. Closing her eyes, she let the soft music drift over her as she lost herself to the feel of him against her. They danced through three more songs before returning to where William stood propped on his crutch between Max and Daniel.

"I'll be right back." Braith kissed the top of her head and left the room.

She watched him go before leaning against the table.

"Where did everyone go?" she inquired as she realized Ashby, Jack, Xavier, and Gideon were no longer present. Aria stepped away from the table. Braith had handled her revelation well, but she knew he'd been furious when she told him about their plan. "I'll be right back."

Daniel stepped in front of her. "We were told to keep you here, something about a surprise."

Was it really a surprise, or was he going to confront them?

She glanced nervously from Daniel to the door Braith had disappeared through. "Daniel—"

"It's fine, Aria."

"I hope so," she muttered.

"It's been over a week since you told him," William reminded her as he leaned forward on his crutches. "Don't you think he would have done something by now?"

"Or he's let the anger fester," Max said.

"Nice, Max," Daniel said brusquely.

Max shrugged as he picked at some cheese and crackers. Aria twisted her hands before her as she shifted from foot to foot and watched the door.

"Getting married soon?" William tapped her calf with his crutch to get her attention.

"I think so," she muttered.

"Becoming a vamp soon?"

The three of them became quiet as they exchanged a look. She had a difficult time meeting William's gaze. It would kill him if she decided to try and make the change and didn't survive. The thought of it caused a hard lump to form in her throat.

"I don't know," she admitted. "I was going to wait till after our birthday before deciding anything."

William nodded, his gaze traveled to the cake. "Who knew we'd be hoping we *did* have vampire blood in us."

Aria chuckled. "Not me. Do you still have Daniel's drawing of us?"

Sadness crept over his features as he hesitatingly met her gaze. "No, dad saw it one day and asked me for it. He, uh, he liked it."

"Oh." The sudden pressure in her chest made it difficult to speak.

William squeezed her arm. "I'll give you away, you know; I've been trying to do it for eighteen years now."

She managed a small laugh as she clasped his hand.

BRAITH RAN the key Ashby handed him over his fingers. "It's all set up like you asked for it to be."

"Good."

"Are you going there to change her?" Jack inquired.

"I'm not sure about anything when it comes to that," he admitted.

"She is stronger and more impressive than any other human I've ever met," Gideon said.

Braith glared ferociously at Gideon. "We believe there is a reason for that. Xavier, if you would please tell them."

Xavier's dark eyes were reproachful as they scanned over Ashby, Jack, and Gideon. In his firm, even tones, he revealed to them exactly what he had told Braith, and what Braith in turn related to Aria. Gideon and Ashby's mouths dropped, Jack seemed to have an ah-ha moment as he placed his hands over his face and began to nod.

"It makes so much more sense now," Jack muttered. "There were so many things..." Jack broke off as his hands fell away. "I should have suspected something like this. The four of them were always so talented with weapons and so fast. We've all seen the way Aria moves through the trees, and she helped bring down Caleb. You've never seen Daniel or David on a horse though, they're amazing, and William may very well be the fastest human I've ever seen when he runs."

"It would completely explain the bloodlink," Ashby breathed in awe. "And your eyesight. You were able to link because she has vampire blood in her, and I am sure of that, even if you're not. Your vision came back when she appeared because something inside of you recognized her as your link, and you *had* to be able to see her to claim her as your soul mate.

"The minute I saw Melinda, I *knew* my life would never be the same. Because you were blind you weren't able to find her immediately, so something inside of you made it possible for you to do so. It makes sense you would have such a reaction to it considering she isn't a vampire but does contain some of the genetics. The sharing of your blood and the increasing intensity of your bond has improved your vision, and for all we know may one day cure it completely. Your bloodline is the most powerful and the purest; your father was the oldest vampire ever. We'll never know what he may have been capable of, and we may never know what *you* are fully capable of, especially when it comes to her."

"How did we miss this?" Jack demanded.

"You were too busy plotting how to take her away," Braith snarled. He had promised Aria not to break anything or lose control, and he would keep his promise, but he hadn't promised to let it go. His gaze fixed on Gideon. "Or even killing her."

Ashby took an instinctive step back as Braith pressed closer to them. Braith's hand shot out, he seized Gideon by the throat and shoved him into the wall. Gideon remained immobile as he stared unblinkingly at him.

"Braith, be reasonable," Jack urged.

"I am being reasonable, Jack; he's still alive." Gideon's hazel eyes narrowed. "For once, I am not simply just reacting, right, Gideon?" Braith inquired.

"You have to admit, Braith, you backed us all into a corner," Gideon grated.

"I admit it, and because of that, I'm not going to kill you. I swear on her life if you ever go behind my back again, if you *ever* think of hurting one hair on her head, I will do things to you even my father would have been jealous of. Do you understand me, Gideon?"

Gideon's eyes were hooded as he stared at Braith. "I understand. It's not like I wanted to kill the girl, and she came to me."

Braith jerked his hand away before he accidentally snapped Gideon's neck. "I know she did."

"If any of you had come to me, this never even would have been an issue," Xavier admonished.

Ashby had the grace to appear chastised; Jack and Gideon wouldn't meet Xavier's gaze.

Braith's hands fisted; he stared down the hall as his stomach twisted. "There will be no more plotting, not amongst us, and not if we are to have any chance of making it a better world than my father did."

"Agreed," Gideon murmured.

"If she does agree to the change, what are you going to do if she dies, Braith?" Ashby inquired.

"Survive," he muttered.

"Braith," Ashby's eyes flickered briefly over the others. "I don't know if that's possible."

"It *has* to be possible. I promised her I would, and I will keep my promise no matter what happens."

"I don't envy your position," Jack said.

"No one would."

"Perhaps someone else could do it if she decides to try," Ashby suggested. "Jack even, he's your brother."

Jack's mouth dropped as he shook his head forcefully.

"No," Braith said firmly.

"For you to be the one who causes her death is a different kind of monster," Ashby persisted.

Braith turned as Aria stepped into the hall; he should have known her brothers wouldn't be able to keep her away for long. Apprehension etched her features as she stared at him. When her gaze flickered over the others, her delicate eyebrow shot up questioningly.

"It will be me," he informed them, unable to take his eyes from her. "No one else will touch her in such a way again."

They exchanged a disconcerted look before Jack turned to him. "I'll be by tomorrow."

"Don't destroy the kingdom while I'm gone, Gideon," Braith told him.

Gideon laughed as he rubbed his reddened throat. "Don't destroy our future queen, Braith."

"You're an asshole," Braith hissed as he shoved past him.

"So I've been told."

Braith didn't look back as he hurried down the hall toward her.

"Is everything okay?" Aria demanded.

"Fine. Are you ready for your surprise?"

She glanced at the men behind him and nodded. He smiled as he held his arm out and waited for her to take it.

CHAPTER TWENTY

"WHERE ARE WE GOING?" she demanded with a laugh.

"I told you, it's a surprise. Keep your eyes closed."

It was impossible to see anything anyway. Braith didn't seem to trust her not to peek as he'd placed his hands over her eyes to ensure her blindness. They were in the woods, and though she couldn't see the leaves, she knew they were beginning to turn as the smell of them hung heavily in the crisp air.

Keegan pressed close to her side, and she felt the goodbye in the gesture before he slipped away. She knew they would see the wolf again, but for now, he was returning to his family.

Braith adjusted his hands to slip one away from her eyes as he pushed back a limb. He stopped suddenly, pulling her back against his chest as he held her. The hum of anticipation raced through her as she practically bounced on her toes.

"Are you ready?" he asked.

His lips brushed her ear as he bent close to her. Her heart pulsed with excitement but she wasn't sure if it was for the surprise, or for him. "Yes."

He slipped his hands away from her eyes. For a moment, she

stared around the darkening forest in confusion as she saw only a fox hiding amongst the trees.

When Braith reached around her, his chest pressed against her back, and his cheek brushed hers as he pointed upward. Aria's head tilted back, and her mouth dropped as disbelief swamped her.

There, nestled in the trees, was a home that spread throughout five towering maples and oaks. The light wood of the building gleamed in the moonlight reflecting in the two front windows. A winding walkway started from the far edge of the woods and curled up toward the large porch. Her hand fluttered to her heart, and she couldn't breathe through the love engulfing her. It was far smaller than Ashby's rambling creation had been, but it was stunning.

"I know you're not at home in the palace. I know this is where you're happiest, that the forest is part of who you are. I told you I'd bring you to the woods as often as I could, but you'll require a place to stay when you come here, somewhere safe, a home."

"Home," she breathed. Tears shimmered in her eyes as she turned toward him. "How? When?"

His fingers caressed her cheek. "I started it after Caleb took you in the hopes it would help to keep me somewhat calmer. It didn't work very well, but it kept me a little preoccupied and from going insane. Jack, Ashby, and Daniel have been working on it lately, and I'm told William hobbled around giving orders."

Aria laughed as she shook her head. She turned back to the tree house; she could barely breathe as she tried to take it all in. She was so unbelievably loved. That love was in every nail, in every piece of wood, and every drop of sweat it took to put it all together. It was amazing, she loved it, but she knew one thing above all else...

"Wherever you are will always be my home."

His arms wrapped around her and turned her within them.

He kissed her briefly before lowering himself to one knee and holding out a small black box to her. She could only gape in astonishment as he opened the box to reveal a small emerald ring inside.

"Will you marry me, Arianna?"

For a moment, she couldn't find her voice; she could only open and close her mouth like a fish as her heart raced and tears of joy burned her eyes. "I thought you didn't have to ask."

Oh how she loved seeing his grin on such a regular basis now, loved how it lit his eyes and revealed the dimple in his cheek.

"Is that a yes?" he asked.

She burst into joyous laughter as he leapt to his feet, wrapped her in a massive hug, and kissed her soundly. She wiggled her fingers as he slid the ring on; it was a little big, but she didn't care.

"I thought an emerald suited you better than a diamond," he said.

"I love it."

He cradled her face as he kissed her again. She melted against him when his tongue swept in to take possession of her mouth. Her legs encircled his waist as he lifted her up and held her against him. She barely felt him moving while he carried her up the walkway and into their home.

ARIA HADN'T TAKEN the time to explore the night before, or at least Braith hadn't given her the time to do anything but explore *him*, but now she relished in every square inch of the rooms. There was far more detail than she would have thought to put into a home in the trees. Daniel must have helped with the features as some of the intricate carvings in the doorframes and cabinets were a work of art.

She smiled as she ran her fingers over the cabinets within the kitchen. She closed the door on some bread, and as her stomach rumbled at the sight of it, she wondered how much longer she would feel hunger for something other than blood.

She wasn't sure if she would be leaving here a human, or if she would even be leaving here at all. It seemed like a perfect time to make the change, to throw caution to the wind and have eternity, but she was terrified of losing this bit of bliss they had just discovered together.

Her whole life had been nothing but arduous, and now it was going so well, she was contemplating her death. And no matter how she looked at it, Braith was right about one thing; she was going to die.

The delicate carvings in the cabinets were ivy leaves she realized as her fingers lingered on them. That must have been William's suggestion; he knew how much she loved the way the ivy grew through the trees in some areas of the forest. Thoughts of Max and her brothers saddened her. They had already lost her father; she didn't know how they would survive her loss too, especially William if she decided to do this and didn't survive.

Aria sighed as her fingers slipped from the cabinet. She had no idea what to do. It was one thing to die for a cause; it was another thing to risk her life when it wasn't *entirely* necessary. At least not yet.

She could wait a few years; maybe even wait till she was twenty-five. It was an age she'd never thought she'd hit anyway; it would be nice to see it.

However, if she waited a few years then Aria wasn't sure she'd have the courage to do it, and what if she accidentally became pregnant? She'd never take the risk of leaving her child behind by doing something that may end her life.

She'd thought this decision would be easier, but she was completely torn. Why did she have to become reasonable and concerned about consequences *now*? She wished her father were here so she could talk to him and seek his guidance in making this decision.

I have vampire blood inside of me; she clung firmly to that thought. *I'm stronger than most, more stubborn. I will survive; I will.*

She traced over the swirls within the soft green countertops as she studied the open, airy kitchen. They hadn't run electricity from the palace, and Aria was glad as she much preferred the flicker of the lanterns hanging above her. It was cozier with the mellow radiance illuminating the picturesque home.

She felt Braith's eyes on her before she spotted him leaning against the doorframe. Her toes curled as her mouth went dry. His eyes were hooded with sleep, and his dark hair tussled across his forehead. He had taken the time to throw on a pair of pants that hung low on his hips to reveal the hair running from the waistband and up to his belly button before flaring out slightly at his chest.

The hard ridges of his abdomen flexed as he crossed his legs and scanned her with the same hunger she was sure had just been in her gaze. A sly gleam lit his eyes when her gaze raked him from head to toe. His full mouth curved in a predatory smile.

He was far more delicious looking than cake, she decided firmly. And he was *hers.* The thought caused her hands to clench as possession shot through her. He would always be hers, no matter what she decided.

"Do you like it?" he asked.

"It's incredible."

"I'm glad. You must be hungry."

Her stomach rumbled eagerly at his words. "Guess I am," she told him as she placed a hand on her belly.

"I'll make you something."

She nodded as he moved away from the door with the ease of someone who was intrinsically aware of every muscle and cell within their body. He opened and closed cabinets as he retrieved supplies and she settled at the table.

"Braith?"

"Hmm," he murmured as he used the knife to slice bread with startling speed.

"Will I, uh, be able to eat human food again if I become a vampire?"

He stopped slicing and stared at the cabinets for a moment before glancing at her over his shoulder. His eyes flickered; something feral crossed his face before he shook it away.

"You can; it's not the same, but I've eaten it before. I don't find it appealing, but it might be different since you have a taste for it; I never did."

"Oh." Her eyebrows drew together as he continued to watch her. "The blood, I'm not so sure about that. I don't know if I can bite someone. I know you've been drinking the blood humans provide, but..."

She shuddered as she thought about the one aspect of this whole thing she had been trying *not* to contemplate.

Braith turned away; she watched as the muscles in his back and shoulders rippled with the deft slices of the knife. He finished cutting the loaf and carried a plate of bread and fruit over to her. Sitting before her, he leaned forward, his hands clasped as his eyes blazed into hers.

"You have consumed my blood."

She fiddled with a piece of bread. "That's because it's *you*. But another's blood, a *stranger's* blood, is an entirely different matter." Her nose wrinkled as revulsion twisted within her. "And after your father's blood."

He stiffened at the reminder as a slight snarl curled his lip.

"It was awful, Braith; I could never describe how awful it was."

"I know."

She leaned closer to enjoy the smell of spices and earth radiating from his body. "Is it that awful for you now, with others? Is that why you don't like drinking other people's blood anymore?"

"I don't think it's quite as revolting to me. The blood isn't forced on me as my father's was forced on you. And its blood, it's always been my staple. I don't enjoy another's blood the way I enjoy yours. It doesn't fill me in the same way, it's not as empowering, and it's nowhere near as pleasant tasting, not anymore."

He shook his head as he leaned back. He was trying to appear casual, but the tension in his shoulders and chest didn't ease. "I don't like touching them either. It's not their fault, but the idea of it has become offensive to me. Ashby doesn't enjoy it either, though he seems more willing than I am when it's necessary."

"What will happen if I'm gone?"

"Don't say that," he growled.

Aria opened her mouth to argue; she hoped he would move on if she was gone even though the idea of it made her want to vomit, but she bit back her words. Rehashing these worries and concerns wouldn't achieve anything except upsetting them both. She forced herself to eat a slice of bread. He wasn't looking at her anymore; his gaze was focused on the windows behind her.

"You don't have to drink anyone else's blood afterward though," he said. "I can provide for you."

She froze with a piece of bread halfway to her mouth. Her brow furrowed as she stared at him in confusion. "What?"

His gaze came back to her. "I can provide for you. My blood will be more than enough to sustain you. I will have to consume more, but it won't be necessary for you to go to another."

Relief flowed through her. "That's possible?"

"It is." His hands seized hers.

"But what about you? Won't it be draining on you?"

"Not if I stay well supplied."

"You just said you dislike the other blood, Braith. I know

you're not feeding as well as you should, you can't hide it from me. If you lose my blood on top of that—"

"But I won't be losing your blood." He brushed the hair back from her neck; his eyes latched onto his new marks on her skin. "I will still have yours; though it won't be enough to sate me completely, I won't lose it."

She took a large gulp of juice to wet her suddenly parched throat. A few months ago, such a proposition would have been revolting. For a reasonable, sane human being it still would be, but he'd helped to make her anything but reasonable and sane. She couldn't take her gaze from his neck, the muscles cording it, and the tautness of his smooth skin.

"Will you..." she had to take a breath before she asked the question. "Will you feed on other women?"

She couldn't look at him as she awaited his answer. She knew it was necessary for him to survive, and possibly her too, but damn if the thought didn't almost break her. He grasped her cheeks as he turned her face to him and tilted his head to peer at her.

"No. I would never turn to a real person again unless it becomes necessary to survive, and even then I would hate it. I don't mind the other blood as much as long as I don't have to touch the person. I will use the donor program, and you can feed solely on me if you decide to do this."

"Yes," she breathed, relieved and strangely titillated by the thought of such a proposition. "Would I be normal after?"

"What do you mean?"

"What will I be like afterward? Will I still be me or will I be a little wild? Will I lose control and try to kill someone, or start trying to feed off everyone?"

He tilted his chair on its front legs towards her. "You think you'll be a monster."

"Yes," she croaked out, horrified by the possibility.

"No. You will be you, Aria. I'm sure it will take some time to get used to certain things, but you will be able to control the hunger, and you will not become a bloodthirsty lunatic."

She couldn't help but chuckle as she shook her head. "I didn't think I'd be a lunatic but how can you be so sure?"

The chair clicked against the floor as he leaned back again. "Because we can all control what we do, and because Xavier has assured me the others he knows of did not lose their minds. They did not go off their rockers and were as normal as any other vampire born of a human."

"What if he's wrong?"

"There are many things about Xavier I don't understand and will never know, but I *do* know that, annoyingly enough, he's never wrong about the histories he speaks about."

"I see," she muttered, slightly more at ease.

When he leaned forward, she thought he was going to kiss her, but instead, he picked up a piece of apple and handed it to her. "Eat up; you're going to need your strength. We have a whole week out here together, and I have it in mind to tire you out."

She glared at him, not at all pleased when he chuckled, kissed her forehead, and rose. She bit into the apple as he grinned at her.

"I have to return to the palace for a bit. There are some things I must take care of," he said.

"Okay."

"I won't be gone long, and Jack is here in case you get bored or want to go for a walk."

"I'll be fine," she assured him. He squeezed her hand and turned to walk away. "Braith, I know you never wanted to change me before, but do you want to know that there might be a better chance I'll survive?"

He froze in the doorway; his hands grasped the frame as he shuddered but didn't look back at her. "I want to do whatever makes you happy, but yes, Aria, I want to change you."

She opened her mouth to tell him that doing this would make her happy, but the words froze in her throat. She couldn't shake the niggling fear she wouldn't survive, and though she craved nothing more than an eternity with him, Aria was terrified of losing the years of happiness they could have if she remained human.

He waited for a minute more before his shoulders slumped and he slipped away from the door. Her heart ached for the torment she felt within him. No matter what he'd said in the past, no matter what he said now, she knew what he wanted most was to make her immortal.

She should eat, but she couldn't bring herself to put one more bite of food in her mouth. The front door opened and closed as he left. She'd never felt more alone in her life. She sat for a while, idly twirling a piece of bread as she tried to sort out the jumbled mess of her emotions.

Shoving away from the table, she rose and grabbed her black cloak by the door. She swung it around her shoulders and opened the door. The crisp air hit her, winter would be arriving soon, and for the first time in her life, she didn't have to worry about freezing to death.

Jack was already on his way up when she stepped onto the porch. He stopped when he saw her, his head tilted to the side.

"I'd like to go for a walk," she declared.

His eyebrows shot into his hairline; his mouth quirked in a small smile. "Already ordering people around, your highness?"

She scowled at him. "You don't have to come with me."

"Well, thank you for the permission to stay behind."

She clasped the cloak more firmly around her neck as it dragged across the ground behind her. "I'm sorry." She was being a jerk, but she felt like a tightly coiled spring about ready to explode. "I need to get out for a bit."

"I can help with that." Though he was smiling, it didn't reach his eyes; eyes that came alive when he was truly happy.

She slipped her arm into the one he offered her and walked with him down the ramp.

"The house is beautiful, Jack, I love it. Thank you."

He patted her hand; uncomfortable with her gratitude. "Yeah, well I was bored. After all the excitement of the past couple months, I had to have something to keep me occupied."

"I'm happy you did."

They slipped into the woods, moving in companionable silence as they traveled through the trees and deeper into the forest. It wasn't until they were almost there that she realized where she was unconsciously leading them the whole time.

"The banquet tree." She tilted her head back to look into its massive, leafy limbs.

There were no apples now, and the leaves had already started to turn subtle hues of gold and orange in the sunlight. She released Jack's arm, grabbed the lower limb and lifted herself into the branches.

She didn't scurry up the tree like she had as a child. Instead, she took her time and savored the feel of the bark and the scent of the tree as it wrapped her in the security of childhood memories. She could almost hear William's laughter floating to her from below as he ran about trying to catch the apples she plucked and tossed down to him.

It wasn't until she was near the top that she saw something shining in the tree. She moved faster and with purpose now. There was only one other person who would have climbed up there and risked the thinness of the upper branches.

Aria burst upward and seized the object entwined in the tree. A sob burned her throat; tears streamed down her cheeks as she opened her hand to reveal the delicate, silver, horse head brooch that was her mother's. It was the same brooch her father had given to Jack on his return to the palace in search of her, the one that let her know she could trust him.

Near the brooch, tied around a branch, was what appeared to be an oilskin cloth. She tugged the strings free from the tree and pulled off the skin. She nearly slipped from the tree in surprise but managed to catch herself and keep her hold on the thin limbs.

She held the drawing Daniel had made for her; the one of her sitting in Braith's lap as he read to her by the lake. Daniel had managed to capture every ounce of the love they shared for each other in the fine lines and details.

She opened her hand to study the brooch and the drawing. Her father had known there was a chance he might not survive to speak with her, to guide her, and this had been his way of doing so. She and William had thought they'd kept the location of the tree secret, but of course, their father would follow them and learn where they were going. He was their father, their protector, and he'd loved them.

She was unable to stifle a sob. He'd known she would come here, and if he didn't survive, she would find these things. This was his way of telling that though he was afraid for her, he supported her, and he trusted Braith.

This was his way of letting her go.

She lifted her head to stare over the treetops at the glittering palace in the distance. She'd looked at it often as a child and questioned what had driven the humans to such depths as to betray their kind in favor of a race who enslaved them. She'd also speculated about that race, and what had driven them to be so cruel and heartless, so brutal and hideous, and she'd hated them with every ounce of her being.

Now, she was going to become one of them.

Rolling the parchment back up, she tucked it into the waistband of her pants and started down. She knew Braith was there before she spotted him below with Jack. His head was tilted back as he watched her descend. She dropped soundlessly from the tree. He looked as if he was going to grab for her, but his hands remained at his sides as his fingers twitched.

She opened her hand to reveal the brooch. Jack's startled gaze darted back to the top of the tree before returning to her. She pulled Daniel's drawing out and handed it to Braith. His eyes stayed on her as he unrolled it; he finally glanced at the sketch. Jack peered over his shoulder at it.

"It's from the lake," she said.

"I remember," Braith murmured, his brow furrowed as he studied it.

"Daniel stumbled upon us by accident. He said that day he realized what was between us was real and more than just love. I gave the drawing to William to keep it safe; my father discovered it and kept it. He put it there with the brooch so I would have it again and know he accepted you and me. That he supported whatever choice I made." She tilted her head back to look into the tree again. "You can see the palace from up there; I used to watch it and wonder when I was a child. I don't wonder anymore."

Braith and Jack both stared at her now. Braith's hands trembled as he held the drawing. She opened the brooch and pinned it at her neck to clasp the cloak together.

"No more doubts," she said. "No more waiting. I'm ready. Today."

CHAPTER TWENTY-ONE

SHE WAS ready for the pain, braced for it. Braith had told her it would hurt, that it may even last for days. She'd experienced pain before though; she could handle it.

She wasn't ready for the bliss that came before the pain. The floating, drifting sensation that came from sustaining him, giving him what he coveted, and so often denied himself.

He'd never have to deny himself again when she wasn't human any longer.

She'd be able to give him as much as he needed whenever he needed it. It may not fill him in the same way as human blood would, but hers would always be the only blood he craved. Her heart hammered with the realization, excitement tingled through her as he drank from her not in greedy gulps, but in gentle pulls that shook her to her very core.

Her fingers curled through his hair as she felt a weakening in her body signaling her life was draining away. She hadn't experienced this, not even the first time when he'd been so eager to have her he'd lost control and nearly killed her.

He would kill her now.

The thought didn't terrify her, she thought she was a little insane for that, but she couldn't find fear in his arms.

She felt the weakening pulse of her heart as he pulled away from her. His fingers were tender on her face when they stroked her. She tried to open her eyes to look at him, but she was tired, and her lids were unbelievably heavy. She felt the press of his wrist against her lips, and she opened them to receive him.

"I love you." The words were whispered in her ear. "Don't leave me, please don't leave me."

They echoed what he'd said to her the first time he'd taken her blood, when she mistakenly thought she dreamt his words. She couldn't find the words to tell him she would never leave him, and this was far easier than he'd said it would be. His fangs sank into her once more as he continued to let his blood flow into her.

Her body stiffened as her heart skipped a beat, *that* hadn't happened the first time. She tried to remain relaxed, tried to keep her body as still as possible so he wouldn't feel her anxiety. She knew he already had though as his hand constricted in her hair and he hesitated. She worried he would retreat, change his mind, and not continue.

Then, with a low growl, he bit down harder, and she realized there wouldn't be any stopping him, not at this point.

Aria inhaled sharply; her body went rigid, and her eyes flew open as her fingers constricted on his head. She was acutely aware her heart had stopped beating, and there was no air within her lungs.

A scream stuck in her chest, she didn't have the breath to release it. She hadn't expected this nothingness, this waiting, this feeling of being trapped within her own body, unable to move, but still fully aware of her surroundings, and thoughts.

He was above her, his eyes searching and petrified. She was looking back at him, she was seeing him, but her eyes were as frozen as the rest of her. They were locked on him and as immobile as if she were dead.

It hit her like a ton of bricks; she *was* dead, and there was absolutely nothing she could do about it.

She took it back; this wasn't easy. She would have far preferred agony over this frozen uncertainty. He'd said there would be rigor mortis, but was this it? So soon?

It took hours after a person died for rigor mortis to sink in; she'd seen it. Although, this wasn't an ordinary death. She wasn't dead, not completely. She was confined to a husk that no longer moved and no longer offered her the life support she had once required.

She felt his fingers on her cheeks; even felt the drop of a tear as it landed on her skin. It left a cold trail on her cheek as it slid toward her neck. Braith was crying. For her, and there was nothing she could do to ease his worry.

She didn't know how long she remained trapped in a world where all she had were her thoughts, none of which were entirely pleasant. She wanted to cry, wanted to do anything other than just lie here like this. Braith sat with her, his arms around her, his hands on her face, and in her hair. The look on his face and the fright in his eyes was almost as awful as this endless uncertainty.

Then a warming sensation started in the tips of her toes and gradually spread upward. At first, it wasn't unpleasant, and she welcomed anything over the nothingness encompassing her.

The tingling reminded her of holding her frozen hands over a fire and heating them too quickly as it pricked at her skin. It became unpleasant, but if she could grit her teeth, she could get through it. Unfortunately, her mouth wasn't unfrozen yet.

The tingling worked its way through her arms, up to her shoulders, across her neck, and into her chest. She tried to fist her hands against the pain; they wouldn't move. Frustration filled her; she tried to scream, tried to cry, tried to do anything other than lay here like a useless lump.

A plea began inside of her; the only problem was she didn't know what she was pleading for at the moment... a true death to free her from this relentless pain or eternal life.

The heat pierced her *non*-beating heart. She'd never experienced anything like this, never expected to hear the silence of the vital organ once pulsating so fluidly within her. She hadn't realized how much of a constant part of her it had been until the heavy cloak of silence blanketed her following its cessation.

Tendrils of heat brushed against the organ as gentle and quiet as a butterfly's wings. The heat retreated for a moment before surging into it once more. It slipped inside and began to spread throughout.

She didn't know what the heat was, but she pictured Braith's blood flowing in to fill the spaces her blood had left behind. Pictured it replenishing her cells and rehydrating them with his life. She tried to keep that image in her mind; it was far more pleasant than the uncertainty threatening to consume her.

The heat filled her deadened heart again; her fingers flickered as she felt a heaving inside her chest before it seeped out again. Hope swelled within her. She'd *moved*! It was only a small bit of progress, but at least it was something different, it was something more than this hideous nothing.

The heat began to increase; her body was on fire as it prickled through her extremities. She lurched, her body jerked as warmth slammed into her heart once more, but it didn't beat again, and she knew it would remain still forever.

The tingling, prickling sensation in her fingers and toes started to worsen as it spread into her torso. A scream welled inside her, but her mouth wouldn't open to release the agony consuming her from the inside out.

Braith's fingers brushed her face as he leaned over her. Her skin felt as if it had been scrubbed away to expose her nerve endings. His silky touch was more than she could stand. She couldn't cringe away from the contact though, couldn't pull away, as her body still wasn't hers. It was this fleshy shell that had become her coffin.

"Aria?"

Just when she thought she couldn't take anymore, her body broke free of its paralysis. Braith leaned over her as she opened her mouth, and the scream she had been unable to release for so long, ripped loose in an unending echo that left her throat ravaged and her body drained as she fell lifelessly back to the bed.

Braith reached for her, but she moved away from him, unable to bear his touch on her brutalized skin. She curled into the fetal position, but even that was almost too much to bear. Her body shook and shivered, she was hot, she was cold, she was dying, she was living, and she was doing it all too fast. Braith's hand fell back to his side; hopelessness filled his gaze as her teeth chattered.

Aria yearned to tell him she would be all right, but she wasn't going to lie, and the mere idea of moving was more than she could handle right now. Every muscle in her body screamed, her bones felt as if they were shattering into a million little pieces. Everything inside of her felt as if it were changing, and somehow rearranging.

What had she done?

The thought was fleeting. It didn't matter; it was done. There was no turning back, and no matter how badly this hurt, she wouldn't have changed it. She forced herself to open her hand toward him.

Seeming to sense she couldn't stand much of his touch, he placed two of his fingers lightly into her palm. The small connection helped to ease her slightly. She kept her eyes focused on him as she struggled to survive her death.

"YOU LOOK LIKE SHIT."

Braith could barely lift his head to look at Jack. He felt beaten and drained in ways he hadn't thought possible. He hated himself and this whole awful mess; he wished he'd never agreed to this.

She'd told him it was his decision to make. He'd been terrified she would die and petrified of losing her, but there had been another part so entirely enthralled with the prospect of having her by his side forever, that he'd talked himself into believing this would be okay. They could get through this.

Now, he knew he'd been completely wrong. He'd do anything to take this from her, but there was nothing he could do. He couldn't even *touch* her without causing her to moan or scream.

He'd seen a lot of wretchedness and death in his long life, but he'd never experienced anything like this. Even the one attempt at the change he'd witnessed was nothing compared to this, but then that person hadn't been Aria, and he hadn't cared about what they'd endured or whether they would survive.

Aria was the strongest person he knew, and she was falling apart before him, swamped within the nightmare he'd created for her. He'd never hated himself more, he didn't have a clue how to make it better, and he would have willingly offered up his own life to go back in time and decide against doing this. What had he been thinking?

He hadn't, and now she was the one paying for his lack of good judgment. Ashby had once said he would end up changing her no matter what and wouldn't be able to resist, but he believed he could have refrained from doing so.

However, he couldn't deny the fact that when she'd agreed to this, the darkest and most primal part of him had thrilled at the prospect and wouldn't have been stopped by anything or anyone.

It was a piece of himself he didn't like, but over the past few months, he'd come to accept there was no denying it, or the fact that the person who brought it out and kept it under control the most, was Aria.

"How bad is it, Braith?"

He tiredly ran a hand through his sweaty, tangled hair. His muscles ached from being tensed at her side all night; he was exhausted from lack of sleep, yet he should be more miserable. His pain was nothing compared to what she was going through.

"Bad, real bad."

Xavier stood behind Jack, his head bowed and his hands enfolded in his voluminous cloak.

Jack placed a jug of blood on the kitchen table. "Did you get any sleep?"

Braith shook his head. "No."

"Did she?"

"She's sleeping now but not well."

"You should take a break. Why don't you let us watch over her while you take a shower, maybe a nap?"

"No."

"Braith..."

He shook his head as he glanced over his shoulder at the shadowed bedroom. He tried to pick up on some clue she had awakened and needed him. He wasn't doing her any good, but he was going to do everything he could for her, especially since any second might be her last. His hands tensed around the door-frame; he had to fight the urge to rip something to shreds. He wanted to tear *himself* to shreds.

"If she dies..." he broke off as he strained to get the words out. "I would have been the one to kill her."

Jack and Xavier exchanged a glance.

"You said you could handle this, Braith," Jack said worriedly.

He shook his head as he fought the urge to scream or destroy everything around him. He'd lost it when she'd left him, but she'd still been alive then. Now he was certain she wouldn't survive whatever was happening to her body. She was strong, his blood was powerful, but so few made it through and she now barely clung to what little fight she had left in her.

How had he ever believed he could endure the consequences of this?

Because he had to, he reminded himself. He simply had to.

There were so many lives hanging in the balance; so much still needed to be done, and he had promised her he would survive. So, he would somehow, but he would never be the same if she died.

She'd entered his life and turned it upside down. He'd had everything he ever required since birth and been empty until he saw her standing on that stage, proud and defiant, even while facing her death. He'd had it all, but he'd had nothing until then.

He would survive without her, but he would never live again. Ashby had been right, after all, he realized dully; bloodlinks couldn't *live* without each other. They simply existed.

"I can handle this," Braith told him.

Jack folded his arms over his chest and leaned back. "You must feed."

"I've fed more than well enough," he muttered.

He'd more than sated himself on her, and for the first time in months, he didn't feel the clawing thirst for blood in his chest and gut. He'd rather be starving.

"You have to keep up your strength."

His gaze slid back to his brother. Jack's eyes were shadowed and dark, his hair tussled and disordered.

229

"Believe me, Jack, I've had plenty, and I've never felt stronger."

It was true, she was at her weakest, shattered and tormented, and he was suffused with the power of her blood.

Jack didn't seem to comprehend what he was saying, and then his eyes closed and his shoulders slumped. "Yeah, I suppose so. I'll leave this here for you anyway."

A whimper, so soft he knew Jack and Xavier wouldn't pick up on it, caught his attention. Braith turned as he waited to see if anything more would follow, but she quieted once more.

"How are things at the palace?" he inquired.

Jack pulled out a chair and dropped into it. "There are still quarrels, but that's to be expected for a while."

"Yes," Braith agreed, but he was barely paying attention.

This time the whimper had been louder. He left his brother and Xavier as he made his way to the bedroom. Even though she was incoherent, he'd left the bathroom lantern lit and the door cracked in case she did wake.

He went to her, knowing better than to touch her as he moved around the bed and knelt before her. She was curled into a ball with her eyes closed and her lips compressed into a thin line. Her hair was lank and damp with sweat as it fell around her unnaturally pale face. He brushed back a piece of her hair and tucked it behind her ear.

Her eyes flew open, for a moment he was frozen as he gazed at her. His body no longer felt like his own as her usually bright blue eyes shone a vibrant shade of red.

"Aria," he breathed.

When she gazed unseeingly at him, he had a feeling she didn't even know he was there. She turned her face into his wrist and her mouth pressed against it. She moved with startling speed as she opened her mouth and bit down.

Braith jerked in surprise as her fangs sank into his vein. He almost instinctively pulled back, but then her deep pulls sparked something primal and possessive inside of him. This had never happened to him before, he had shared his blood with her, but he'd never actually had another vampire feeding on him. His heart swelled; pleasure and love swamped him, but they were swiftly doused.

Her torment engulfed him as her mind flowed forward to blend with his. She was new, she had no idea what she was doing to him, but he was ensnared within the agony consuming her, and he allowed himself to be drawn into it. He couldn't stand the thought of her facing this alone, bearing it all herself.

He pushed her hair back and nuzzled her temple as tears burned his eyes. "Aria," he breathed in her ear.

Movement caught his attention. Jack hovered in the doorway, his eyes troubled and apprehensive. A surge of protection washed over Braith; a low growl escaped him as he waved Jack back.

This was *their* moment alone, and for all he knew, it might very well be one of his last with her. He wasn't going to share it with anyone, especially not his brother. Jack slipped into the shadows, disappearing from view as Aria abruptly released her hold on him.

A violent scream erupted from her as she fell upon the bed. Braith lurched upward; he lunged for her shoulders but pulled himself back. He ached to touch her, but he didn't dare when he knew it would only hurt her more.

Jack reappeared in the doorway with his mouth ajar and his eyes wide. Xavier nervously hovered behind him.

"Get out!" Braith roared at them.

Jack took a step forward before taking a small one back.

"It is almost done; one way or another, it will be over shortly," Xavier assured him as he pulled Jack away.

Braith stalked over and slammed the door shut; it did nothing to ease the knot of tension and terror that constricted his

ERICA STEVENS

chest. He was shaking as Aria moaned and tears spilled down her face.

He curled onto the bed beside her; his two fingers rested lightly on the palm of her extended hand. Her eyes, now their beautiful sparkling blue again, met his. Love shimmered in them before death rose up to drag her back into its overwhelming depths once more.

232

CHAPTER TWENTY-TWO

ARIA WOKE SLUGGISHLY, her eyes barely drifted open before slipping shut again. She ached everywhere; muscles she didn't even know she had were cramping. Knots twisted through her body as she lay entirely still, fearful of moving.

Even her eyelashes hurt and felt far too heavy, but it wasn't the same as the pain she'd been going through for the past few days, weeks, hours...? She didn't know anymore; she'd lost all track of time.

"Aria." The word breathed, so hopefully, held so much love that her deadened heart broke. It was different now, completely still, but it was his and always would be. "Aria."

"I'm alive," she whispered.

His two fingers on her palm twitched a little. Her eyelids fluttered open again to find him lying across from her. He was magnificent, beautiful, and heartbreakingly lost as his gaze searched her face. The world was brighter; he was brighter. The scars around his eyes were more clearly visible; *everything* was clearer.

For the first time, she noticed that flecks of sapphire and azure filled the beautiful blue band encircling his irises.

"Aria?"

Those two fingers were featherlike against her cheek, just a whisper caress that made her crave more. He was hesitant to touch her though, and she didn't blame him for everything.

The faintest touch was too much before. It had grated on her nerve endings to the point it felt like hot coals were pressing against her skin. She'd been wearing a nightgown, but at one point she knew she ripped it off, unable to take the thin material against her skin anymore. She still felt raw, but it wasn't anywhere near as bad as it had been.

"I think I'm okay; I think I made it," she said.

He reverently searched her face; he seemed almost afraid to believe what she said was true. He looked nearly as broken and beaten as she felt. Lines she'd never noticed before etched his face; there were dark shadows under his eyes, and his hair stuck to his forehead.

They both smelled, she realized dimly, and almost laughed out loud at the realization. She'd been hideously smelly when he'd first claimed her as his blood slave, and she was as bad now that he'd claimed her again. This time, forever.

"How do you feel?" he inquired.

"Like I died," she answered honestly.

His fingers skimmed over her cheeks as he traced a line to her lips. Shock flickered through her as she felt a tingling, prickling sensation in response to his tender prodding at her canines. Amazement filled her when they lengthened and sharpened against his finger. Her gaze flickered to his wrist and the two red marks marring the inside of it.

She traced the bite mark as she frowned. "Did I do this?"

"You did."

She didn't know what to make of that, part of her wanted to

cry, and the other part was strangely titillated. She didn't recall doing it, but she had a dim memory of something sweet and delicious filling her. She vaguely remembered something breaking through the anguish for a brief moment, and now she understood why.

"Did I hurt you?" she asked.

"Nowhere near as much as I hurt you."

"You didn't do anything I didn't ask for. We both wanted this." She managed a wan smile. "And it worked."

He still looked as if he wasn't convinced. "It appears to have."

She seized his hand and winced as the motion made her abused muscles throb.

"You're still in pain," he accused.

"I'm sore," she admitted. "But it's *much* better than it was."

His hand spread out across her face as he cradled it. "Perhaps a bath."

"Sounds incredible," she agreed eagerly.

He moved gingerly from the bed, careful not to disturb her as he left the room. She listened as he walked around the attached bathroom, surprised by the intensity of the sounds, the acuteness with which she heard them.

She'd been so determined to get it over with, to do it, that she hadn't thought about what it would be like afterward. What the world would become to her newly deadened yet enhanced body. It was as frightening as it was astonishing.

Water was turned on; she could almost feel the heat of it already blessedly encompassing her tender body. He was back beside her; his eyes troubled as he knelt next to her.

"Can I?" he asked as he held his arms out to her.

Aria remained unmoving as she warily stared at his arms. She desperately longed to be in them, but the memory of the pain was still fresh in her mind. She gathered her courage as she managed a small nod.

She braced herself as his arms gingerly slid underneath her. It was a little uncomfortable, but the rush of pleasure flooding her sensitized skin buried it. Her toes curled as she pressed closer to him and felt his bare skin against hers. Skin, she was beginning to realize, that might always feel this electrified by his touch.

"It's different," she breathed. "It's all so much more... intense."

His brow furrowed and he stopped walking to study her. "Is it unpleasant?"

"No, just somewhat overwhelming. The world is clearer and louder; my skin feels as if lightning bolts are zapping through it. It's an amazing feeling, but it's, ah it's..."

"It's inhuman," he supplied.

"Yes," she whispered. "Is this what you feel like all the time?"

"I was born this way, Aria, I've never known anything different. I'll help you through it though; we *will* get you through this."

"I've no doubt," she replied with a small smile as she wrapped her arms around his neck and leaned her head into the warm hollow of his throat.

"Can you stand?"

The question, asked days ago, would have offended her. Now she had to think about it. "I'm not sure," she hated to admit.

He sat her on the edge of the tub. Steam rose around her, warming her as it floated in the air. He knelt before her and reached around to test the heat of the water. His hands rested on her knees as he leaned closer to her. The feel of him enveloped her; it warmed her more than the heat of the bath on her back.

He pushed the hair over her shoulders; his fingers lingered on his marks on her skin. The bites left by his father and brother had faded rapidly during her transition and were barely visible anymore. She didn't think she'd be able to see them anymore if she was still human.

His hands were gentle as he helped ease her into the tub. A

moan of pleasure escaped as the blessed heat of the water engulfed her.

"We stink," she mumbled.

"We do," he agreed as he grabbed a bar of soap and shampoo from the sink. "It's been an endless three days."

"Is that how long it was?"

"Yes."

"It seemed like forever."

She swallowed heavily as he came back to her. She watched as he placed the shampoo and soap down and quickly shed his pants. Her mouth went dry when she took in his magnificent body. He slid into the large tub behind her and his legs clasped her sides.

Pulling her into his lap, he rested her back against his chest as he leisurely began to rub and massage her aching muscles. She leaned into him, savoring the tender way he touched her and the exciting new way he felt against her skin. He worked steadily over her body, rubbing and kneading her with a tenderness no one else had ever seen from him or ever would.

"You stayed with me," he whispered as his fingers worked over her arms.

"I told you I would."

His hands stopped moving over her as they enfolded her against him. "I was still worried."

"I know; so was I," she admitted.

He turned her head toward him and nibbled on her lower lip as he kissed her. Heat sizzled through her as a rocking sensation, unlike anything she'd ever experienced, shot through her. His kisses had always melted her, but this was different, it felt as if she were dissolving against him.

She needed to feel the reality of the press of his lips against hers, of the warmth of his tongue caressing her mouth. She'd been frightened she would never feel anything like this again.

He pulled away slowly, his eyes intense and fiery as they bored into hers. The dark shadow lining his jaw made him appear harder and more dangerous as her fingers trailed over the bristly hairs. He was glorious though, and he was hers, forever.

Everything she had endured was entirely worth it.

His fingers started to work over her muscles again; he washed her hair and cleaned the shampoo from it before washing his own and helping her from the tub. Her legs were shaky, she felt like a newborn colt, and she supposed in some ways she was. She was able to stay on her feet as he towel dried her, wrapped a robe around her, and loosely knotted the belt.

"Do you want me to brush your hair for you?" he asked.

Though it sounded appealing, she didn't like feeling this helpless and needy. "No, I think I can handle it."

He nodded but leaned against the counter to watch her. She felt slightly uncomfortable with his scrutiny.

"I'm not going anywhere," she assured him.

"I don't know that yet, Aria, not for sure."

"I'm sorry for what you went through."

He frowned at her as he folded his arms firmly over his chest. "What I went through was nothing compared to what you went through. I would do everything in my power to take away what you just experienced."

"It was worth it."

He remained doubtful looking as his eyes scanned her.

"I would do it again for this result, Braith. Don't ever doubt that. The memories of the pain will fade; the millions of memories we'll make together will last forever. Life is so fragile and delicate all the time, we have to seize every moment we have together and cherish every gift given to us, and this is one such gift. We can be together forever."

She didn't realize she was crying until he leaned across the counter and wiped the tears away with the pads of his thumbs.

"I do cherish it," he whispered against her lips as he rested his forehead on hers. "And you. I look forward to every one of those memories."

"Good. Now, can you stop watching me as if you're afraid I'm going to go toe up again at any moment?"

He laughed as he kissed her. "Okay."

She reluctantly pulled away from him and wiped the steam from the mirror. She stared at her reflection, surprised by the sight of the woman staring back at her. It was her still. She was tired, drained, and beaten looking, but it was still her. Relief filled her.

Despite what Braith had said about her being the same, she'd still been terrified she would turn into a half-crazed beast with red eyes and fangs, or become a shadow of the person she'd been. Instead, it was merely a girl with auburn hair made darker by the water, brilliant blue eyes, and a face that had thinned out from grief staring back at her.

Braith rested his hands on her shoulders. "Are you okay?"

"It's still me," she breathed.

"It is." Her fingers slid over the mirror as she traced her features. "Let me."

She didn't argue when he took the brush from her hand and began to work it through her hair.

"Were you expecting someone else?" he asked.

"I didn't know what to expect," she admitted. "I half feared I'd be a monster."

He met her gaze in the mirror, holding it for a poignant moment. "You could never be a monster, Arianna."

She smiled shakily at him, acutely aware that when it came to him, she could be a monster to ensure he survived. She closed her eyes and relished the comforting feel of him pulling the brush through her hair.

She was also becoming aware of a new scent and an unfamiliar discomfort growing in her belly. She didn't understand what it was though, and as she hesitatingly scented the air, she couldn't place the delicious aroma.

Braith placed the brush down and led her into the bedroom. She slumped onto the bed, tired and still a little sore. That growing twinge in her stomach was starting to spread outward. It was becoming uncomfortable when she shifted on the bed in an attempt to ease some of the discomfort growing within her.

Braith's eyes narrowed. "What's wrong?"

"I don't know," she admitted. Her hand fluttered to her chest, and a rush of saliva filled her mouth. "But I don't feel right. There's something; it's here and aching." She pressed her hands to her stomach and chest. She couldn't find the words to describe the growing distress of her body.

"Ah," he said with dawning realization. "You're hungry."

She frowned at him as she shook her head. "No, I'm surprisingly *not* hungry."

His smile was sad and understanding. "Yes, Aria, you're just not hungry for mortal food, not anymore."

She felt like an idiot as her mouth parted. "Oh," she breathed as understanding filled her. "I see."

Her gaze strayed to his neck, the solid muscles cording it, and the vein she saw running just beneath the surface. She tore her gaze away from his dampened skin as the discomfort bloomed into a scorching fire.

"Is this what you experience all the time?"

"Not all the time."

"Since you met me?"

He brushed the hair back from her face. "Not all the time."

She ached for the torment he had gone through and that she wasn't able to understand until now. "It's an awful feeling, how did you deal with it?"

"Years of experience, and you. Just being with you made it all worth it."

She forgot her discomfort as love streamed through her. She kept thinking it wasn't possible to love him more, but he always managed to prove her wrong.

"I'll teach you how to control it, but if you feed well and often, it will be easy to control. You won't have to feel this way again, Aria," he vowed.

Her gaze drifted back to his vein. She shuddered as desire tore through her and left her shaken. It was not his body she hungered for right now but something more, and it frightened her. She'd fed on him once, but she didn't recall it and didn't know how she'd done it, or if she'd even done it right.

"Braith," she gasped.

"It's okay." His hands were on her waist; he lifted her and eased her onto his lap. "It's okay, Aria."

His hand wrapped around her head. She remained unyielding in his grasp as uncertainty, dread, and a coil of disgust warred incessantly within her.

"What if I hurt you?" she asked.

"You won't."

She licked her lips and started in surprise when she felt the sharp prick of her teeth. A whimper involuntarily escaped her.

He turned his wrist over, revealing the marks to her. "This didn't hurt," he said.

"I was completely out of it; I didn't know what I was doing."

"You knew what you were doing then, and you'll know what you're doing now. Just let your instincts take over; they'll guide you through this."

He guided her head to the hollow of his neck and rested it there. She could smell the sweet scent of his blood as it wafted out of him. It was delicious, enticing as it ensnared her within its scent of spices and earth and *her*.

She pressed her lips against his warm skin; he tasted of soap and something more, something masculine and dark and powerful. Something she craved with a driving frenzy that frightened her, but it wouldn't be denied.

How had he ever controlled this consuming thirst around her?

She tried not to think as she let the instincts he spoke of take over. Her lips pulled back, her teeth—no they weren't just teeth anymore, they were razor sharp fangs, and right now they were aching to be buried in his tender skin.

A small shudder of anticipation rocked him as she pressed her fangs against his skin. She kissed him before she bit down. His hands clenched on her back; a low groan escaped him as she pulled his blood from him.

When pleasure swamped her, she pressed closer as the sweet flow of his blood filled her mouth. She didn't feel repulsed; she wasn't sickened by the flavor and heat of it within her mouth. It was the most delicious thing she'd ever tasted as she felt their minds surging forth to mingle together.

Her fingers dug into his back as his joy mixed with hers. She'd experienced it as a human, but now, as a vampire, it was more profound and more open. There weren't any barriers between them. He was completely bared to her; she felt the ebb and flow of the darkness within him. Felt the lengths and depths of brutality he would go to for her and the others he sought to protect. He revealed to her the true depth of his fear for her, the extent of his instability within The Barrens, and when Caleb had taken her.

It shook her, humbled her, and brought her to tears. She'd always known he was powerful, always known it was stressful for him when it came to her, but he hadn't revealed the true depth of that strain until now. He hadn't shown the depths of his dislike and lack of pleasure and satisfaction he experienced with anyone else's blood.

Aria pressed closer, unable to get enough of this glimpse into him, of this complete baring of the soul of the man she loved so desperately. She couldn't get close enough as she exposed everything she had and revealed all her love and concerns to him as he did to her.

She was enmeshed in his pleasure and caught up in his love as she nestled closer. The soreness in her body eased, and her muscles loosened further the more she consumed. She bit deeper into his neck and relished the blood and energy infusing her.

A low groan escaped him; the headboard crashed off the wall as he slammed his hand against it in an attempt to curve the burgeoning desire she felt swirling up through his body and into hers. She whimpered as he released the headboard and buried his hand in her hair.

His mouth pressed against her shoulder; his fangs nipped at her skin before biting. If she had any doubt he wouldn't find her blood as appealing, it was squashed by his intense delight as it engulfed her.

She wrapped her legs around his waist as he shifted her in his lap. Aria was consumed with love as she lost herself to the touch and feel of him. The pleasure he took from her engulfed her, she couldn't separate her ecstasy from his as his infinite wonder and fulfillment consumed her.

The rest of the world faded away as, for the first time, she gave herself to him with no fear of what the future held. For the first time, she knew complete safety and security. She knew nothing could ever tear them apart again.

CHAPTER TWENTY-THREE

Aria fiddled anxiously with the sleeves of her shirt. Braith quirked an eyebrow as he grabbed her hands and held them in his own. "It will be fine."

She gulped and managed a small nod as Braith opened the door to his newly fixed and refurnished apartment. The furniture was a deep forest green now, and the carpet had been replaced with a gleaming wood floor. The apartment was beautiful before but more masculine. Now, it was more feminine, and she suspected Melinda had a hand in picking out the furniture and the colors.

"I thought you would like to pick out the paintings," Braith told her.

She nodded as she glanced at the bare walls. She hadn't put much thought into what the apartment would look like, or how it should be decorated. She'd been too consumed by her grief and uncertainty. As she glanced at the walls, she itched to cover them with some of the beautiful paintings and artwork Daniel had created since moving into the palace.

Braith pulled the drawing of the two of them free of his coat.

Tears burned her eyes, but she kept them suppressed as she took it from him. It would be the first thing she put on the wall. A subtle knock on the door reminded her of what she'd been so nervous about just moments ago. She rolled the drawing back up and placed it on the desk.

Braith opened the door to William, Daniel, and Max. If she still had a heartbeat, she knew it would be thumping riotously in her chest. The stillness was a little unnerving, but nowhere near as unnerving as facing the three of them. Braith grabbed her hand as she started to fiddle again.

Aria worried they'd be mad at her, not because she was a vampire now, but because she hadn't told them she was going to do it. She worried Max would resent her. He'd been doing so much better, but she still didn't know how he was going to react to this news.

William, finally free of his crutches, grinned at her as he swooped into the room, lifted her into the air, and gave her a crushing hug. He dropped her down and seized her hand, seemingly oblivious that she wasn't human anymore.

"Nice ring," he remarked.

"I'm glad you approve," Braith commented dryly.

Aria smiled shyly at William as he grinned at Braith and twisted her hand within his. Max and Daniel came forward to hug her and offer their congratulations. She went to fiddle with her hands again but thought better of it as Braith shot her a look. She didn't know how to tell them, did she blurt out, 'oh by the way I died?' Or perhaps the, 'I'm not a human anymore' approach would work better.

"I uh...I'm..." the words caught in her throat, she couldn't stop her gaze from going to Max.

Max's forehead furrowed as he stared at her questioningly. Then his brow cleared as realization dawned in his eyes. "A vampire."

William and Daniel's heads snapped toward her; their eyes perused her. Braith took her hand and encased it in both of his.

"You did it?" William asked.

Aria winced at the upset in his voice. "I didn't know I was going to," she told him. "And then I found the drawing dad left behind for me."

"What do you mean?" Daniel's blue eyes narrowed at her.

She filled him in on what she'd discovered in the banquet tree. "I didn't go out there with the intention of this happening," she told him.

She shifted uneasily under their intense scrutiny.

"You're okay though?" William worried.

It was a little disconcerting, but she heard the difference in William's heartbeat as he circled her. His pulse sped up; there was a faint knock in it as adrenaline spurted through him. It didn't entice her, but the fact she could hear it unsettled her. It was going to take her a while to get used to all the new sights, sounds, and sensations her new status offered her.

Braith slid his arm around her waist and pulled her against his side as he seemed to sense her discomfort.

"I'm okay," she assured William.

"So I guess this means we do have some vampire DNA in us?" William asked.

"I would assume so," Braith confirmed.

"Max?" Aria inquired nervously.

His gaze focused on the window behind her. Her fingers clenched on Braith's back as tears burned her eyes. *Please,* she pleaded silently. *Please don't hate me again.*

Max finally looked at her, and though it was sad, he offered her a small smile. "I'm glad you survived. I'm happy for you," he assured her.

A low sob escaped her as she released Braith and stepped forward to hug Max and her brothers again. Another knock on the door drew her apart from them. Melinda poked her head in; she scented the air before she broke into a brilliant grin. She flung the door open and bounded across the floor to them. Free of the cloak of her father's oppression, and her separation from Ashby, Melinda had turned into a lively, exuberant woman.

William shot her a disgruntled look as Melinda elbowed him out of the way, seized Aria's hand, and jerked it toward her. Aria's eyes widened as Melinda released a joyous squeal. Ashby had entered behind her and now stood beside Braith, grinning in amusement as Melinda started speaking.

"We have so many plans to make!" Melinda gushed. "So much to do! It's going to be amazing!"

"I'd actually like a small ceremony," Aria told her.

"A queen's wedding can never be small!" Melinda retorted.

Aria cast Braith a pleading look as his sister began to propel her toward the sofa. He jumped forward, smiling pleasantly at Melinda as he extricated Aria's arm from Melinda's death grip.

"We can do both," Braith placated.

She knew arguing would be pointless; Melinda was right, and if Aria still got to have the ceremony she wanted, she didn't see what difference it made as long as she got to marry Braith.

CHAPTER TWENTY-FOUR

OVER THE NEXT FEW DAYS, Melinda kept her occupied with endless details, most of which she never would have considered. It was overwhelming on top of trying to adjust to her new vampire abilities. She accidentally ripped the handle off the door in the library and broke a saddle when she forgot her strength. She kept trying to breathe, missed the beat of her heart, and was still trying to adjust to the unfamiliar sensations of her over-sensitized skin.

Even though she felt overwhelmed, she'd also never felt this secure and happy. She fell asleep in Braith's arms every night and woke to find him beside her every morning. When Melinda wasn't demanding her time, she would go out with Max, Xavier, Jack, and William to help in rebuilding the town.

Daniel and Braith were entrenched in the intricacies of establishing the new government, and dealing with the problems that arose from the people and vampires struggling to assimilate to the changes.

Melinda had told her the building wasn't something a future queen should be doing, but Aria didn't care. She didn't want to be involved in the running of the household, and planning a wedding was beyond tedious. Besides, with her newfound strength, she was far better at building, and faster at it than she ever would have been in the past.

Maybe it wasn't what the other queens had done, but *she* was going to, and nothing was going to change that. She was willing not to be in the woods every day and wear the silly undergarments and dresses when they were required.

Once queen, Aria would tend to the things she had to, but she was *not* going to be trapped within the palace, and she would not be relegated to running the household. Melinda enjoyed doing it, and Aria preferred to be with all the people and vampires in the town.

She listened to the problems they were having, what they needed, and she did her best to resolve the issues herself, or by bringing it to Braith and The Council's attention. She enjoyed working side by side with them toward a common goal as they all tried to assimilate into their new lives.

It also helped to ease the grief, helped take her mind off the empty hole in her life. She knew her father would have been thrilled to see all the changes taking place, and his children helping to make those changes.

Aria stepped back as she handed the last of the boards up to William and studied him with a heavy heart. He'd told her this morning he planned to go with Jack, when the rebuilding was done here, to help build up the towns in the outlying areas. They wanted to expand the territory, search for water, and create a burgeoning world of prosperity and hope where now there was none.

She'd assumed William would stay with Daniel and learn more about the way things were going to run, but he'd been showing less interest in it every day and had asked Max to step in to take over for him yesterday. She knew it was because of their father's death, but she also knew he wouldn't talk about it. Maybe when he came back from his journey, but not now. She understood his urge to run away, but it was still tearing her up inside, and she prayed he found whatever he was looking for and returned to her soon.

It had taken everything she had not to cry when he'd told her, and she could feel tears burning her eyes again. She longed to ask him to stay; she needed him, but he'd never confined her or disapproved of her decisions. This was something he had to do, and she wasn't going to try and dissuade him no matter how much she wanted to.

"You're the one who likes heights, shouldn't you be up here?" he protested from the roof of one of the new homes being erected in the bailey.

Aria grinned at him as she wiped her hands on her dirty pants. "I have a wedding to help plan," she reminded him. "Unless you want Melinda to come out here to retrieve me again?"

He made a face as he shook his head briskly. The last time Melinda came out here to retrieve Aria, she'd forced William and Max into the palace to be fitted for tuxes. They'd both gone out of their way to avoid her since.

"Go! Go!" he urged with a quick wave of his hand before hastily retreating from sight. His hand reappeared to wave her briskly away once more, but he didn't look over at her again.

She laughed as she turned away from the house and made her way to the stables with her constant companion at her side. There was a colicky horse she wanted to check on before retreating to the palace.

"Are you ready for more wedding planning?" she asked Xavier.

Xavier crooked an eyebrow at her as he shook his head. "I never knew there were so many different flowers before."

"Neither did I."

Xavier followed her into the stable and waited as she entered the mare's stall. She was relieved to find the horse more relaxed and some fresh manure in the corner. Patting the mare's back and neck, she moved slowly around her as she spoke softly with her for a few moments.

"Xavier, can you bring me some hay? I think she might be ready to eat now." Aria rested her hand on the horse's neck as she waited for an answer, or for her guardian to appear. She heard nothing though, and the stable remained oddly hushed. "Xavier?"

The dim light danced and swayed as shadows flitted around the dark interior of the barn. A chill slid down Aria's spine; her hand fell from the mare's neck as a rustle of movement drifted to her.

"Xavier?" she called, trying to keep the nervousness from her voice.

Silence continued to greet her. The scent of hay, straw, and horse seemed even more acute as she remained immobile. Her body became still in ways it never could have been if she was human. For the first time, she didn't miss the beat of her heart as her ears picked up sounds it would have muted. A calmness settled over her; her heightened senses opened as she searched the surroundings outside of the stall.

A smell she'd never experienced before reached her. It was body odor, decay, and rot all rolled into one disgusting blend. It was old and decrepit but also strangely compelling. The image of a walking corpse filtered through her mind as a soft rustle reached her. She opened her mouth to call out to Xavier again but thought better of it. Whatever was out there, it wasn't Xavier.

A shadow fell across the stall door seconds before feet shuffled into view. If she still had a heartbeat, it would be on the verge of exploding. She couldn't tear her gaze away from those filthy feet with their overgrown toenails and ragged cuts. The bottom of the pants were tattered and so incredibly soiled she couldn't discern the color of them anymore.

A lump formed in her throat, tears burned her eyes as she arrived at the disgusting shirt that was in much the same condition, but the hole and bloodstain on it were still clearly discernible.

It took every ounce of courage she had to force her eyes to continue upward. The haggard features, obscured by dirt and decay, were almost indiscernible. The grayish skin sagged, the outline of the skull was visible as cheekbones stood out severely and the eyes had sunken. A piece of the bottom lip, right ear, and half the left side of the nose were gone.

Nausea twisted through her as she realized they'd probably been eaten off while he was buried. Perhaps, even more had been missing, but as she watched the lesions on his face and arms knitted together and repaired themselves.

Her nose wrinkled, she recoiled from the smell radiating from this *thing* standing across from her with blazing ruby eyes. The mare snorted, she shifted nervously in the stall as a low whinny escaped her and she spun suddenly. Aria just managed to avoid being knocked over as the mare shoved her toward the hideous creature at the front of the stall.

A scream surged up her throat; she drew on her recently acquired vampire strength to lunge back. She wasn't quick enough though, even partly decayed and slightly rotten the king was still faster than her. He seized her throat, propelling her backward as he slammed her into the wall with enough force to shake it. Pain lanced through her back, the mare squealed and bolted from the stall.

Aria envied the horse greatly as the monstrosity holding her lowered his face to hers. His lips skimmed back to reveal his pointed teeth and black, *black*, gums. A shudder of revulsion rippled through her, she tried to twist her head away, but he clasped her cheeks and squeezed.

The reek of putrefaction entrenched her. A small whimper escaped her as she finally managed to get her hands in between them.

Beneath the shirt, she could feel the pliancy of his skin, and for a moment she thought her fingers were going to sink right into it. She gagged involuntarily, even if she couldn't breathe, she felt herself spiraling toward a panic attack.

This couldn't be possible! She'd seen Caleb kill him! She'd *been* there for it! Yet as his fingers dug into her cheeks to force her lips out, and his black tongue slithered out to brush against her mouth, Aria couldn't deny the reality. She nearly vomited on him as he pushed against her.

"Someone's no longer human," he murmured against her ear as he sniffed along her neck. A shudder rippled through her; bile surged up her throat. "My son thinks he can keep you, but he's wrong. *I'll* be keeping you."

"How?" she croaked as he forced her head to the side.

"You think a simple stake is going to kill me? I'm over a thousand years old; there's plenty you don't know about me, *bitch*. I know plenty about you though, especially where you are, always." His fingers flitted up and down her neck before resting on the marks Braith left on her last night. "I'm going to make you pay, and I'm going to make my *son* pay. No one can defeat me."

Pain, unlike any she'd ever known, exploded through her as his teeth sank into her neck and he replenished his depleted strength with hers.

⚜

GIDEON HANDED Braith the truce agreement written with the border towns. He knew most of the concessions and promises made within the deal, but even so, he read it carefully to make sure everything met his approval.

The border towns would be sending an elected representative to join The Council next week. In exchange, they would consent to representatives from the palace moving into the towns for an unspecified amount of time to ensure all slavery ended.

Braith nodded as he grabbed the pen and hastily added his signature to the document. His hand cramped from the endless signatures, but they were finally reaching an end and forming a stable union with everyone involved in the war. He flexed his fingers as he sat back in his chair and surveyed the room.

Things weren't perfect, far from, but they were better than he'd thought they'd be at this stage. They'd formed alliances, they were rebuilding, the donation center wasn't thriving, but more people were coming around to the prospect of giving their blood. There were still fights, and there would be continuing violence for a while, but even that had started to slow as stability was beginning to return in the form of homes, businesses, and a solid government.

He also had Aria.

It was more than he ever could have hoped for. He was going to have an eternity to enjoy their marriage and *her*. The thought caused a small smile to tug at his lips.

He knew she would be coming in soon to meet with Melinda; he thought he might be able to slip away for a few minutes to intercept her. Unknowingly, he tapped the pen harder as he planned his brief escape.

He didn't realize his foot had dropped to the floor as an uneasy feeling twined through his stomach.

"Easy there, fidgets," Daniel said as he signed the document and passed it on.

The pen cracked in his hand, the ink ran out to coat his fingers as he stood slowly. A sense of doom slithered like a serpent through him as he scanned the room for whatever danger he felt licking across his skin. Even as he searched, he realized whatever was wrong wasn't coming from in here, but from somewhere else.

It was Aria; something was wrong with *Aria*. Braith didn't know how he knew or why he was so confident of it, but he knew that something wasn't right with her.

"Braith?" Gideon asked.

An involuntary snarl ripped from him as Gideon rose from his chair. Gideon took a startled step back.

"Aria," Braith growled.

He didn't look back as he raced from the room faster than he'd ever ran in his life.

AFTER THE INITIAL burst of agony nearly drowned her within its dark depths, Aria managed to regain enough control of herself to begin to put up a fight. Her hands fisted as they were ineffectively pinned against his mushy chest.

She squirmed against him as she tried to bring her legs up between them to get some leverage against his savage attack. Using the palm of his hand, he pressed it flat against her face as he pushed it hard against the wood of the stall.

She kicked at him, but with his body flat against hers she was unable to get a good shot at him. She finally managed to break one of her pinned hands free. He blocked her from punching him, but her fingers hooked into claws she raked down the side of his face. A choked scream escaped when she felt the bugs beneath the squishy skin she'd managed to tear free. His skin broke away with a vile odor that nearly overwhelmed her.

Her struggles increased, but it was like pitting a lion against a lamb as he growled low and bit down harder. Even half dead, he was ten times stronger than she was, and his strength was increasing as hers weakened. She put every ounce of power she had into her legs and arms as she gave one final attempt to shove him off her.

A startled cry escaped, she dropped onto her butt as the king abruptly released her. She looked up in time to see Braith heaving him one-handed across the stall by his shoulder. The wooden wall gave way beneath the impact of the king's body when it shattered around him. She stared in disbelief at the wreckage as ruined wood continued to topple down on the king.

Aria's hand fumbled at the trail his teeth had raked across her throat as she tried to staunch the flow of blood. Braith was suddenly before her, his hands on her cheeks as he turned her head toward him.

"Are you okay?" he demanded.

"I'm fine," she assured him. "I'm fine."

"Who did this?" His upper lip curled as his eyes shimmered red.

"You didn't see?" she gasped. He shook his head as he pulled her hand away to examine her neck. "Braith, it's your..."

She broke off as the broken fragments of wood exploded outward. Braith enveloped her with his body as splinters, boards, and beams rained down around them. He grunted beneath the impact of the debris as he protected her from the dangerous wood crashing against him.

Silence filled the broken stall as the last board clattered to the ground. Braith's face was warm against hers, the stubble rough on her cheek as he waited to see if there was anything more coming at them.

"Hold onto me," he commanded.

Her hands encircled his biceps; his muscles flexed beneath her grasp as he lifted her against him and surged back to his feet.

Releasing her, he planted both hands on either side of her head and pressed closer as he turned his head to face the new threat.

The muscles in his arms vibrated beside her head as his fangs extended over his bottom lip. He did a double take when his father stepped from the wreckage with far more aplomb than Aria expected from a man wearing rags and still missing part of his nose.

The king appeared refreshed and better than he had before, thanks to her blood. He wiped the blood from where she had gouged his face, but the marks were already gone. Straightening the remains of his shirt, he eyed them both with amusement.

"Father," Braith finished for her.

CHAPTER TWENTY-FIVE

BRAITH COULDN'T KEEP his astonishment hidden as his father took another step away from the ruined wall. It was a sight he'd never even imagined he would ever see, never mind actually *experience*.

Part of him felt like a child again, cowering beneath his father's heavy hand, and unable to defend himself from the repeated blows and the abuse his father so jovially inflicted on him.

Another part of him, the adult one, the *king* one, the one shielding Aria, wanted to rip the entire barn down and shred the man looking at him with such delight. Red shadowed his vision as the scent of Aria's blood drifted up to him, and a snarl curled his lip.

He'd dared to touch her again, and Braith was going to make him pay for that. After everything this man had done to Aria, to him, and countless other innocents, Braith knew he could not let him survive this. There was no way he would allow this man to touch her again or be in charge; no way he would allow him to unravel all the good they had already created here.

Braith just wasn't sure there was any way to stop him. His father had taken a stake to the heart, and with no sustenance to sustain and revitalize him, the wound had still somehow managed to heal itself.

It was apparent his father hadn't had much nourishment before returning to the palace, but Braith suspected he'd looked far worse than this when he first crawled from his grave. Braith didn't know how long he'd been wandering around, but the fact he'd returned here meant he believed himself strong enough to be a threat to Braith and anyone else he came across.

He looked like a decomposing corpse, but beneath the rotten exterior, Braith felt the vibrant pulse of power he still possessed. His body was rapidly healing itself; his shoulders were straightening as he thrust them back and quirked an eyebrow in amusement.

His upper lip curled to reveal long fangs glistening in the dim light of the stable. Even though her chin lifted, and her eyes narrowed, a small shiver ran through Aria and into him as his father leveled her with his gaze and licked his lips.

A low growl rose in Braith's throat as he pushed Aria back a little. The tension in his body notched higher; bloodlust curled through him as he shielded her. He had far more control over his more primitive instincts now, but even so, he would slaughter the creature across from him before he ever allowed his father to touch a hair on her head again.

"Xavier!"

His father's head tilted to the side as Gideon's startled cry echoed through the stable. Braith had seen Xavier's prone figure in the shedrow, but he hadn't taken the time to learn if the vampire was alive or not. Judging by the marks on Xavier's neck, and his father's rapid healing, Braith suspected Xavier was gone. Aria's blood alone couldn't have caused the changes rapidly transforming his father.

"He was delicious," his father murmured.

"Xavier," Aria breathed.

"Almost as good as your whore here," his father purred.

Aria's hands tightened on his arms; he refused to rise to his father's baiting as he pulled her closer to him. Pressing her flat against his body, his hands splayed across the hollow of her lower back. He stood for a moment, savoring the feel of her while he still could.

Aria's gaze darted behind him at the sound of feet skidding to a halt outside the stall door.

"Holy *shit!*" William blurted.

"Atticus?" His father's head swiveled to the side, a smile twisted his lips at Calista's disbelieving question.

"You look as beautiful as I remember, Calista, perhaps when this is over we can reunite," he said suggestively.

Braith's grip on Aria eased. If there was one thing he knew for sure, no vampire came back from having their head ripped off. Her eyes were wild as they came back to his, her fingers clenched around his arms before her grip reluctantly loosened. He stared at her before she gave a subtle dip of her head and her fingers stroked briefly over his biceps.

She let go of him as he sprang into motion. His father turned toward him, bracing for the impact as Braith lowered his shoulder and collided with him. His father's hands came down on his shoulders; his fingers dug into his skin as Braith propelled them both backward. They crashed through the already ruined stall divider and into another wall.

Everything about the hideous creature who had once been a king was repulsive. Yet Braith hadn't been prepared for the strength in his hands. The walls gave out, and he lost his balance as they tumbled into the shedrow. They rolled over the top of each other as they each sought to gain the top.

Braith managed to get a few blows into his father's lower

ribcage, but it felt as spongy as the rest of him. He'd been decaying when his body came back to life, Braith realized. He wasn't just starved and emaciated like his pitiful trophies; his body had started to break down.

Braith's nose wrinkled as he lifted his father with his feet and flipped him over his head. He jumped back to his feet, but even in his state, his father was faster and back on him in an instant. They had been about the same size once he hit maturity, but he had a good thirty pounds on his father now. Even still he was knocked backward by the force of his weight and momentum.

They slammed into the back wall with enough force to crack the wood. Dust rained down as bits of the beams fell over top of them. A loud grunt escaped Braith as his father dug his fingers into his stomach and tore through his flesh. He struggled to unhinge his father's hold on him, but he continued to rip and dig until fire erupted within Braith's gut and rapidly spread through his limbs.

A bellow of fury erupted from him. He drove his elbow into his father's nose hard enough to knock him slightly loose. He seized the hand working its way steadily into him and yanked it back. His father screamed in his ear; his fetid aroma washed over Braith as bone and skin cracked within his grasp. Braith took advantage of his father's slackened hold to get his legs in between them and thrust him off.

He crashed into the wall, but Braith didn't take time to recuperate as he charged at him, grabbed his throat, and propelled him into the wall again. It gave way with a loud crash as they plunged out of the barn, bounced across the ground and bounded back to their feet.

He was dimly aware of screams and shouts as humans and vampires scrambled to get out of their way as they ran full speed at each other. Braith felt as if he'd run into a brick wall as his shoulder dislocated with the reverberating crack of a bat hitting a ball. His teeth clenched as a low hiss escaped him.

Braith tried to seize his father's throat, but his father grabbed his hand. Before Braith knew what he intended, he sank his fangs deep into the meaty part of his palm. Braith grunted at the unwelcome invasion, and reacting on instinct he delivered a crushing blow that collapsed his father's eye socket. It only made him bite down harder.

Infuriated, Braith released a rapid series of punches on him, but he clung like a dog on a bone as he gained strength from Braith's blood. Gritting his teeth, Braith ripped his hand back. Skin and sinew tore, but he was finally able to extricate himself from his father. Lowering his head, he charged at the man, wrapped his arms around his waist and propelled him back a good fifty feet before they hit a house.

It shuddered from the impact but held firm as his father somehow managed to get him turned around and underneath him. Braith didn't see the piece of wood in his father's hands until he was plunging it downward.

He managed to get his arm up to deflect the blow somewhat, but his father's weight continued its downward trajectory. It slammed into his upper chest, dislocated a shoulder, and tore through flesh and bone as it burst out the other side.

A grunt of pain escaped him; his legs reflexively kicked up as his body instinctively tried to curl inward to protect itself. Red filled his vision as he swung his arm up and caught his father harshly under his jaw. Knocking his father aside, Braith managed to push himself up with his good arm.

Reaching up, he snapped the end of the board off and tossed it aside. He rose into a crouch as his father launched at him again. Braith's hands grasped his back as they fell into one of the newly constructed houses.

"LET GO OF ME!" Aria shouted as she tried to rip her arm free of Gideon's hold.

She didn't know what possessed her, or perhaps she did, but she'd never experienced it before as a ferocious snarl ripped from her and her teeth elongated instantaneously. A strange shimmering rattled through her as the line between light and dark seemed to spread out before her. A line that made her realize what it was Braith had been so fiercely struggling with all this time.

She could take one step over the line and let it all go; she could embrace the power lurking just beneath the surface and let the darkness take over. Destroy, as she so badly wanted to destroy the man who had hurt Braith.

How had Braith controlled this so well? She felt like she was going to fall apart as if she wasn't herself anymore. Her skin crawled with the energy sizzling up and down her body. She knew the only thing that would make it better was death.

"Easy, Aria," Gideon urged. He released her and held his hands up as he backed away. "Easy."

She spun away from him and took a step forward before she stopped abruptly. Braith and his father had disappeared into the house; the walls were shaking from the force of their fight.

She started to run forward, but faster than she could blink, Jack appeared in front of her. She didn't know where he'd come from, Jack hadn't been in the stable with the others, but he was here now, and he wouldn't let her go as he grasped her arms.

"Let go of me, Jack!"

Jack bent so he was eye level with her. "You are of no use here, Aria. Stay out of the way; you're only a distraction."

He pushed her gently back as he released her arms. Hands seized her, and it took everything she had not to kick Ashby in the shin as he gripped her. Jack turned and ran toward the house. Aria fought against Ashby, but the harder she struggled, the tighter he held her.

"Aria, please, stop," he pleaded against her ear as he pulled her down to the ground and enfolded himself over her.

A scream welled in her throat, tears burned her eyes as she continued to struggle against him, but it was useless. Gideon and Calista ran past her, followed by Daniel, Max, and William. A low moan of anguish escaped her; she rocked forward as Ashby kept her on the ground.

A loud crash echoed from within the house. It sagged precariously for a minute before collapsing.

THE BOARDS CAUGHT him hard in the back and drove him to his knees. Braith threw his good arm up as he tried to protect his head from the roof crashing upon him. He was buried beneath the weight, pushed down under the force battering his already bruised and broken body.

It took him a moment to recuperate as the last of the beams fell with a dull clatter upon the heap. Gathering his strength, he pushed back some of the boards as he drew upon his determination to end this once and for all.

He crawled out from under the boards, shoving them off as he surveyed the ruins of the house. The front of the building was still standing, but a stiff wind would knock it over with ease.

In all the confusion, he'd managed to lose his father. Pulling himself free of the jumbled mess surrounding him, Braith spotted him. He'd already extricated himself from the rubble and was trying to make an escape when Braith launched to his feet and raced after him.

If his father were able to get free now, he would bide his time and grow stronger as he tried to recruit an army. Braith suspected he'd come here with the intention of claiming Aria and trying to control Braith.

It didn't matter what he'd expected; he wasn't going to leave here alive. He was never going to have the chance to touch Aria again. Drudging up some of the last remnants of his strength, he surged forward, grabbed his father's shirt, and yanked him back.

Braith didn't realize his father was holding a board until it smashed into the side of his face. Stars burst before his eyes as his cheekbone cracked and his jaw broke. Blinking away his blurry vision, Braith wrenched the board from his father's hands, spun it around and swung it against his father's side. He staggered sideways from the force of the blow; his hand flew to his collapsed ribs.

Jack appeared on the other side, encircling their father as a cruel smile curved his lips. Braith had never seen that look on Jack's face before or the vindictive gleam in his eyes.

"Father," Jack greeted, moving to intercept him as he tried to go in another direction.

Gideon grinned as he stepped forward, blocking another pathway as Calista moved to block another. Max, William, and Daniel blocked the other side. His father's eyes spun crazily before focusing on something in the distance.

Braith followed his gaze to Aria as she slowly approached the circle. Ashby was hot on her heels, looking chagrined as he rubbed at his reddened jaw. Braith had never seen it before, but Aria's eyes were glistening rubies when they met his and then his father's. He sensed the unraveling beneath her outwardly calm exterior and moved to intercept her as she reached the circle.

"I'm fine." Her crimson eyes focused on the board protruding from his shoulder. His fingers brushed briefly over hers as he looked to soothe her. "Really, Aria."

William and Max flanked her. They wouldn't be able to hold

her back, not anymore, but their presence seemed to have a further calming effect upon her as her fingers wrapped briefly around his hand.

"What was your plan here, Atticus?" Gideon inquired with a tilt of his head and a quirked eyebrow.

"He planned to recapture her or kill her," Braith answered flatly.

"I plan to do many, *many* things to her, son. All of which I will truly enjoy."

A gleam on the other side of the circle caught Braith's attention. Jack had managed to retrieve a honed ax from one of the building sites. He twisted it in his grasp as he met Braith's gaze over the top of their father's head.

"You can't kill me!" Their father laughed as he flung his arms wide and spun in a circle. "Look at me! I'm invincible! You can't stop *me!*"

His father was still laughing as Braith lurched forward. His father wasn't fooled though, instead of meeting Braith head on, he spun to confront Jack. Jack's fangs flashed as he threw the ax to Braith and dove at their father with unrestrained glee.

Braith had anticipated the action as he leapt into the air and seized the handle with his good hand. Jack rammed his shoulder into their father and shoved him back. On his descent, Braith swung the ax downward with the full force of his might.

Atticus turned toward him as the ax whistled through the air. Braith had to grab it with both hands as the impact of metal against flesh and bone jarred his arm. Atticus's mouth parted in an O; his crimson eyes widened as the ax cleaved his neck.

Braith stepped back when the head bounced across the ground and the body collapsed. There was no satisfaction in the deed, but rather a strange sense of completion and relief as the ax slipped from his fingers. Disgust coiled through him as he wiped the splatters of his father's blood from his face.

"Not that fucking invincible," Jack spat as he nudged the head away with his foot.

Braith's shoulders sagged; now that his adrenaline wasn't pounding, and the threat eradicated, it took everything he had to stay on his feet as blood loss started to take its toll.

Aria was beside him in an instant. Her arm wrapped around his waist as she pressed against his side. He grabbed her hand when she reached for the broken piece of board jutting from his shoulder. He couldn't be weak in front of so many.

He pressed her hand flat against his chest. His broken bones and wounds were throbbing, and he desperately needed some blood, but there was something he had to do first.

"Caleb," he grated. "We have to make sure Caleb and Natasha are still in their graves."

"Braith, you need blood," she whispered.

He glanced down at her, relieved to find her eyes back to their crystalline, sapphire color. "We can't take the chance Caleb may be out there right now."

"I'm coming with you."

He started to protest but decided against it. He'd feel better having her with him just in case his siblings were out there. His hand tightened on her arm as Saul emerged from the barn with Xavier's arm draped around his shoulder. Xavier was pale beneath his dark complexion as he held a hand to the still bleeding wound on his neck.

"He's okay," Aria breathed.

Tears shimmered in Aria's eyes as she watched Xavier. Braith had to admit he was relieved to see him still alive. Xavier still managed to irritate him once in a while, but he was an asset and had become Aria's friend.

Melinda pushed past the crowd as she arrived at the edge of the circle. Her mouth dropped, and her eyes flew wildly around before landing on Ashby. A small cry escaped her as she raced across forward and threw herself into his arms.

Aria went to take a step toward Xavier but stopped as she glanced nervously at Braith and wrapped her other arm around his waist.

"Saul, gather the remains and place them in the stable. We'll burn them later." Saul nodded agreement to Braith's command. "The rest of you grab shovels, something to light a fire with, and come with me."

Aria's fingers dug deeper into his skin as the crowd that gathered during the fight parted to let them pass. "I think there is no longer any doubt you deserve to be king," she said.

The crowd bowed their heads and began to kneel as they started forward. At least something good had come from this awful mess, Braith realized as he pulled her closer to his side. Though he couldn't understand how his father had returned.

"It appears so," he agreed.

Aria eased against him as they moved past the gates and into the town beyond. When they entered the woods, she released him and turned to face him.

"Let me look," she commanded.

"We have to check on Caleb and Natasha."

"They're either still dead, or they're already roaming the earth again. A few minutes isn't going to change the outcome either way. Now, let me see."

He could behead his father and take on twenty men at once, but he still found it difficult to say no to her. He forced himself not to wince as her fingers gently prodded at the wood embedded in his shoulder.

"We need to get that out," she said.

"Later."

Her eyebrows drew together as she frowned at him. "If Caleb

did crawl out of his grave, you'll be in better shape to face him if you're already healing."

"Fine," he relented, knowing she was right. "Jack."

He released her as he grabbed the trunk of a tree. With clenched teeth, he braced himself as Jack stepped beside him. Jack placed a hand briefly on his back before seizing the board and pulling it free in one hard yank.

A low groan of pain reverberated off Braith's teeth as he stood with his head bowed and his shoulders heaving. His fingers dug into the bark of the tree as he fought against the bellow threatening to erupt from him.

Aria rested her hand on his arm, but it was a few moments before he could open his eyes to look at her. Ducking under his arm, she stepped between him and the tree. With nimble fingers, she pulled back the tears in his shirt to examine the jagged wound.

Blood still seeped from the hole, but with the beam removed he could already feel his body working to heal itself. The jagged tear in his stomach was already almost closed.

"You need blood," she murmured.

"It can wait."

Aria pressed her back against the tree as she unwaveringly met his gaze and pulled down the collar of her shirt. His gaze latched onto the marks his father had left, an involuntary snarl escaped as he wrapped his arm around her waist and pulled her against him. Using his body to shield her from the others, he bent his head to the side of her neck that wasn't wounded.

"I'm fine," she told him when he hesitated.

He briefly nuzzled her before sinking his fangs into her. Her hands curled around his arms as she melded against him. He took enough to regain some of his strength before pulling away and offering his wrist to her. Her eyes closed in pleasure as she bit into him. Releasing him, she lifted her eyes to his.

"How was that possible?" she murmured.

Braith shook his head as he released the tree and stepped away from her. Though he would still require human blood, he could already feel the strength of her blood healing his broken bones and other injuries.

"I don't know," he admitted.

"He told me he was over a thousand years old and a stake wasn't enough to stop him."

Braith's jaw clenched, his hands fisted at the reminder his father had a chance to tell her such a thing.

"Has anything like this ever happened before?" she asked.

"I have never heard of such a thing," Xavier said. Xavier was starting to regain some of his color, and the bites on his neck had almost completely healed as he stepped closer to them. "But Atticus was the oldest of our species, ever, and his line is the purest. He must have been far more powerful than any of us realized. I never heard him coming; I didn't know he was there until he was on top of me, and by then it was too late."

"He tracked me," Aria murmured.

Braith wrapped his arm around her waist and pulled her to his side. "He'll *never* be able to do that again."

She nodded as she tilted her head back to study him. "You might also be able to survive such a thing?"

"It *is* a possibility," Xavier said.

"I'm not willing to find out," Braith told them.

"Neither am I." Aria shuddered against his side.

"We will probably never know what you're capable of, or Jack and Melinda." Xavier's gaze landed on Aria as they made their way steadily up the hill to where Caleb had been unceremoniously buried. "Though it's obvious it's more than the rest of us."

At the top of the hill, Braith led the way toward a barren and dark area of the woods. Nothing grew beneath the high bows of the pines shadowing the forest floor. The inhospitable environment had seemed like the perfect spot to place his father and siblings. Dirt had been heaved up around the hole his father had pulled himself from, but the other two graves appeared undisturbed.

Calista smiled as she handed the shovels to a scowling Gideon and Ashby. "Dig away, boys," she said.

They didn't protest as they broke ground and began to uncover a creature Braith never thought he'd see again. Caleb's hands appeared first and then his chest and face. His face was sunken in, his skin grayish and missing chunks. Aria's hand tightened around his; she shuddered and turned away when they began to uncover Natasha.

"Burn them," Braith ordered gruffly, unwilling to take the chance that a month or two from now they may reemerge also.

Calista and Gideon lit the torches and tossed them into the graves. Braith didn't care to see the result; he didn't want Aria there for any longer than necessary.

"If they're still in their graves, does that mean you wouldn't survive a stake?" she whispered as he led her through the woods.

"I don't know. It may have been my father's age which allowed such a thing to happen, it may have taken more time for them to rejuvenate, or it may have simply been my father's bloodline." Aria nodded as she leaned against his side. "Are you sure you're okay?"

Her hand absently fluttered to her neck; her eyes darkened as she nodded briefly. "I'll be fine. The darkness, Braith, I don't know how you handled it."

He kissed her temple briefly, inhaling her sweet scent beneath the hay, blood, and sweat. "Because of you."

"Yes, because of you," she murmured.

"I understand the darkness, Aria. It will never rule *you* though; you don't have to fear that."

She glanced at him from under lowered lashes as he squeezed her shoulder. "Unless something happened to you."

"That's not going to happen," he assured her. "Apparently, there's a chance I might be even harder to kill than any of us thought."

A small laugh escaped her. "Apparently."

He fought against the waves of anger suffusing him as he brushed the blood from her neck. "This will never happen again."

"I hope not. If he comes back from a beheading, I think we can give him his crown, throw him a party, and admit defeat."

"Thankfully, that's not a possibility."

"Good, there are only so many shocks my heart can take, beating or not." He chuckled as he kissed the top of her head and they reentered the town.

CHAPTER TWENTY-SIX

THROUGHOUT THE REPAIRS AND REBUILDING, the golden chains were salvaged from the wreckage of the town and placed where the stage once stood. That night, after taking some time to recuperate and consume some blood from the donation center, Braith gathered all occupants of the palace, towns, and forest together to burn the chains with the remains of his father.

The sun was beginning to set as he lit a torch and handed it to Aria. "I thought you would like the honors," he said.

The flames heated her cheeks as she twisted it in her hands. She smiled at him before stepping forward and tossing it onto the pile of kindling. She'd never seen anything as satisfying as watching all those chains, and the king's remains, spark and catch fire. Braith reached into his pocket and pulled out something. She leaned over him as he opened his hand to reveal the signet ring symbolizing the House of Valdhai he'd worn when she first met him.

"Braith?"

"It's a new beginning all the way around, Aria."

He stepped forward and tossed the ring into the flames.

Sliding her arms around his waist, she rested her head on his chest and savored the moment. The fire spread throughout the vast amount of wood and rose higher. Sparks shot and leapt into the air as smoke curled high into the darkening night. It had been an awful day, but this moment made it all worthwhile.

A cheer erupted from the crowd as the last symbols of oppression from the old regime turned to ashes. Food and alcohol were brought forth; music filled the air as the crowd of vampires and humans laughed and danced in celebration.

There was still a lot of work to be done, and a long way to go before trust was fully established, but as the heat of the flames beat against her skin, and Braith twirled her into the merriment, she knew they could do it. That together they could conquer anything; they could make a world neither of them had envisioned, but both of them were willing to sacrifice anything for.

She thought of the darkness that threatened to drag her under earlier, but instead of being afraid of it, she found strength in the power coursing through her. A strength that would help her get through the days and years ahead. Days and years she couldn't wait to experience with him.

THE NEXT DAY, Aria agreed to give Melinda her undivided attention until the wedding and coronation ceremony was over. Melinda bombarded her with endless details, and Aria was reaching her breaking point when Maggie strolled into the apartment with an armload of dresses.

"I asked her to come," Melinda whispered in Aria's ear.

It took Aria a moment to get over her surprise at seeing Maggie again. "You don't have to wait on me," she said.

Maggie grinned at her as she placed the dresses on the arm of the sofa. "I'm not here as a servant. I came willingly."

"Every queen requires a lady in waiting," Melinda said flippantly.

Aria was even more uncomfortable with that prospect. Melinda started pawing through the dresses Aria now realized were wedding dresses.

"I've ordered the tailor to come up also," Melinda said.

Aria winced at the prospect. She had to adjust to these things if she was going to spend an eternity within these walls, but even so, she couldn't help but dream about escaping with Braith to their tree house soon. Maggie watched in amusement as Melinda held dresses up to Aria, shook her head, and tossed them aside with rapid precision.

They were almost to the end of the pile when Melinda seized one that caused Aria to lurch forward. She pulled it closer to her as she gazed at the beautiful dress in awe. "This one. *This* is the one."

Melinda's gray eyes twinkled as she grinned at her. "I knew you'd like it. Didn't I tell you this would be the one?" she demanded of Maggie.

"You did," Maggie agreed.

"Let's get it on you before my brother decides to snoop."

Aria helped them to maneuver her into the striking dress. Standing before the mirror, she was unable to believe it was her as she gazed at herself in amazement. It was the only dress she'd loved, and not only could she not wait to wear it, but she didn't want to take it off.

Melinda fluffed out the bottom of it and took a step back to scrutinize it. A radiant smile lit her beautiful face as she nodded approvingly. "You're not the most conventional queen, but you can pull off a dress when it's necessary."

Aria laughed as she twirled in front of the large mirror. Feeding on Braith had added curves to her that hadn't been there since her first captivity within the palace. His blood had given her a glow of health and a rosy blush to her skin.

She was amazed by the drastic change her life had taken. As a motherless, wild child, she never would have dreamed she would one day be standing here, a fatherless vampire, surrounded by more loved ones than she ever dreamed of having and marrying a king.

Though it took all her self control, she managed to stay still, and not fidget, as the tailor made a few adjustments before nodding his approval.

Melinda clapped her hands enthusiastically together as she eyed Aria with approval. "Are you ready to get married?"

"More than ready."

"Good. The wedding is tomorrow." Aria gaped at her as Melinda smiled mischievously and shared a pointed look with Maggie. "I've told Braith to stay away for the night, as we have a lot of plans to make, and also because I like to torment him."

"It's too soon for such a big wedding," Aria protested.

"Not the big one, Aria, tomorrow will be *your* wedding. The one *you* dreamed of having. The other one can wait until the end of the month."

Tears burned her throat and eyes as she threw her arms around Melinda. Her future sister was nearly her exact opposite, but Aria couldn't have asked for a better friend. She hugged Maggie afterward; grateful to see the young girl who was the closest thing to a friend she had while a blood slave. She'd never been so nervous and excited in her life, but she couldn't wait to be a queen.

EPILOGUE

WILLIAM GRINNED at her as he grasped her hands and held her arms out before her. "Might not be wearing heels, but the dress alone is worth it," he said.

Aria rolled her eyes as she slid her arm through his and smiled. "Don't get used to it."

"I don't plan on it," he assured her. "You look beautiful, by the way."

"Did you just offer me a compliment?"

His eyes sparkled as he squeezed her hand. "Don't get used to it."

"I don't plan on it," she told him laughingly.

"Are you ready for this?"

"I'm pretty sure this is the smallest step I've taken recently."

"Yeah but you'll be a queen after this one, that seems a little more intimidating than dying."

Aria burst into laughter as she leaned against his side. "I think you might be right."

His expression became sober as he studied her. "You'll be good at it though."

"I hope so. You'll do well also, with Jack."

He shrugged as he anxiously pulled at the edges of the light green tunic he wore. Though it was of more exceptional quality than the clothes they'd worn in the forest, it was the same style. "I'm looking forward to it."

"I'm going to miss you," she could barely get the words out through the sudden constriction in her throat.

"I'm not so sure your future husband will."

Aria laughed again as she shook her head. "He'll miss you too, but I'll annoy him enough for the both of us until you return though."

"Of that, I have no doubt."

She leaned forward as she tried to peer out to where Braith waited with the others by the banquet tree. She was nervous about the larger ceremony at the end of the month, but pure excitement filled her with this one.

Today was just for them.

William pulled her back and shook his head reprovingly. "No peeking."

Aria frowned impatiently but resigned herself to waiting a little longer. Though most of the leaves were still in the trees, they had started to flutter down. The clearing was alive with the swirling oranges, yellows, and reds floating lazily toward the ground. The air was crisper, but she didn't feel the cold as acutely as she had as a human.

She shifted the simple bouquet of pale yellow roses and orange baby's breath in her grasp. Max approached from where the others waited for her, he was smiling and handsome in the same color shirt William wore. Amusement gleamed in his eyes as his gaze ran over her and he nodded approvingly.

She'd been blessed with eternity, but it had come at a price. She was reminded of this fact as she looked between Max and her brother. One day, she would lose them, but for now she was going to savor the small moment of perfection she'd found in a life she'd never expected to be blessed with.

"They're ready if you are," Max informed her.

She grinned at him as she nodded enthusiastically. She'd never been more ready for anything in her life. "Completely," she replied as she slipped her arms into Max's and William's.

Someone, she suspected Melinda, had instructed the colorful leaves be gathered and spread out to serve as the aisle she would walk down. There were no decorations except for the splendid color of the fall day surrounding them as she stepped onto the makeshift aisle. Gideon, Xavier, Saul, Calista, Adam, Frank, Ashby, Melinda, and Maggie were adorned in simple garb as they stood beside the makeshift aisle, but her eyes were immediately drawn to Braith with Jack at his side.

Pride bloomed in her chest; love swirled and built within her as tears burned her eyes. He was magnificent with his dark hair brushed neatly back, and his hard jaw shaved clean. The dark green tunic he wore fit perfectly over his large frame.

She had to admit she enjoyed him in such simple clothing; he appeared more at ease in the attire of the forest people. And that smile, well she'd never get tired of the smile lighting his face and causing his eyes to sparkle.

Max and William stepped aside when they arrived at the end of the aisle with her. Braith couldn't stop himself from smiling as he held his hand out and took hers. She was beautiful, with a glow of happiness and love radiating from her as she stared up at him with tears of joy shimmering in her eyes.

She hated dresses, but the simple gown she'd chosen was ideal for her. The cream color was flattering against her sun-kissed skin. Woven across her stomach, through the dress, were subtle strands of gold and orange that accented her slender waist.

More strands of color ran throughout the form-fitting bodice, and the off-the-shoulder sleeves. Her hair fell about her shoulders in thick, red ringlets interwoven with tiny yellow and gold flowers.

She was a vision of fall and earth, and she was his.

Daniel cleared his throat to draw their attention to him. Her other hand enfolded his as Daniel began to recite the vows he'd written. Though they weren't traditional, Braith recognized them as belonging to the people of the woods, as belonging to Aria and her loved ones.

Daniel spoke of the trees and the seasons, of growth and loss, of the changes they all had to endure. Braith found himself enraptured by Daniel's speech, the emotion swirling within the words, and the enthusiasm radiating from his gaze.

"Though you may weather tough times, may your love be as durable as the swaying oak, as steadfast as the rising sun, and as evolving as the changing moon." Daniel stared expectantly at them before clearing his throat and blushing slightly. "You can kiss her now," he said as he realized he'd forgotten this part.

Dim laughter accompanied his statement, but Braith heard none of it as he pulled her against him and kissed her. Her mouth was pliant against his as her arms wrapped around his neck and she melted against him. Loud cheers and applause resounded around them as he broke the kiss before he couldn't.

She grinned up at him, her eyes sparkling and mischievous and her mouth slightly swollen from his kiss. He wasn't entirely certain forever would be enough for him. He knew that no matter what, this woman, once his blood slave, then his greatest downfall, and finally his salvation would never fail to amaze him, never fail to bring joy and love to his life, and would hold him captive for eternity.

Turn the page for a sneak peek of *Redemption*, book 5 in The Captive Series.

SNEAK PEEK

REDEMPTION, THE CAPTIVE SERIES BOOK 5

SMOKE DRIFTED through the tavern as Jericho took a step inside and looked around. He didn't know the man he was looking for but even so he glanced at every table within the cluttered room. There was no one sitting amongst the tables or tucked into the shady recesses of the establishment that immediately grabbed his attention. He thought that perhaps he would somehow just *know* the leader of the rebels by some aura of power surrounding the man, but they all appeared to be ordinary humans.

But then, all humans were ordinary and rather boring to him.

He snaked his way through the crowd of unshaven, unwashed and drunken men to an empty table near the back. His nose wrinkled, he'd smelled better things in the dungeons of his father's palace. These men didn't seem to care though, and neither did the women that were throwing themselves at them with the hope of a little extra coin or food. He'd lived amongst the humans for two years now and though he survived on their blood, and took pleasure in what their bodies had to offer, he felt no sympathy for the plight they faced.

Grabbing hold of one of the rickety chairs, he pulled it out from a table. Years of too many beer mugs sat down with a heavy hand, and too many fights, had left the table surface covered with nicks and gouges. He sat down carefully, worried that the wobbly chair might not support his weight. Leaning back, he forced himself not to sneer as he surveyed the scene with his arms folded over his chest. He was supposed to be on the human's side in their battle against the evil vampires; he couldn't show his open disdain of them right now.

He almost chuckled aloud, but managed to keep it suppressed, as a buxom brunette shimmied up to him and asked for his order with a saucy grin. Though he wasn't overly fond of human food, he found he had a taste for the darker ale that the taverns served, so he ordered a mug. The woman's eyes practically stripped the clothes off of his body as she leisurely took him in. She sauntered away with a swish of her hips that would have been far more tempting if she'd possessed all of her teeth. He enjoyed women, and the pickings had been slim lately, but no matter how slim they were he still had his standards. They weren't as high as they had been when he lived in the palace, but a full set of teeth were still mandatory.

"I think Kelly likes you."

Jericho had been so lost in his thoughts that he hadn't realized the young blond man at the table next to him had tilted back in his chair to speak to him. He was so close that Jack could smell the spearmint leaf he was chewing on. Though the man was smiling at him, and seemed friendly enough, his youthful appearance was out of place in this world of prematurely aged men and women.

"She doesn't bite I assure you," the stranger continued.

"I imagine she would have trouble doing so," Jericho replied with a chuckle.

The young man laughed as the legs of his chair plopped back down. "That she would."

"You know Kelly well?" Jericho inquired.

"Not that well," he assured him quickly. "But I've heard the tales."

"You seem a little young for such tales."

The stranger's bright blue eyes twinkled with amusement as he leaned further away. "Not everything is as it seems."

"So I've been told." So he *knew* for a fact.

"I haven't seen you around here before."

Jericho shrugged and tossed a coin to Kelly after she returned with his ale. Money was scarce in these areas but he'd come into a windfall yesterday when he'd killed and robbed some of his father's own men in order to continue with his subterfuge. It had been the final test that he'd had to take in order to prove his loyalty to the rebellion enough to be led to this place, and the people he was supposed to meet. *If* they ever showed up.

It was easier than he'd anticipated, killing and taking money from vampires while pretending to be a mere human. However, he was beginning to realize that what the humans lacked in strength and speed, they made up for by being creative. They were devious little critters and he now knew why his father was having such a difficult time squashing their rebellion.

He'd never seen such intricate traps designed and carried out, and though he'd had to dispatch of the two surviving troops, the other six guards had been slaughtered when hundreds of wooden stakes had exploded from the spring lever traps hidden within the trees. The two wounded men had been impaired enough that it had been easy for him to take them out, even while having to pretend to be a mere "human."

"I'm new to the area," Jericho informed him as he took a sip of ale; it warmed him from his throat all the way to his belly.

A strand of blond hair fell into the young man's eye as he tilted his head to the side. "We don't get many new people around here."

Jericho shrugged and wiped the foam from his upper lip. "I needed to get away from the confinement of the palace walls and the vampires there. I've been doing some traveling, meeting different people, trying new things."

"I see." The young man turned away and waved to Kelly, she came back with a tankard of the amber colored ale and set it before him. "You've had problems with the vampires at the palace?"

"Haven't we all?"

The man raised his mug to Jericho. "That we have stranger, that we have. What brought you to this town?"

Jericho sensed something more behind the young man's twinkling eyes as he studied him attentively. As the man leaned closer to him, Jericho sensed an acuity that went far beyond this human's youthful years. He was struck with the realization that he'd just waded into treacherous waters and he would have to tread carefully. It had taken him years to get to this point, he couldn't ruin it now. He didn't know who this man across from him was, but the playfulness that he'd first exhibited was now gone.

"A man they call Neil told me to stop by here," Jericho answered.

The blond took a sip of his ale. He was smiling again, but Jericho wasn't fooled by the carefree demeanor anymore. "I've heard of Neil, but then I've heard of a few men called Neil over the years."

"As we all have." Jericho looked around as he realized things had begun to change in the tavern. Though conversation, drinking, and the clatter of dice and dominoes continued from the tables surrounding them, there had been a shifting amongst the crowd. Most of the attention was now focused upon them, upon *him*. He wasn't afraid of anyone in this room and though it would blow his cover, if it came down to it, he could destroy each and every one of them. "Neil told me his cousin would be here."

The young man's eyebrows furrowed as he studied the room. "Timber over there has a cousin named Neil."

Jericho didn't have to ask who Timber was, or why they called him that; the sheer size of the man was enough to rival the sequoias that he'd once seen in the Sierra Nevada Mountains. Ok, so maybe he'd have a tough time taking down *that* guy, Jericho thought as he turned away from the giant who was currently grinning at the woman seated in his lap. Jericho had a suspicious feeling that Timber was more aware of him, and the man he was talking to, than the woman though.

"I don't think that's the guy I'm looking for," Jericho told him.

"What makes you say that?"

"I only received a vague description of the man, but I imagine part of that description would have included the fact that he could rip my head off with his bare hands."

The blond chuckled and real amusement filtered back into his eyes. "Do you know the name of the man you're looking for?"

"David."

The young man nodded and gulped down his tankard of ale. "I know many a David too." He lifted his hand in the air and gestured to Kelly with a subtle flicker of his long fingers. The tips of his fingers were streaked with black. Jericho frowned as he tried to figure out what the blackness was. It didn't appear to be dirt but he didn't know what would have stained the boy's fingers like that.

Jericho watched as Kelly reappeared with another tankard for the boy and one more for him. The sound of a chair scraping out form the table drew his attention from the boy and Kelly. He turned as a man settled with ease into the chair across from him. The man's arms folded over his chest; his face was expressionless as he studied Jericho with shrewd green eyes. His reddish brown hair was tussled but clean for someone that lived amongst this area of the woods.

Out of the corner of his eye, Jericho saw that the young blond was holding the newly delivered tankard in his hand. From his vantage point, he spotted the gleam of something tucked into the boy's sleeve. Kelly may have been eyeing him like a fresh piece of meat she wanted to devour, but she had still surreptitiously slipped the blond a knife with her last drink delivery. There was no amusement in the blond's eyes anymore as they met and held his gaze.

Rebel, the thought blazed across his mind.

The wisdom and horror of the rebel's everyday life was now on full display in the subtle lines on the younger man's face. The rebels wore the knowledge of those that had lost too much on their faces and in their eyes. The sand slipping rapidly through the hourglass of their lives was something that they endured every day they awoke. He'd only met a handful of the true rebels over the past couple of years, but he realized now he was nestled amongst them.

He was a snake within a den of rats.

"I've also known a David or two in my lifetime," the older man across from him stated.

He was younger than Jericho had anticipated, but he knew without having to be told that *this* was the man he had been searching for, the man he'd been sent to help destroy. He fought the urge to shift in his chair as his fangs pricked with anticipation. He could kill this man right now and put a nail in the coffin of the entire rebellion. He'd been sent to infiltrate the rebel group though, to learn as much as he could about the rebellion before reporting back to his father, the vampire king.

He steadied his impulse to leap across the table and break the man's neck by taking a small sip of ale. Finally he would have a chance to prove himself to his father, a chance to show that he wasn't simply the unnecessary, easily kicked around youngest prince. He would have a chance to prove that he was just as ruthless as his middle brother Caleb. That he could be just as determined and relentless as his oldest brother Braith.

He took another sip and placed the mug down on the table. He was so close, he couldn't ruin his chances now, but he wasn't entirely sure how to proceed. "I see," Jericho murmured.

The man smiled at Kelly as she placed a bowl of steaming soup and a mug before him. "Thank you Kelly." She flashed a smile that showcased her remaining teeth and strode away with an even more inviting sway of her hips. The man shook his head, lifted his spoon, and blew on the soup. "So a man named Neil sent you here?"

"Yes," Jericho answered.

"What did he tell you about this David?"

Jericho was growing tired of the subterfuge and games. He'd had enough of that with his father; he wasn't going to play those same games with this man. "He told me that *you* were the leader of the rebellion."

The man paused with his spoon halfway to his mouth, for a minute he remained unmoving and then a smile slipped over his face. "I see. What's your interest in the rebellion?"

"I would like to join. I'm strong, fast. I'm a good hunter and an even better fighter. I'll be a valuable asset."

"I'll be the judge of that." The man dropped the spoon and leaned back in his chair to survey Jericho with eyes that though they weren't as callous as his own father's, they were every bit as astute. Jericho bristled at the thought of being judged by this human; he'd been judged and found lacking by his father his

288

entire life. He wasn't about to be sized up by a man he could kill in the blink of an eye if he so chose.

The tingling in his fangs increased as he met David's persistent stare. It would piss his father off, and ruin everything he'd worked for over the past couple of years, but he was extremely tempted to give into the urge to rip this man's throat out.

Then the man leaned forward and thrust out his hand. "I'm David and this is my son, Daniel."

Jericho glanced at the blond beside him who flashed him another arrogant grin. Jericho's fingers tingled as he resisted the rising desire to take down father and son, which would rather effectively cripple the rebellion. But that would be like cutting off the head of the hydra wouldn't it? He would take two down only to have more grow back.

"And you are?" David prompted as Jericho leaned forward and took hold of the hand extended toward him. As he returned the firm handshake, he could feel the large calluses on the man's palm and the numerous cuts that marred his skin.

"Jack," he answered without thought. He didn't know where the name had originally come from, but it had slipped easily from his tongue the first time he'd encountered a rebel two years ago. He didn't think the rebels had much knowledge of the royal family, and even if they did, he wasn't the only man in the world named Jericho, but it wasn't a name he wanted to use. Not here, not amongst these people.

David smiled at him and brusquely shook his hand. "Well then Jack, are you ready for your life to change?"

He'd been ready for over nine hundred years for his life to change, but he never could have expected the amount of change that David and his family would bring to his life.

Continue reading *Redemption*, The Captive Series book 5: ericastevensauthor.com/Redwb

Stay in touch on updates and new releases from the author by joining the mailing list!

Mailing list for Erica Stevens & Brenda K. Davies Updates: ericastevensauthor.com/ESBKDNews

FIND THE AUTHOR

Erica Stevens/Brenda K. Davies Mailing List:
ericastevensauthor.com/ESBKDNews

Facebook page: ericastevensauthor.com/ESfb

Erica Stevens/Brenda K. Davies Book Club:
ericastevensauthor.com/ESBKDBookClub

Instagram: ericastevensauthor.com/ESinsta
Twitter: ericastevensauthor.com/EStw
Website: ericastevensauthor.com
Blog: ericastevensauthor.com/ESblog
BookBub: ericastevensauthor.com/ESbkbb

ABOUT THE AUTHOR

Erica Stevens is the author of the Captive Series, Coven Series, Kindred Series, Fire & Ice Series, Ravening Series, and the Survivor Chronicles. She enjoys writing young adult, new adult, romance, horror, and science fiction. She also writes adult paranormal romance and historical romance under the pen name, Brenda K. Davies. When not out with friends and family, she is at home with her husband, son, dog, cat, and horse.

BOOKSHELF

Books written under the pen name

Erica Stevens

The Coven Series

Nightmares (Book 1)

The Maze (Book 2)

Dream Walker (Book 3)

The Captive Series

Captured (Book 1)

Renegade (Book 2)

Refugee (Book 3)

Salvation (Book 4)

Redemption (Book 5)

Vengeance (Book 6)

Unbound (Book 7)

Broken (Book 8)

The Captive Series Prequel

The Kindred Series

Kindred (Book 1)

Ashes (Book 2)

Kindled (Book 3)

Inferno (Book 4)

Phoenix Rising (Book 5)

The Fire & Ice Series

Frost Burn (Book 1)

Arctic Fire (Book 2)

Scorched Ice (Book 3)

The Ravening Series

The Ravening (Book 1)

Taken Over (Book 2)

Reclamation (Book 3)

The Survivor Chronicles

The Upheaval (Book 1)

The Divide (Book 2)

The Forsaken (Book 3)

The Risen (Book 4)

Books written under the pen name
Brenda K. Davies

The Vampire Awakenings Series

Awakened (Book 1)

Destined (Book 2)

Untamed (Book 3)

Enraptured (Book 4)

Undone (Book 5)

Fractured (Book 6)

Ravaged (Book 7)

Consumed (Book 8)

Unforeseen (Book 9)

Forsaken (Book 10)

Relentless (Book 11)

Legacy (Book 12)

Coming 2021

The Alliance Series

Eternally Bound (Book 1)

Bound by Vengeance (Book 2)

Bound by Darkness (Book 3)

Bound by Passion (Book 4)

Bound by Torment (Book 5)

Bound by Danger (Book 6)

Coming 2020

The Road to Hell Series

Good Intentions (Book 1)

Carved (Book 2)

The Road (Book 3)

Into Hell (Book 4)

Hell on Earth Series

Hell on Earth (Book 1)

Into the Abyss (Book 2)

Kiss of Death (Book 3)

Edge of the Darkness (Book 4)

Historical Romance

A Stolen Heart

Printed in Great Britain
by Amazon

18044086R00180